"Sherry Harris is a gifted storyteller, with plenty of twists and adventures for her smart and stubborn protagonist."
—Beth Kanell, Kingdom Books

"Once again Sherry Harris entwines small-town life with that of the nearby Air Force base, yard sales with romance, art theft with murder. The story is a bargain, and a priceless one!"
—Edith Maxwell, Agatha-nominated author of the Local Foods mystery series

Praise for *Tagged for Death*

"*Tagged for Death* is skillfully rendered, with expert characterization and depiction of military life. Best of all Sarah is the type of intelligent, resourceful, and appealing person we would all like to get to know better!"
—*Mystery Scene Magazine*

"Full of garage-sale tips, this amusing cozy debut introduces an unusual protagonist who has overcome some recent tribulations and become stronger."
—*Library Journal* on *Tagged For Death*

"A terrific find! Engaging and entertaining, this clever cozy is a treasure—charmingly crafted and full of surprises."
—Hank Phillippi Ryan, Agatha-, Anthony- and Mary Higgins Clark-award-winning author

"Like the treasures Sarah Winston finds at the garage sales she loves, this book is a gem."
—Barbara Ross, Agatha-nominated author of the Maine Clambake Mysteries

"It was masterfully done. *Tagged for Death* is a winning debut that will have you turning pages until you reach the final one. I'm already looking forward to Sarah's next bargain with death."
—Mark Baker, Carstairs Considers

Also by Sherry Harris

Agatha-Nominated Best First Novel
TAGGED FOR DEATH

THE LONGEST YARD SALE

ALL MURDERS FINAL!

A GOOD
DAY
TO BUY

Sherry Harris

KENSINGTON PUBLISHING CORP.
http://www.kensingtonbooks.com

KENSINGTON BOOKS are published by

Kensington Publishing Corp.
119 West 40th Street
New York, NY 10018

Copyright © 2017 by Sherry Harris

All Kensington Titles, Imprints, and Distributed Lines are available at special quantity discounts for bulk purchases for sales promotions, premiums, fund-raising, and educational or institutional use. Special book excerpts or customized printings can also be created to fit specific needs. For details, write or phone the office of the Kensington special sales manager: Kensington Publishing Corp., 119 West 40th Street, New York, NY 10018, attn: Special Sales Department, Phone: 1-800-221-2647.

Kensington and the K logo Reg. U.S. Pat & TM Off.

ISBN-13: 978-1-4967-0751-2
ISBN-10: 1-4967-0751-6
First Kensington Mass Market Edition: May 2017

eISBN-13: 978-1-4967-0752-9
eISBN-10: 1-4967-0752-4
First Kensington Electronic Edition: May 2017

10 9 8 7 6 5 4 3 2 1

Printed in the United States of America

To Bob

4

Chapter 1

Love fades. People change. It's happened to me. I'll fall in love and buy something, but in a few years, I'm ready to move on. Fortunately it happened to other people as well, which was what kept my garage sale business growing. But today my client was a story all her own.

"Sarah Winston, are you going to sell my Pyrex for so little? You might as well give it away." Not only did Mrs. Spencer's voice shake but her whole body did too—even her rigidly hair-sprayed, gray curls. She snatched the red Pyrex bowl out of my hand and thrust it at the startled woman standing in front of me.

"Go ahead, take it. Just take whatever you want." The woman looked at me with raised eyebrows. I gave her a small nod before turning back to Mrs. Spencer. Out of the corner of my eye, I saw the woman hurry to her car. Happily, we were having a lull in the Spencer garage sale so there weren't a lot of people to witness the outburst or decide to help themselves to items based on Mrs. Spencer's comment.

I'd tried to be patient with Mrs. Spencer over the last two weeks since the Spencers had hired me to run a garage sale for them this Saturday. Mostly because I loved her husband, a Vietnam vet. He'd decided it was time to downsize and head south to Florida to be near their son and grandchildren. Mrs. Spencer was on board with the move to Florida, but not with the downsizing. While I wouldn't call her a hoarder, she was definitely an avid collector and she didn't want to part with anything.

Her cupboards and closets bulged with everything from old aluminum foil pans to plastic Dunkin' Donuts cups to embroidered samplers her ancestors had made. Her biggest problem was not knowing which things had value, like the samplers, and which didn't. I sighed and shook my head. Actually that wasn't true. Her biggest problem was that she was just a piece of work. I didn't know how her husband, a gentle, patient man, put up with her. I'd have killed her long before now.

Not long after they'd hired me, I'd called Mrs. Spencer by her first name, Velma. She'd laid into me about respecting my elders and knowing my place. I was the hired help. Since that day, I'd called her Mrs. Spencer and her husband Mr. Spencer, even though he'd asked me to call him Verne. Better to be overly polite than to incite more of Mrs. Spencer's wrath.

I smiled as Mr. Spencer came outside just then, taking Mrs. Spencer's elbow. He was looking especially spiffy this morning in a bomber jacket, newsboy-style hat, pressed khakis, and a plaid shirt. He winked at me over her head. "How about a cup of coffee, dear? I brought you some of those Italian cookies you like from DiNapoli's." Her body relaxed and she allowed herself to be pulled away from the sale and into the Cape-style house.

A man approached me, carrying the last of the five wooden lobster traps the Spencers had for sale. "I'll give you ten bucks for this."

In your dreams. I had it priced at a hundred and twenty-five dollars, and that was a bargain. It was a real, wooden vintage trap. People loved to use them as bases for coffee tables. I could picture setting one on its end, adding some shelves, and using it as a nightstand. Or adding long legs and turning it into a small desk. Inwardly, I'd hoped they wouldn't all sell, but that was as much of a dream as this man's offer.

"I can do one-twenty," I countered. The other four had sold first thing for full price. Earlier, two people had argued over one and an interior designer had offered to pay fifty dollars over the asking price. Mr. Spencer had brought this one out when he'd seen how much they were going for. It made me wonder what else he had stashed that I hadn't seen.

"You aren't even taking ten percent off." He glared at me.

Better men than you have tried to intimidate me.

Ten percent was standard in lots of cases. "It's the best I can do."

"I ain't paying that much for something at a garage sale."

It was a common problem. Just because it was a garage sale didn't necessarily mean it was cheap. I understood where he was coming from though. Everyone wanted to find something of value and pay next to nothing for it. "Sorry. It's my best offer."

A woman came over and stood next to him. "We'll take it." She opened her purse and pulled out the cash as the bargain hunter beside her stood with his mouth open. It took all my strength not to smile. This woman got pricing.

"Did you see the wooden lobster trap buoys?" I asked the woman. Now I was trying to upsell. "There are only a few of them left."

She whipped her head around when I pointed at a table. Mr. Spencer had an extensive collection, which he'd winnowed down to seven that he wanted to keep. Mrs. Spencer didn't like them so they'd been banished to the garage, where they hung by thick ropes on a pegboard.

"What the heck are you going to do with those?" her husband asked.

"I've seen them turned in to the base of a lamp," I said. "Or stuck in a trap like yours for decoration." If I had a bigger place, I would have bought some myself.

"Or hung on a wall—inside or out," the woman added as she snatched two off the table. She didn't even ask for a better price. As they walked off, I heard him say, "Some negotiator you turned out to be." His wife snapped something back, but I couldn't hear what.

The lull gave me time to straighten things up. I'd tried a new system today because I found pricing every single item tedious and time consuming. Today I'd color-coordinated plastic tablecloths to bright matching circle stickers. All the dollar items had yellow stickers and sat on tables with yellow cloths, five-dollar items had red stickers and cloths, etc. Anything over twenty-five was priced individually. I'd also posted signs showing the color of the item and the price.

The stickers on clothes had been a bit tricky because they tended to fall off. They worked best when stuck to a tag with the size or washing instructions. I'd priced some of the more valuable items in two places. One that was obvious and easy to see and one less obvious, like inside a vase or on the bottom of a chair. I hoped this would impede sneaky people who moved stickers from one item to another. It happened all too often at garage sales, but I couldn't control everything. Which is one of the reasons I'd hired Lindsay, a high school girl, to help keep an eye on things. She was a former neighbor when I'd lived on nearby Fitch Air Force Base. She was already straightening and reorganizing.

"Thanks, Lindsay," I called. "Help yourself to some coffee and donut holes." Lindsay nodded. Her long, golden-brown ponytail swayed as she worked. Hopefully, we would have a few minutes before more people descended. Mr. Spencer was getting rid of lots of tools, camping equipment, and hunting and fishing gear, which meant there had been more men at the sale than usual. Mentioning all of it at the beginning of the online ads I'd placed had worked out well.

I looked across the yard as rock music played from speakers I'd hooked my old iPod to. I'd bought colorful balloons to pass out to kids, plus some wash-off tattoos and a big box of Dunkin' Donuts coffee and donut holes. Mrs. Spencer had complained vehemently about me wasting money until I'd explained I'd done it all on my dime.

This was my first big sale of the season, and I wanted it to be fun, not only for the Spencers but for the people who came. And it was working. People bopped their heads to the beat of the songs and smiled. One group of women had even stopped shopping to sing part of Meat Loaf's "Paradise by the Dashboard Light." I would have joined in if I hadn't been so busy.

I hoped it would help my business too. So far, so good. Three people had asked me to organize sales for them and merchandise was moving fast. The warm early May weather lent to the overall party atmosphere. Forsythias blossomed with bright pops of yellow. The air was scented with lilac and warming earth. I was thankful because May in Massachusetts could be dicey. Although I'd learned since I'd moved here three years ago that any month in Massachusetts could be dicey. In my book that's just another reason to love living here.

By ten, the sunny skies had lured more people out, making the lull short-lived. Several groups of friends stopped by, but with the crowds, I only had time to say hi. Soon, I was negotiating the price of an oil painting of a harbor scene with a man who enjoyed bartering as much as I did.

A shrill shriek pierced the crowd. I jerked my head up and looked around. *Oh no. What now?* A little girl pointed up, emitting a sound that would have dogs cowering, as her lime-green balloon drifted away. Lindsay rushed another balloon to the girl, tied it securely around her wrist, and the shrieking mercifully stopped.

My heartbeat dropped back to the normal range as I countered the offer on the painting. The man and I went back and forth until we agreed on a price. Both of us left smiling—that was the fun part of the sale.

While I did all the bargaining and kept all the money, Lindsay continued to help people find things and did a great job of putting items back as they were moved from table to table. I was grateful Mr. Spencer had taken Mrs. Spencer inside to keep her out of my hair. It was hard to bargain with Mrs. Spencer watching my every move and giving people the evil eye when they bought something. I empathized with her difficulty in parting with her possessions. As a former Air Force wife, I had parted with many things over the years, as well as places I loved, dear friends, and even my husband.

While someone paid me for a captain's chair, a woman headed toward the part of the garage that was off limits to the public. I'd hung sheets with clothespins to divide the public and private space.

"You can't go back there," I called to the woman.

It didn't stop her, so I hurried after her. Mr. Spencer had a lot of expensive tools stored in a work space at the back of the garage. Mrs. Spencer resented he wasn't selling more of "his crap" as she called it. I'd heard numerous arguments on that topic over the past two weeks. The woman parted the curtain anyway.

She screamed and stumbled back, pulling one of the sheets down. I gasped, taking in the scene. The Spencers lay sprawled across the concrete floor. Mr. Spencer was on his stomach, head turned to one side, eyes open. Blood pooled under his head. Mrs. Spencer was curled into a fetal position near his feet.

Chapter 2

I raced toward them, pulled my cell phone out of my pocket, and dialed 911. Lindsay ran over to me.

"Keep everyone back unless someone thinks they can help. No one else comes in the garage. And don't let anyone leave if you can stop them." It was a lot to ask a seventeen-year-old, but I knew Lindsay could handle it.

"Okay." Lindsay hustled to the front of the garage. "Is anyone here a doctor or nurse?"

I glanced back as a crowd of people stood at the garage door gawking. "Unless you can help, get back," I shouted. No one came forward. Lindsay put her arms out and started shooing them back.

As soon as the 911 dispatcher came on the line, I gave her the address. "This is Sarah Winston. I've got two badly injured people. One may be dead."

"I'll make sure Chief Hooker knows what's happened." Sadly, the 911 operators were all too familiar with me. I checked for pulses as I talked to the dispatcher, but couldn't find one for Mr.

Spencer. I hoped it was because I wasn't trained to find it, but the way his eyes looked blankly at the wall didn't give me much hope. A faint beat pulsed from Mrs. Spencer's neck when I pressed my cold fingers to it. But she didn't move when I called her name.

"What's the extent of their injuries?" the dispatcher asked.

"I'm not sure. Mr. Spencer has blood near his head. I can't imagine what happened."

I looked around. The back door of the garage was open. The backyard stretched to one of the many wooded paths that wove around and through Ellington. I saw a brown blur of movement, the impression of a man running. There were popular trails through much of the conservancy land, but that wasn't a jogger. It was someone fleeing.

I started to rise to go after him. But I quickly sank back to the floor next to Mrs. Spencer. Chasing a possible murderer through the woods was a terrible idea. I told the dispatcher what I'd seen. Maybe the police could catch him at the end of the trail. I stroked Mrs. Spencer's arm as we waited. I told her everything would be all right, even though I knew I was lying. With her beloved husband dead, her world would never be the same.

I studied the garage, trying to note what, if anything, was different from how it had been early this morning. On the workbench, a few tools were askew, as was the pegboard hanging above it. Maybe there had been a struggle. It couldn't have been too prolonged or loud, or surely I would have heard something.

The song "Help" by The Beatles boomed from the speakers outside. It made me realize the music must have blocked any sounds of fighting. I'd never imagined the music would allow a bad person to do something horrible. It was supposed to be fun.

Both of the Spencers had multiple bruises. Mr. Spencer's plaid shirt was askew and his hand was out as if he was reaching for something. There were some tools scattered on the floor, along with a brightly painted wooden lobster trap buoy on a thick rope, Mr. Spencer's Purple Heart medal, and a white business-size envelope with cash spilling from it. I squinted and saw most of the bills were hundreds. That couldn't have been money for the sale because I always asked my clients to get an assortment of small bills. What could possibly have gone on back here? It must have been an attempted robbery, but somehow the word "payoff" popped into my head.

Why? I realized how little I knew about the Spencers other than that they wanted to move to Florida. I'd grown fond of Mr. Spencer over the past two weeks I'd been working at their house. What a contrast he was to his wife. But other than having a fairly intimate knowledge of their household goods, I knew almost nothing about them.

* * *

The EMTs and police converged at once. I hurried over to Lindsay after a police officer ordered me out of the garage. Someone re-hung the sheet for privacy.

"Are you okay?" I asked her. Quite a few people still stood on the front lawn. Some huddled in groups. Others talked on their cell phones. A few filmed everything like this was a sporting event. I hated to think this tragedy might go viral online.

Lindsay jabbed a finger at the street. "A few people left even though I told them not to."

"Don't worry about it," I said. "It's not like you could sit on them." I pulled off the light sweater I'd worn this morning for our eight-o'clock start.

"I couldn't believe it. What's wrong with people?" Lindsay said. "But I took pictures of them and their license plates." She held up her iPhone.

I smiled at her. "Good thinking." It was possible whoever attacked the Spencers might have blended back into the crowd. Could someone be that cold? I thought about the man I'd seen near the woods. Maybe he had a good reason to be there, but he certainly seemed suspicious to me. "Will you send the photos to me?"

Lindsay nodded, and in a few seconds, my phone vibrated in my pocket as each picture came in. "You'd better call your mom," I told her.

"I already did." Lindsay's father had deployed last fall, and she'd come to me for support when she and her mom were fighting. When I'd asked her to help out with the garage sale, I'd never imagined anything like this would happen. Her mom wouldn't be happy.

Two EMTs hustled by with Mrs. Spencer on a gurney, an oxygen mask covering part of her pale, frail face, and an IV stuck in her arm. This was the first time I ever wished I could hear her voice berating me for not valuing her things. I waited but couldn't see what was going on behind the sheets. Soon enough, another set of EMTs came out. They walked slowly and lugged their equipment. I knew it meant Mr. Spencer was dead. I dug my nails into the palms of my hand. *Keep it together.*

More police cars arrived, and officers Pellner and Awesome, whose real name was Nathan Bossum, climbed out of a car. Awesome had joined the Ellington police force last winter after leaving the New York City Police Department. He dated my friend and landlady, Stella Wild. Pellner had been with the force for years. We'd had a rocky start when we first met last spring, but had slowly eased into a friendly-ish relationship.

Pellner headed over to me, and Awesome hustled over to the garage and disappeared behind the sheets I'd hung so carefully earlier this morning. If only I hadn't, maybe none of this would have happened, at least not in the garage where they couldn't be seen. I should have cordoned the back off with a rope and a sign that said PRIVATE. But no, I had to hang the sheets. It was the one thing I'd done Mrs. Spencer had approved of. That in itself should have been a sign.

"Sarah, would you come with me?" Pellner asked.

Lindsay shivered beside me. I put my arm around Lindsay's waist. "I'm not leaving Lindsay until her mom gets here."

"I'll get an officer to stay with her," Pellner said.

Lindsay leaned into me. Now that the immediate action was over, for us anyway, the emotion of what had happened was starting to sink in. Kids with parents in the military weren't unfamiliar with death, but it didn't usually happen in front of them. We huddled together. I didn't know which of us needed the other more, but I did know I had to stay calm as long as she was here.

"No. She's with me." I looked at Pellner with a steady, don't-mess-with-me gaze.

He gave a quick, unhappy nod. He had five kids, and I think he understood how protective I felt. "Wait here then," he said. "You'll have to give statements before you leave."

"Lindsay, tell Officer Pellner about the pictures you took."

She explained about the people leaving, taking pictures of them and their license plates, and then forwarded the photos to Pellner. Lindsay's mom arrived and joined the small crowd at the bottom of the driveway, which was strung with yellow crime scene tape. She argued with a police officer who was keeping track of who came and went from the scene. She gestured toward Lindsay. But she wasn't allowed to pass by.

"Pellner, Lindsay's mom is here." I pointed down to the bottom of the driveway.

"Okay, I'll take your statement now then." He pulled Lindsay off to one side. They talked quietly and Pellner did a lot of nodding while he took notes.

Pellner slapped the notebook shut, and they walked back over to me. "You can go," Pellner said to her.

Lindsay gave me a hug.

"I'm sorry you had to go through this," I said.

"It's not your fault." She glanced at Pellner. "It was kind of cool being able to help the police." Lindsay gave me one last hug and trotted down to where her mother waited on the other side of the crime scene tape near the street. While Lindsay might be forgiving, her mom's stiff posture said something else entirely. I'd have to talk to her later.

One by one, the police took statements and let people leave. While I waited for my turn, I scrolled through the photos Lindsay had sent me. No one stood out. I actually recognized a few people because I'd seen them around our small town or had talked to them during the sale. When Pellner headed back over to me, I flicked off the photos. He wouldn't be happy if he knew I had them.

"Where's CJ?" I asked when he arrived by my side. CJ was my ex-husband and the chief of police of Ellington. Our relationship was beyond complicated. We'd divorced over a year ago after being married for nineteen years. For most people, that was it, but we were taking baby steps back into a relationship.

"Chuck's helping coordinate the search for the man you reported seeing in the woods."

I hated it when people called CJ *Chuck*. Sure his first name was Charles but that didn't fit him either.

"Our department is strained to the limits because of you."

"*Me?* I didn't do this." The guilt I'd felt earlier disappeared faster than the woman with the free Pyrex. "What are you talking about?"

Pellner rubbed his hand over his eyes. "Sorry. I've been working a lot of extra assignments. I'm tired."

It was a common practice for the Ellington PD officers because it gave them extra money. I looked at him more closely. "Everything's okay?"

"Ready to give your statement?" Pellner asked.

I nodded and filled him in on what I knew, which wasn't much. He jotted down notes in his notebook while I talked.

"Do you know anyone who'd want to harm the Spencers?" he asked.

I mulled it over for a few moments. "Not really."

"What do you mean?"

"Mrs. Spencer wasn't easy to get along with, but Mr. Spencer was a doll." I shook my head again at the image of them lying on the floor of the garage. "I don't know anyone who would harm them. Any news on Mrs. Spencer?"

Pellner's dimple deepened, but not because he was smiling. "Nothing yet."

We both turned at the sound of car doors slamming. Seth Anderson, the district attorney for Middlesex County, stood with a couple of his assistants, scanning the yard. I hadn't seen Seth since February when I'd realized my heart belonged to CJ. But now he was here, as handsome as ever with his dark hair and broad shoulders, dressed in a tailored suit that was bound to be custom made. He noticed me standing there and our eyes met. I'd like to say I felt nothing, but, oh, I felt something. I just wasn't sure what it was.

Pellner watched me as Seth approached us. I tried to keep my face as neutral as possible, but a betraying warmth crept up my cheeks.

Seth stopped a few feet shy of us. "Are you okay, Sarah? I'm sorry you're involved in a situation like this."

My eyes filled with tears. Something about Seth had always made me feel vulnerable. With Lindsay gone, I no longer had to keep it together, although I really didn't want to fall apart in front of Pellner and Seth. Seth took a step toward me, hand reaching for me. The crack of a car door slamming stopped him. CJ had arrived. He spoke to the officer at the bottom of the drive and ducked under the crime scene tape. As he strode up the driveway and noticed us, his jaw tightened.

Seth dropped his hand and took a step back. He nodded toward CJ before turning to Pellner. "Show me the scene?" He started to turn, but let his gaze sweep over me before moving away.

CJ shoved his sunglasses on his head, mussing his hair. It was longer than when he'd served in the Air Force. His pale blue eyes studied me as his long legs shortened the distance between us. He pulled me into his arms as soon as he reached me. I buried my face in his chest for a few moments. He pulled back and tipped my head up.

"I'm okay," I said before he asked. "Go do what you need to do." I nodded my head toward the garage. "Find who did this."

"You're sure?"

I flicked my head toward the garage. "Go."

I walked down the block to my Suburban, carrying the Spencers' money from the sale with me. CJ had promised to secure the rest of the outside stuff when they were done with the crime scene. I indulged in a pity party as I drove the winding, narrow roads typical of New England. Why me? It was like a black cloud hovered over me, except instead of a direct hit of lightning, I kept getting singed. I tried to concentrate on avoiding the unforgiving granite curbs, but a couple of angry tears rolled down my face. I gripped the steering wheel with one hand and swiped at the tears with the other.

I pictured the scene in the garage again. It jolted me out of self-pity mode and back to thinking about the Spencers. I replayed the horror of seeing their bodies sprawled across the floor and the realization that Mr. Spencer was dead. His son would be getting a knock on the door or phone call sometime today. The kind of call no one ever wants to get.

It was after one by the time I flung my keys, sweater, and purse on my grandmother's rocker and moved to the living room window beside it. Home. I loved this place. My second-story apartment was one of four in the old house and overlooked the town common. A white clapboard church sat at the south end of the common, and a long lawn used for community events stretched to Great Road, the main thoroughfare of Ellington. My favorite restaurant, DiNapoli's Roast Beef and Pizza, sat on the north side of Great Road waiting for me, not only with good food but good company in the form of Angelo and Rosalie DiNapoli.

I sighed because I wasn't ready for company. Instead, I went to the kitchen to make a Fluffernutter sandwich out of Marshmallow Fluff and peanut butter on white bread. They didn't appeal to everyone, but there was a reason people balked when someone suggested they should be removed from the school lunch menu. The reason being they are delicious.

I set my plate on the small kitchen table and ran a hand across CJ's leather jacket, which hung on the back of one of the two kitchen chairs. Part of me felt like he'd left it there on purpose, staking his claim or marking his territory. There wasn't any reason for him to do that anymore. I'd thought I'd made that clear to him.

Just as I took the first bite, I heard a knock on my door. I chewed fast while I headed for the door, unable to savor the gooey sweetness of the Fluff or the salty peanut butter. The whole bite felt like it was stuck on the roof of my mouth. I swallowed as I yanked open the door, hoping it was CJ with some good news. Instead, I dropped my sandwich and stared.

Chapter 3

I blinked my eyes a couple of times before I launched myself into the man's arms. At first, he didn't hug me back, but then his arms wrapped tightly around me. My eyes filled with tears as I pulled away. "Luke? What are you doing here? How did you find me? Have you talked to Mom and Dad?"

My estranged brother stood there in worn jeans and a flannel shirt. A brown leather backpack was slung across his shoulder. His tawny brown hair settled below his shoulders, and a scraggly beard added to the weary look on his face. He hadn't even been able to grow a beard the last time I'd seen him, nineteen years ago.

Luke glanced around. "Can I come in?"

I stepped back. "Of course. Are you hungry?" *Hungry?* Where the heck had that come from? I must be channeling CJ's mom's Southern girl hospitality, calling up some long unused manners required in an uncomfortable situation. If I didn't watch it I'd be making sweet tea and apologizing for my bare feet.

"Can you cook now?" he asked with a slight smile.

I gave him a look and cocked my head. "Things haven't changed that much." Adrenaline was surging through my body for the second time today. "But I make an excellent Fluffernutter sandwich. Trust me, you'll like them."

Luke followed me into the kitchen but froze when he spotted CJ's jacket. "Whose is that?"

"It's CJ's." Luke looked around again. "He's not here," I said.

Luke's shoulders sagged and he collapsed into one of the kitchen chairs. I busied myself making sandwiches, my hands unable to keep up with my thoughts. The last time I'd seen my younger brother was when he'd joined the Marines a couple of weeks after CJ and I had gotten married. He'd been so involved in his new life and I had been so busy with mine, I hadn't realized for a while that we'd drifted apart. Way apart. When I'd tried to call or write, there had never been a response. I'd finally quit trying. Luke had only called me twice in all that time. The last call had been over ten years ago. There'd been recriminations and accusations. My hurt at his disappearance from our family had come out as anger. Both calls had ended with him hanging up on me.

I glanced over my shoulder at him. His eyes were closed and his head was tipped back against the wall. But I could still see the baby brother I'd always defended, even with the long hair, broad shoulders, and lined face. Last time I'd seen him, he'd been a lanky boy. He'd done one tour with the Marines, gone home for bit, and then nothing but the two calls.

His eyes popped open and he smiled. "How many sandwiches are you going to make?"

I looked down and realized I'd made nine. I grabbed two plates and put two on one and three on the other. I handed the plate with three to Luke. I watched as he powered through the first two.

"You're right, these are good. Aren't you going to eat?" Luke asked.

I took a bite, but my hunger had disappeared. "Do you want something to drink? A beer or water? I could put on a pot of coffee." Did he even like coffee?

"Remember the last time we had a beer together?" he asked.

I smiled at the memory. "I was eighteen and you were seventeen."

"Dad was furious when he realized we'd gotten into his stash of Sierra Nevada Pale Ale."

"And even though we were both sicker than dogs the next morning, he woke us at sunrise and made us do yard work all morning." I laughed at the memory.

A *knock, knock, knock* sounded on my front door.

Luke jolted out of the chair. "Who is it?"

Why was he so jumpy? "It's probably CJ. Or Stella, my landlady. She lives right downstairs."

"I can't see anyone right now."

Even though he was looking down at me, I saw the

little kid who used to look up at me. Eyes pleading silently for me to get him out of whatever mess he was currently in. I nodded, hoping I was wrong and he had a good explanation. "There's an attic space off the living room."

"The small door I noticed?"

Observant. One side of the living room had a slanted ceiling that met a four-foot-high section of wall. Behind the wall was the storage space. "Yes, go in there. I'll close the door behind you." Luke snatched his plate and the other sandwich, taking them with him.

There was a *bam, bam, bam* on the door that shook it. I yelled, "Just a minute." I hoped it was Stella and not CJ. I latched Luke into the attic.

"Are you okay?" I heard CJ shout. The doorknob rattled.

I hurried to the door and flung it open. "Yes. Why ask?"

CJ pointed to the sandwich I'd dropped out in the hall. I picked it up. "*Yeesh.* I wondered what happened to it. I must have dropped it when I checked to see if the mail had come." I hated lying to CJ about Luke, although it was more omission than lie.

"What took you so long to answer?" he asked.

"I didn't want to answer the door in my undies."

"I wouldn't have minded." He grinned.

"What if it hadn't been you?" I turned my back to him and hustled inside to the kitchen, wanting to preempt any questions about the stack of Fluffer-nutters. "I made some Fluffernutters in case you stopped by." Lies kept popping out. Covering for Luke came back to me as easily as getting back on a bike. It's what we'd done for each other from the time we could talk, on the playground, in the classroom, and at home. Especially at home.

CJ backed me up against the counter and gave me a long, breathtaking kiss.

"Are you all right?" he asked again.

"W-why wouldn't I be?"

He ran a hand through his hair, and the lines around his mouth deepened. "Someone was murdered at your garage sale this morning."

Good heavens. Luke's appearance had driven everything else out of my head. "It's stress." At least that wasn't a lie. "I'm still in a bit of shock." The murder hadn't been the only shock of the day. "So it's definitely a murder?"

"Because it's an unattended death, it's treated as if it were a homicide."

"Have you found who did it?" I didn't really expect they would have at this point, but needed to get the focus off me.

CJ shook his head. "We don't have much to go on. Your sighting of a man and one report of someone speeding off in a light-colored sedan at the end of one of the trails." He snagged one of the Fluffernutters off the counter. After eating it in five bites, he poured himself a glass of water and gulped it down. "We're following up on the license plates Lindsay took pictures of." He looked down at me with his cop look. I hoped anything he saw in my face could be taken as worry from the events of the day. CJ pulled me back into his arms for another sizzling kiss. It felt really awkward knowing my brother was hidden mere feet away from us. "Maybe we have time for—"

"No. You have to find out what happened to the Spencers. Who did this." It came out louder and more vehemently than I'd planned. I hope he didn't hear the note of panic in my voice. If kissing him felt awkward, anything else would feel like I was back in my parents' house and about to get caught doing something I shouldn't have been doing. I kept myself from shuddering at that.

CJ sighed. "You're right. I'll try to make it back later tonight. Please take care of yourself." He kissed me again before he left.

I leaned back against the door for a minute, my heart pounding madly. I hurried across the living room to the window and watched CJ climb into his official police SUV. He waved as he took off. I pulled the curtains shut and let Luke out of the attic.

"Now you have to tell me what's going on." I said it in the "I mean business voice" I'd used on him when he was little. Strange how things came back even after years apart. Luke nodded and sprawled across the couch, a yard sale find that my mom had made white slipcovers for. I pulled the rocking chair closer to him, sat, and leaned forward to hear him out.

"I'm here investigating a story."

I took that in. "You're a reporter?" Luke nodded. "What kind of story brought you to Ellington?"

Ellington was just under thirteen thousand residents, although it abutted Bedford, Concord, and Fitch Air Force Base. As part of the greater metropolitan Boston area, it seemed much larger.

Luke narrowed his eyes. I knew that expression. It was the one that said, "How much do I have to tell her to keep me out of the most trouble?"

"Spill it." How easily I dropped back into the role of older sister.

"I can't give you all the details."

"Can't or won't?" This had been one of Luke's classic moves as a kid.

"Can't. Seriously. I'm not ten anymore. I'm an adult and my job is important. Don't pigeonhole me in the past."

It was my turn to narrow my eyes. When we were kids, he would always look away when he was lying, but he didn't now. I noticed the deepening lines around his blue-gray eyes, the shadows under them. His hair had strands of grey running through the brown.

"What brought you here?" I asked again.

"I'm doing a story and it led me to this area. That's all I can say."

There were lots of tech companies in the area, and universities. There were lots of active-duty military and veterans living here. Fishing industry, tourism, local politics—without more to go on, I'd never figure it out. "Did Mom tell you I lived here?"

"No. I haven't talked to them." He looked down at his clasped hands. "Not in a long time. I Googled you once in a while. Your divorce popped up and the website for your garage sale business. Plus there were articles about CJ and his troubles. They mentioned you too."

"I guess running from your past is almost impossible these days." I hadn't done a computer search on myself for a while. I'd never seen the articles Luke mentioned. "Can I tell Mom and Dad you're here?" I'd never understood the rift between Luke and the rest of us. We'd all always gotten along. He'd idolized CJ. Luke had enlisted in part because of him, but after his enlistment, he'd disappeared from our lives. And he was very good at covering his tracks because I'd tried to find Luke more than once.

"Please don't tell them, for now anyway."

"Why? Are you working undercover or something?"

"Yes. I am." He paused. "It's an investigative piece. I don't want anyone to get wind of it. That's why I'm asking—no, begging you—not to tell anyone I'm in town."

I stood and roamed the living room. A worn Oriental rug topped the wide plank floor I'd painted white when I first moved in. There wasn't a lot of furniture, just the couch, the rocker, an end table, and a trunk I used as a coffee table. There was room for more, but I hadn't found the perfect thing.

Sadly, nothing in life was perfect. I wanted to know what had happened, what had made Luke leave our family. Only knowing what had driven him away would ease the empty spot in my heart. This might be my sole chance to find out. If I honored his request for privacy, maybe I would finally get some answers. Oh, how I hoped I would. I turned back to Luke. "I won't tell for as long as I can. And I'll let you know if I can't keep it a secret. It's the best I can do." I sat back in the rocker, stroking the smooth broad oak arms.

"That's fair. Thank you." His tone didn't match his words. He sounded disappointed, and I had always hated disappointing Luke.

"Where are you going to stay?" I asked.

He shrugged. "I don't know. Not here with CJ coming around."

"The apartment next door is empty. The Callahans, who live below it, aren't back from Florida yet, but they will be any day." I considered my options. "You can at least stay next door tonight. The last person left a bit of furniture. I think there's a bed." I'd make it up to Stella later by cleaning the place.

"I'm used to roughing it. A floor and my backpack as a pillow are usually it. If I'm lucky. Do you mind if I shower?"

"No, go ahead." I grabbed a fluffy, white towel from the hall linen closet and put it on the pedestal sink. The bathroom was small, but the large clawfoot tub had sold me on the place when I'd first looked at it. I came back out. "It's all yours."

* * *

As soon as I heard the shower go on, I went over to where Luke had left his backpack on the couch. It was covered with peace signs and patches from different cities—Paris, London, Rome, and many more. I unzipped the first section. Going through his things felt wrong, but what did I really know about Luke? He'd shown up out of the blue and acted cagey. He hadn't sold me with his reporter story. I wanted to make sure there wasn't anything illegal in there. I unpacked a pair of jeans, socks, underwear, a plaid flannel shirt, a denim jacket, notebooks, and some stubby pencils. He still chewed his pencils.

I found a phone at the bottom. Not a fancy one—it looked like a burner phone. I opened it, but didn't find any incoming or outgoing calls listed. Okay, I could see a reporter having a burner phone to prevent sources from obtaining his personal number. Maybe this confirmed his story.

I stuffed everything back the way I'd found it, then rooted around in another pocket. Tissues, wallet, and an iPhone. The phone was password protected. Darn, no snooping through it. I reached for the wallet but heard the water shut off. I repacked the backpack, put it against the couch cushion where he'd left it, and went into the kitchen to make coffee. Full-on caffeine was required even though it was after three. Luke might not need any, but I sure did.

Chapter 4

Sunday morning, I woke up a twitchy mess. After Luke's shower yesterday, he'd been engrossed in his phone and then left to go to sleep next door. He hadn't told me anything of substance. Then I'd spent too much of the night awake listening for CJ, for Luke, or for Stella to discover Luke. Around midnight, CJ had sent a text saying he wouldn't be over, which was a relief and a disappointment all wrapped in a ball of confusion. I wanted to be held but wouldn't have been able to keep the secret of Luke from CJ. Once I knew CJ wasn't coming over, my worries turned to Mr. Spencer and Mrs. Spencer. Who would hurt them? And then my fear turned back to Luke. Why show up now? My mind whirled like a carousel until I finally fell asleep after four.

It was almost eight when I heard footsteps trotting up the stairs. I flung open my door. "Stella. What are you doing up this early?" Normally, she wasn't one to show her face before nine. Beyond being owner and landlady, she taught voice classes at Berklee College of Music in Boston and was starting to rebuild her career as an opera singer. She often stayed up late practicing.

She flicked her head to the apartment I'd stashed Luke in. *Oh no.* Had she heard something?

"I'm showing the apartment today. I decided it was time for a new tenant. I wanted to make sure it's clean enough before I show it at ten."

Seriously? Today of all days. With one exception the place had been empty for over a year. "It must be clean enough as it is," I said, noting the high, cheery note my voice had taken on. "Come over for coffee so we can chat. The apartment will be fine." My voice boomed out of me—I hoped Luke would hear me and do something. What, I wasn't sure, because we were two stories up.

Stella tilted her head and studied me with her deep green eyes. They were stunning against her olive, Mediterranean skin and dark hair. I always felt a bit paler when I was with her, like my blond hair was suddenly washed out and my blue eyes almost clear. Nothing exotic in me, just good English stock. I smiled at her, knowing her BS meter was on high.

"Sorry. I'm a mess. Did you hear what happened at the garage sale I was running yesterday? I barely slept."

"Of course I heard. This is Ellington, after all. I should have come and checked on you." Stella blushed, a little something she rarely did.

"Was Awesome over?"

"Yes, but he shouldn't preclude me from checking on a friend."

"So, coffee?"

"Right after I check on the apartment."

There was nothing else I could do. I followed her in, trying to think up an explanation of why Luke was there. But Luke wasn't there. It was like he'd vanished into thin air. I glanced over at the door to the attic crawl space. This apartment was almost a copy of mine. He must be in the crawl space. Or had he taken off again without telling me?

Stella sniffed the air. Could she smell him? I didn't remember him wearing aftershave. Any scent would be from my soap. My apple soap. Could she really smell it? I sniffed too but only smelled dust.

"I'll open a couple of windows to air the place out a bit. Otherwise it looks fine," Stella said.

I nodded like a bobblehead figurine on speed. "Want that coffee while it airs out?"

"Sure."

Thirty minutes later, I shut the door behind Stella and waited. I heard her water go on and sprinted back over to the other apartment, assuming she was taking a shower. I went in and hissed, "Luke, are you still here?" If he wasn't, I'd be furious and sad, but the little door to the attic opened and Luke crawled out. Tension washed out faster than a tsunami. Tears filled my eyes.

"What's wrong, Sarah?" He brushed some dust off his worn jeans as he asked.

"Nothing. I'm just happy you're here."

"You thought I left again without telling you."

"Maybe."

Luke glanced down at his boots. The heels were worn to the point they needed to be replaced. "Look, you promised not to tell anyone I was here unless you told me first. I promise I won't leave without telling you. Okay?"

I swiped at the tears. "Okay." My voice cracked. "We've got to leave. Someone's coming to look at it."

"How about your place?"

"No. CJ could come over any time." I pursed my lips but didn't like my solution. "I'll let you into the Callahans' apartment. They won't be home for several more days." I'd gotten that bit of information out of Stella over coffee. "But tomorrow we have to figure something else out."

"Couldn't you tell CJ you're sick and not to come over?"

"No. Because CJ would tell someone, who'd tell someone else, then someone on base would find out and I'd have a constant stream of people bringing me soup, flowers, and cards." It made me smile. It was why I loved living here, one of the reasons I hadn't moved back home to Pacific Grove, California, after CJ and I divorced.

"What happened to the unfriendly New Englanders stereotype you always hear about?"

"People here are like lobsters. They can be tough shells to crack, but once you do . . ." I smiled again, remembering the first few times I'd gone into DiNapoli's. Rosalie's smile had been warm, but Angelo hadn't had the time of day for me as he'd cooked and watched over the restaurant. It had taken a while to win them over, but they were family now.

Luke followed me downstairs. I felt around for the key on top of their door.

"How'd you know it was there?" Luke asked as I unlocked the door and shoved him into the apartment.

"I water their plants for them if Stella's out of town. You're going to have to be really quiet so Stella doesn't hear you. No lights. Stay away from the windows."

"I get it." Luke pulled me into a hug. "Thanks. I'll be out of your hair in a day or two."

"I don't want you out of my hair. I want to show you off. My brother, the investigative reporter." I opened the door a crack and peeked out. "I'll bring you some food later." I shut the door and hurried back upstairs before he could answer.

At ten, I left my apartment again to go buy some groceries. I was hoping to time my departure so I'd run into whoever was planning to look at the apartment next door. It would be nice to have a quiet neighbor that could be a friend. As I trotted down the stairs, two guys came in from the street. One had long, pale blond dreads and heavy-lidded blue eyes. Bob Marley smiled at me from the front of his T-shirt. The other guy was almost his twin minus the dreads, and they both looked completely stoned. I rapped on Stella's door and yelled, "I think the guys interested in the apartment are here." I couldn't help but smirk when she came out.

Stella walked out, took one whiff of them, and said, "Sorry. It's been rented."

"Dude," the guy with the dreads said. His friend jerked his head toward the door, and they both shuffled back out, leaving a waft of pot-scented air behind them.

"I don't think that's legal," I said to Stella. "But thank you."

"Quick, give me a buck."

I dug around in my purse and handed her the dollar. "Why?"

"You just rented it for the day. Not that they look like the type to sue me."

"But you never know who has a parent who's a lawyer."

Stella nodded.

"I'm heading out to the grocery store. I'll buy the Callahans some milk and bread since they're coming home soon."

"Flossie wrote and said they'd be home the day after tomorrow. Would you mind watering their plants and maybe opening a window to let the place air out a bit?"

"I'd be happy to." I felt myself relax a little. Luke could stay there overnight before he'd have to move. And paying the dollar rent made me feel a little less guilty about stashing him in the empty apartment in the first place.

* * *

I nudged the Callahans' door open with my hip since my arms were full of groceries. Stella's car was gone, which meant Luke and I were the only ones in the building. As soon as I closed the door and called out, Luke popped out of the bathroom and helped me unpack. Some of the food was for him, some for the Callahans, and some for me. We stood in the kitchen and shared the three lobster rolls I'd bought at the Stop & Shop for our lunch. They weren't as good as the ones from West Concord Seafoods, but they'd do for now. It felt awkward standing here, but I didn't want to risk us being seen by going up to my apartment and back.

I looked up at him. The last time I'd seen him, he'd only been a bit taller than my five-six. Now, he topped me by several inches. I had a ton of questions I wanted to ask him. Why had he disappeared from our lives after he left the Marines? Where had he been? What was with the burner phone in his backpack? But I was afraid to. Afraid, if I pried, he'd take off and I'd be heartbroken all over again. With all I'd been through the past year, I didn't know if I could take it. For now, I'd savor these moments together.

"What?" Luke asked, catching me studying him.

My voice caught and my eyes filled with tears for the second time today. "I've missed you."

Luke pulled me to him in a brief hug. "I missed you too."

We finished eating and I stuck the trash into a bag to take back to my place. Luke leaned his elbows back against the counter. "You were involved in a murder yesterday?"

"Sort of. How did you know?"

Luke held up his phone. "I read about it online. Why didn't you tell me?"

"I guess seeing you drove it out of my head."

Luke scratched his bearded chin. "I feel terrible. Do you want to talk about it?"

Luke and I were only ten months apart, and while I had often lorded my elder status over him, we'd been closer than lots of siblings until he'd left for the Marines. I nodded. "I do want to talk about it." My response surprised me, but I started talking. Luke listened attentively, asking questions when I faltered, and patting my arm when I choked up. My spirits lifted after spilling not only the details but my reactions to all of it. Sharing things with Luke felt like home in a way nothing else did in my life.

"It sucks," I said when I was all talked out.

"Death is never pretty."

It made me wonder what Luke had seen when he was in the Marines, why he'd quit instead of staying in. I wanted to ask but held back a flood of questions. For now, I'd just enjoy having him around.

Luke kissed me on top of the head. "I have to work tomorrow. What's a good time to leave?"

"If CJ spends the night, he usually leaves to go to the gym around five. Stella rarely pokes her head out the door before eight-thirty or nine. The only wild card is Awesome."

"Who's Awesome?"

"Stella's boyfriend, Nathan Bossum. He's a cop too. I have no idea what schedule he's on, and he's over at Stella's a lot these days."

Luke pursed his lips like he always did when he was thinking something over.

"I'm going to be busy most of the day," I said. "I have to meet with a new client this afternoon and then go on base to help at the thrift shop this evening."

"I'll work from here today, and I'll be very careful when I leave in the morning."

I nodded and then headed back to my apartment.

I made a quick marinara sauce and pasta for dinner tonight, stuck it in the refrigerator, and cleaned the kitchen. On my way out to see my client, I dropped some off to Luke. The rest of the day, I rushed from one place to the next until I settled on the couch around 9:30 PM. It had been a long day, especially after tossing and turning the night before.

The work at the thrift shop was endless lately. My friend Laura Nicklas and I had been spending a lot of evenings there the past few weeks as we prepped for PCS—permanent change of station—season. Or, as civilians called it, moving. The busiest moving time for military members was during June and July. It meant in May people donated things they didn't want to move to the thrift shop. It was great for the shop but created a lot of extra work for the volunteers who ran it. I loved keeping up with my friends on base, and volunteering at the thrift shop was one way I could do it now that I didn't have any official status there. With that work done for the evening, I had some research to tackle.

I grabbed my computer and Googled Luke Winston. I couldn't wait to see what kind of articles he'd written in the past. I frowned at my computer because I didn't find anything. I tried again. Unfortunately, both Luke and Winston were very common names. I ended up scrolling through a lot of pages of Luke Winstons. Some were too old, others too young—those were the easy ones. I looked at profiles hoping I'd find something. But my Luke didn't have a footprint when it came to the Web. No Facebook, Twitter, or LinkedIn account. No articles.

I checked the less well-known sites, like the PopIt photo-sharing app, but wasn't surprised when he didn't have an account there. I drummed my fingers on the edge of my laptop trying to decide if I should pay one of those places that said they could find anyone. But without more than his name, age, and birthdate, they probably wouldn't have much more luck than I did. Luke had hidden himself not only from my family but from everyone else too. I wondered why. I'd ask him tomorrow.

I decided to research the Spencers too. There were a couple of articles about Mr. Spencer's death and Mrs. Spencer being at the hospital. But nothing else showed up. Spencer was almost as common a name as Winston. I did find a brief mention that Mrs. Spencer was part of the local garden club.

CJ slumped in just as I gave up my search.

"I cooked," I said, leading CJ to the kitchen.

"I'm not very hungry. Do you have a Sam's?"

The Sam he was referring to was a Samuel Adams beer, brewed locally in Boston. I put a hand on my hip. "I made pasta and it's *delizioso.*" I put my fingers to my lips and kissed them. CJ might be afraid to eat something I'd fixed because he'd suffered through enough of my meals over the years. "Just pasta with marinara sauce. What could go wrong?"

CJ smiled and I threw a dish towel at him because I knew he was remembering his first birthday after we were married. I'd wanted to throw a big party and do all of the cooking myself. I'd known nothing about cooking for a crowd and little about cooking at all. The pasta had bonded faster than a group of sorority sisters and had come out as a glutinous mass. The sauce had tasted like burnt garlic water, the salad had been soggy, and the bread extra crispy. Thankfully I'd had the good sense to order a cake so at least something was edible.

"Okay, something could go wrong, but it didn't." In the nick of time, I bit back a comment that Luke had loved it.

I grabbed a Sam Adams Summer Ale, my very favorite of the Sam Adams beers, out of the fridge and opened it for CJ. He found a glass I'd bought at the brewery and poured the beer in.

He took a long drink. "Okay, I'll risk your cooking."

I cocked my head.

"Please?" CJ asked. "I was teasing."

After CJ finished a second plate, he wrapped his arms around my waist as I washed the dishes. "What brand of sauce was it? We should stock up." He nuzzled my neck with his lips.

"I made it from scratch." As soon as I said it, I regretted it.

He pulled back. "Wow. I'm even more impressed. Where'd you get the recipe?"

Damn. I didn't want to tell him Seth had taught me to make it last February. He was so sensitive at any mention of Seth. It was understandable. I didn't want to hear about whom he'd dated when we were apart.

"Carol." I was glad I wasn't facing him. Carol was a great cook and friend. I'd met her soon after I'd met CJ, when she and her husband Brad, along with CJ, were all stationed in Monterey. We'd been overjoyed when they had been stationed at Fitch. Then all of us had moved to Ellington because we loved it here. She'd cover for me if the subject ever came up.

We settled on my couch after I grabbed two more beers. Shoulder to shoulder, hip to hip, and thigh to thigh. But I could feel the tension in CJ's body. I knew his mind must be on the Spencers. We'd talked about him being more present when we were together. As a military spouse, I was used to coming second. The Air Force and its demands always came first. But I was tired of living that way.

I flipped on the Red Sox game and took a drink of my Sam Adams. Spring filled the air with hope in Red Sox nation. The Red Sox were playing well, and the promise of making the playoffs kept everyone optimistic. I glanced at CJ. He stared at the TV, but it looked like his mind wasn't on the game. He was frowning and the Red Sox had just scored. Apparently, cops' families came after the job too.

"How's Mrs. Spencer doing?" I asked during the first commercial.

"No change. I wish she could tell us what happened." His leg started jiggling next to mine.

"It must be frustrating."

CJ shrugged instead of answering and took a pull of his beer.

"Is there a cause of death?" I asked.

"No. It will be a while before we find anything out."

"I was thinking about the lobster buoy and the scratches on Mr. Spencer's arms. It looked like there was some kind of fight. Was the buoy the murder weapon?"

CJ leaned forward to watch the next play. Base run.

"Any idea who did this to the Spencers?"

"Nothing I can share."

I'd gone from feeling ignored to trying to interrogate CJ. "Do you think it was a robbery gone wrong? All that money was on the floor." I shuddered as I pictured the Spencers sprawled across the floor of their garage.

CJ slung an arm over my shoulders and pulled me closer. I was halfway on his lap. "Let's not talk shop." He took the beer out of my hand and kissed me.

Later, when I woke up next to CJ, the curtains in my bedroom puffed out with cool night air. I snuggled closer to him. CJ used to talk cases out with me when he was commander of the security squadron at Fitch. Unless they were classified. I'd even solved a case for him once. It was a he-said/she-said domestic violence dispute. According to everyone, the young officer had come back from Afghanistan a different man. What they didn't know was he'd found out his wife had had an affair. She had gone berserk when he'd asked for a divorce and beat the crap out of him.

I'd found all that out by working the wives' network. I'd tracked down their former neighbor, who'd witnessed the wife's outburst. She'd been shocked to hear the accusations against him. Without my digging, the truth might have never come out. He would have, at the very least, been kicked out with a dishonorable discharge, but could have served time. Why wouldn't CJ talk this case over with me?

A scream bolted me out of a deep sleep Monday morning. It was still dark out but not middle-of-the-night dark, more almost dawn. I glanced toward CJ's side of the bed, but he was gone. I heard another scream, followed by a shout. It sounded like it had come from right below me. *Oh no, the Callahans' apartment.* My heart pounded as I thrust my arms into the sleeves of my robe. I tied it as I ran down the stairs. Stella almost crashed into me as she flew out her door.

Chapter 5

I looked in horror as I saw Mr. and Mrs. Callahan standing in the hall. They'd arrived hours earlier than I'd expected. Their apartment door was open, as was the front door of the building. I went over and flicked on the entryway light. Everyone blinked a couple of times. I shut the front door to keep the cool air out.

"What happened?" Stella asked Burt and Flossie.

"Someone or something was in our apartment. Looked like a yeti," Flossie said.

"Hunchback," Burt corrected. "A giant. Charged out when Flossie opened the door."

Oh no, oh no, oh no. I knew it was Luke. If his backpack had been over his shoulder, he might have looked like a hunchback in the dark. I don't know where the hell the yeti reference had come from— Luke wasn't that tall or hairy. What should I do now? I'd promised him I wouldn't tell anyone about him being here without letting him know first.

"Is Awesome here?" I asked Stella. I figured he

wasn't or he'd be out here with us, or worse, chasing Luke down the street and catching him.

"No. CJ?" Stella asked.

"No." I vaguely remembered him kissing me good-bye and leaving for the gym on Fitch. Stella's black and white cat, Tux, meowed. He'd wandered out in the entryway with us. Tux came over to me, rubbing against my leg and meowing. Stella scooped him up, put him back in her apartment, and closed the door. It gave me a couple of seconds to think.

"Okay, let's all take a deep breath," I said. "I'll go in and check the apartment, but it sounds like whoever was in there is gone. And they couldn't have been there for long because I watered your plants and aired the place out for you yesterday. No hunchback then." My hands trembled. I shoved them in the pockets of my robe.

I overruled the chorus of nos. "CJ taught me how to do this. I'll leave the door open. If anything happens, you can call the police."

"You'd better call anyway, Burt," Flossie said.

There was no way to stop them from calling without sounding crazy. Burt talked into his cell phone while I walked through the apartment, knowing it was safe. I wiped down a few surfaces with the hem of my robe and made sure Luke hadn't left anything behind. As much as I wanted to clean the front doorknobs, I couldn't without getting caught and I hoped Luke hadn't ever touched them. A couple of minutes later, I returned to the hallway. "It's fine. No one's in there."

We all trooped into the apartment. Burt and Flossie collapsed on the couch. They were tanned, wrinkled, slender, and short. Almost bookends with their gray hair, khaki shorts, and Hawaiian-print shirts.

"What are you doing back?" I couldn't help asking. They weren't supposed to be home.

Flossie jerked her head toward Burt. "Mr. Big Shot here bragged about how we could make it home in two days. It was a stupid idea."

"Could have if it weren't for that huge traffic jam in New York City."

"I told you not to go through it. You should have listened to me when I said to stay in New Jersey and go over the Tappan Zee Bridge," Flossie said.

"The governor in New Jersey is the problem. He caused the traffic." Burt crossed his arms over his chest.

"Oh, that's a load." Flossie shook her head. "I caught him nodding off in Connecticut, and I insisted we stop. He woke me hours ago. Technically, we made it in two days." She made air quotes when she said technically.

Burt looked at us. "Wanted to get home before rush hour started."

"I suppose the traffic in Boston is the New Jersey governor's fault too," Flossie said.

"Oh, don't be ridiculous, Flossie."

"Should you check to see if anything was taken?" Stella asked.

The Callahans stood and moved with swift efficiency around the apartment.

"No, everything's as it should be," Burt said.

"That's not true," Flossie said.

I braced myself for what would come next.

"There's fresh milk and some other groceries in the refrigerator," she said. It came out *refrigeratah* with her Boston accent.

"I brought those over yesterday. I hate having to rush out to the store right after a trip," I said.

"It was very thoughtful of you, dear," Burt said.

If he knew the truth, Burt would be calling me something other than thoughtful.

Thankfully, Awesome walked in the door. "Everyone okay?"

We all nodded.

"Except for the fact a yeti was in here when we got home," Flossie said.

Burt shook his head. "It was a hunchback."

Awesome looked over at Stella and me, eyebrows up, but we just shrugged.

"Have either of you seen anyone strange hanging around?" Awesome asked us.

"Not me," Stella said.

Here was my chance. "Two guys came to look at the vacant apartment yesterday. Maybe they were casing the place." If there was such a thing as karma, I was piling up trouble to rain down on my head at some point in the future. I'd thrown those poor guys under the bus for no good reason.

"Do you have their names?" Awesome asked Stella.

"Not really. I think the one who called said his name was Drake."

"They called each other 'dude' while they were here." Sarah Winston, now playing the role of Miss Helpful. I was starting to hate myself. "But neither of them was tall enough to be a yeti and they weren't hunchbacks." Trying to balance the scales of karma by deflecting suspicion from them, I almost hung my head in shame.

"Was anything taken?" Awesome asked.

"Nothing," Flossie said. Awesome asked us a few more questions, which didn't provide him any more answers. After promising to drive around the neighborhood looking for a hunchback or yeti, he hugged Stella and left.

"Do you want me to have the locks changed?" Stella asked the Callahans. "I'll pay for them."

"It's a good idea," Flossie said just as Burt said, "It's not necessary." They glared at each other.

"Let me know," Stella said. We waved and walked out into the hall, closing their door behind us.

"Wow. They're a trip," I said. They hadn't been around much since I'd moved in. They spent most of their time in Florida and a lot of time in Vermont with their daughter.

"They are, but since they're hardly ever here, it's not that bad." Stella shook her head. "Half the time, we have two cops in the building. Figures this happens when they aren't around."

Thank heavens it had happened when they weren't around. I wondered where Luke had gone. He'd told me he had to work today, but I had no idea where. I started up the stairs. "See you later, Stella."

"Are you okay?" she asked.

"It's been a rough couple of days."

"It has," Stella said. I didn't hear her go back into her apartment until after I got to the landing. Intuitive friends were a pain.

By ten, I'd showered, dressed, and formulated a plan. I needed help and decided Mike "The Big Cheese" Titone was just the man for the job. I wouldn't exactly call him a friend, but he'd helped me out of a jam in February. Mike had a reputation that often went with being an Italian in the North End of Boston. I wondered about the crazy things I'd read on the Internet about him. I mean, really, who would put a piece of cheese on someone's doorstep as a threat? It wasn't exactly a horse head in a bed. Or maybe I ignored those things when I needed him. I hoped Mike would stash Luke someplace for a few days. Although, the last time he'd helped, it had come with a heavy price—a promise that I'd never tell anyone he'd helped me. I couldn't tell CJ, especially not CJ. But trying to hide Luke in Ellington was too stressful.

I'd decided going in person would be better than calling, because I thought it would be harder for him to say no to me. The drive to the Alewife T station in Cambridge took almost a half an hour. T was short for trolley, which was what they called the Boston subway system. I settled onto a hard plastic seat and watched the rough tunnel walls rush by on the oldest subway system in the

U.S. The ride to the Government Center took twenty-five minutes with one stop to switch lines.

After emerging from the tunnel, I stopped for a quick look around. The Government Center was one of the ugliest buildings in the city. A cement monster made uglier by the contrast of sitting across the street from one of the most beautiful buildings, Faneuil Hall, which had been built in the late 1700s. Boston's history fascinated me. The golden grasshopper weathervane on top of Faneuil Hall sparkled in the sun as I trotted down the steps and headed toward the North End. The sky behind the white cupola on top of Faneuil Hall was a bright New England blue.

I turned left to head to the North End—the old Italian section of town. I passed by the Union Oyster House and the six glass towers of the Holocaust Memorial. Thinking about all the great Italian restaurants made my mouth water. But there was no time to go today.

After double-checking the directions on my phone, I walked partway down Hanover Street, took a left on a side street and a right on another until I found Mike's shop, Il Formaggio. It was in a line of stores set in brick buildings with five or six floors of what looked like apartments above them. Across the street, an elderly woman dressed in black sat by a window, watching people pass by. I pushed open the old wooden door. I didn't know what I'd been expecting, but it wasn't this bright, modern space filled with a vast selection of cheese, olives, and crackers.

A girl with a pierced eyebrow and nose stood behind the counter. "Can I help you?" she asked. Her bright smile countered the spiky-haired tough look she had going on.

I'd been expecting an Italian grandmother like the woman across the street or a wise guy. "I need to talk to Mike." I looked behind the girl, at a scarred door marked EMPLOYEES ONLY. I pictured a dark, smoky room where Mike and his associates played poker. But the door swung open as a well-built man hefted out a tray of cheese. Instead of the room I'd pictured, I glimpsed a clean pantry with stainless-steel shelves holding products. The girl said something to the man in what sounded like Italian. He looked at me, shrugged, and answered.

"He's not here," the girl said.

"Oh." My face must have expressed disappointment that went way beyond the "oh" because the girl studied me.

"What is it you need?" she asked.

The man took care placing the cheeses from the tray into the cases. He artfully arranged things, which surprised me. Those giant hands were very gentle with the cheese.

"It's a private matter. My name's Sarah Winston." I didn't notice any sort of recognition in her eyes when she heard my name. The man kept putting the cheese from the tray into cases. The two of them had another conversation in Italian.

"I'll give him a call and see if he can come over," the girl said.

"Thank you. Or I could go to wherever he is."

This time, the girl exchanged a look with the man who'd been refreshing the displays. He shook his head as he swung through the door to the back room.

"Have a seat," she said. She grabbed the handset of an old black phone that was attached to the wall with a long, curly cord. She turned her back to me and spoke in Italian again.

I should learn another language. I sat at a tall round table by a huge plate-glass window while she made the call. After she hung up, she brought over a plate of cheese, olives, and house-made crackers. She also set a glass of lemonade down in front of me. "This is on Mike. He'll be over in a few."

Mike came in as I popped the last olive in my mouth. He was tall and slender, an avid runner. I jumped up, but he motioned for me to sit back down. He perched on the edge of a stool like he didn't plan to stay long. His deep blue eyes looked serious.

"You okay?" he asked. "I was kinda surprised when I got the call saying you were here."

"I need a favor."

Mike leaned away from me. I was no expert in body language, but I surmised he wasn't happy with me.

"You sure you want to ask me for another favor?"

The price of his last favor weighed on my soul, but more than anything, I wanted to help Luke. "I wondered if my . . ." I almost blurted out *brother*, but

I couldn't do that. "If my friend could stay with you or someone for a few days."

"No."

"No?" I hadn't been expecting Mike to say no. I'd assumed he'd at least ask me a few questions. Or maybe I'd thought he would do whatever I asked since he'd helped me in February. "Why?"

"First, you're lying about something. I'm not sure what. And I don't want to know."

I obviously needed to work on my poker face.

"Second, someone in Ellington will help you. And that will be better for you." I started shaking my head. Mike put a hand on my arm. "Look, I know I told you to call me if you needed help with something, but not this time. Just because I did you a favor once doesn't mean I'm the favor bank and you can withdraw one whenever you need to." Mike stood. "You might want to remember that deposits come at a high cost. Wait here."

He went in the back room. Maybe he was going to find someone else to help me. But he came out with a large, linen tote bag. BRIE GOOD was printed on the front. He hefted it onto the table. The back side was printed with HAVE A GOUDA DAY.

"Cheese humor," Mike said. "So I heard there was another murder in Ellington."

That surprised me. "It has nothing to do with why I'm here."

"I didn't say it did. But it happened at a garage sale you were running."

I supposed it was all over the news, another

thing I hadn't been paying attention to since Luke showed up.

"I'm just sayin' it must have been rough on you. I'm sorry." He gave me a nod and strode out of the store.

I wondered if the store was bugged and there'd be a phone or a note or something else in the bag that would help me out. I opened the bag and rooted through it. Lots of cheese, a bottle of Titone olive oil, olives, a bottle of wine, and more of the house-made crackers—nothing that would help me help Luke. I grabbed it by the handles, sighing.

"It's our premium cheese gift bag," the girl behind the counter said helpfully.

"Great. Thanks."

As I lugged the bag from Il Formaggio back down Hanover Street, the sign for Mike's Pastry (no relation to Mike Titone and his cheese shop) drew me like a beam to the mother ship. I wasn't down here very often so I might as well buy some cannolis. People had strong opinions about the best place to buy a cannoli in the North End. For that matter, people in Massachusetts had strong opinions about everything. You either liked Dunkin' Donuts or you despised them. You had your favorite pizza place and would argue relentlessly why it was the best. You liked the Red Sox or—wait, no, everyone liked the Red Sox. But cannolis were a whole different thing.

Mike's Pastry was the first place I'd ever had a cannoli. I'd led a sheltered life when it came to Italian pastries. And no one ever forgets their first cannoli. Others argued it was a tourist trap and that Modern Bakery up the street had fresher cannolis. Then there were the smaller bakeries off Hanover, which some claimed were where the people who lived in the North End went. But I'd seen plenty of Italian mamas standing in line—well, pushing their way past the line—at Mike's.

I went in. The lines were short, the cases were full, and the selection was dazzling. Cakes, cookies, pastries, so many different kinds of cannoli—my eyes feasted on it all. I kept looking around as I waited my turn, expecting Mike or one of his guys to show up. Part of me still didn't believe he wasn't going to help me. I wanted to give him ample time to think this through and turn his no into a yes. But by the time it was my turn to order, no one had approached me. I picked out a selection of cannolis, added a lobster tail, a flaky pastry shaped kind of like an actual lobster's tail and filled with a sweet, delicious ricotta-based cream. I left the store with a cannoli in my mouth and disappointment in my soul. Mike was nowhere to be seen.

Chapter 6

An hour and a half later, I stood next to a very tan Tim Spencer at the end of his mother's hospital bed. He'd flown up from Florida as soon as he heard the news of the attack.

"There's still no change." Tim's shoulders slumped. A thick, red beard covered his jaw and mouth, making it difficult to spot a resemblance between him and his parents.

"It's only been two days," I said.

"They think she had a stroke."

"Oh no." Mrs. Spencer looked so much smaller in the hospital bed without her big, blustery personality on display.

"Her doctor told me the prognosis is good." He patted his mom's foot through the thin hospital blanket.

"Is there anything I can do?" I asked.

"I'd like to ask you some questions, but not in front of Mom."

I nodded and followed Tim out of the room to the patient lounge. Several other families sat in groups, but we found an unoccupied corner. They'd tried to make the lounge cheery with bright-colored abstract paintings on the walls and comfortable chairs to sit in. It didn't ease the tension in Tim's face though.

"Do you have any idea who did this to my family?" He looked at me with red-rimmed deep brown eyes, the irises almost indistinguishable from his pupils. They had dark circles underneath them, which contrasted with his light red hair. Light and dark seemed to be what my life was all about these past few months.

"Why do you think I'd know?"

He jiggled a knee. "You've spent a lot of time with my parents the past couple of weeks."

I stared at him, trying to figure out if there was a way I could help. If I had any information tucked away in my brain somewhere. I didn't remember any neighbors or friends stopping over. The phone had rarely rung, and when it had, I'd heard Mrs. Spencer grumbling about telemarketers. Things had been quiet during my time there.

"My mom emails me every day. The last two weeks' worth of emails were full of you being there and trying to toss or 'give away' her things."

I relaxed a little. "Your mom was very attached to her whipped topping containers even after I told her we could sell them at the garage sale."

"People buy used containers?"

"Oh, the stories I could tell you about what people buy and sell."

Tim smiled for a moment. "Did you notice any change in my parents' behavior?"

"It's hard for me to judge. I didn't know them before they hired me."

Tim looked disappointed. "You spent more time with them the last two weeks than anyone else. Can you describe how they were acting? Maybe I'll be able to pick up on something."

Wow, that was a minefield.

"I know my mom is prickly sometimes."

Sometimes? Most of the time, but I kept it to myself.

"But she was a good mom and didn't deserve this." He rolled his shoulders back.

"You're right. She didn't, and neither did your dad." I thought for a moment about how to phrase what I'd observed. "I had carte blanche to roam most of the house. Your parents had packed a lot of what they planned to move and marked the bigger pieces they'd decided to keep." I remembered a big fight they'd had over a beaten, raggedy-looking couch down in their basement. "Your mom wanted to keep a couch that was the first thing they'd bought as a married couple."

"The awful plaid thing?" Tim asked.

"That's exactly what your dad said." We smiled at each other, and then Tim's face drooped. "They were pretty upset about it. And when I told your mom I couldn't sell it, she told me I was fired.

Your dad intervened and hauled the couch off to the dump."

"One of the reasons they were moving closer to me is because Dad was worrying about Mom's temper. She's never been the calmest woman, but over the past six months, he said things had gotten worse."

"He was patient with her. And very loving."

"That's my dad for you. It sounds like you didn't have access to the whole house. Any place in particular?"

"Your parents' office. But it's understandable. Who wants someone nosing around in their financial records or personal papers? I went in the first day I was there with your mom and visited with your dad a couple of times. I loved his stories."

"He could have been a writer." Tim stood. "I should get back to my mom. If you think of anything else, will you let me know?"

"Of course. I'm sorry I'm not more help. Let me know if there's anything I can do."

"There is something. I'd like to finish the sale. I'm hoping to move Mom down to Florida as soon as possible, and the less I have to deal with here, the better."

"I'm not sure. Your mom was having a hard enough time getting rid of things, and right now she can't speak for herself."

"I get it. What if you sold what was already out and go through the house for stuff you know isn't worth anything?"

"Like her plastic Marshmallow Fluff jars?"

"Exactly."

"I guess I could. Do you have a time frame in mind?"

"Soon."

I dug around in my purse and found a business card. I wrote my cell phone number on the back. "Here. Call me when you're ready."

Tim shook my hand and headed back toward his mom's room.

The hospital doors swished open as I was about to leave. Brad Carson, Carol's husband, almost ran me over. Brad was an administrator at the VA hospital in Bedford. What was he doing here?

"I'm sorry," he said over his shoulder as he started to move past.

"Brad," I called after him. His military-short hair had grown out since he'd retired. It hung over his collar in the back and needed a trim.

He paused and turned.

"What are you doing here?" I asked him. He'd lost weight to the point where his suit hung loosely on his shoulders. Something I hadn't noticed the last time I'd seen him.

I don't think he recognized me until then. I hurried over. His gray eyes looked worried. "Are the kids okay?" I asked.

"Sarah. Sorry. I was a million miles away. Everyone's fine. Are you? Why are you here?"

"I stopped to see Mrs. Spencer. You must have

heard her husband was killed during a garage sale I was running for them on Saturday."

Brad took my right hand, sandwiching it between his two big ones. His skin was cool and smooth. "Of course I heard. I was there that morning, remember?"

I frowned at him. "That's right. Yeesh. It was such a busy morning, and then with what happened . . ." Who else had been there that I'd forgotten?

"Don't be so hard on yourself." He let my hand go.

"If everyone's okay, why are you here?" I asked.

"A meeting. A hospital administrators' thing." He looked down at his watch. "And I'm late." He leaned down and kissed my cheek before taking off. Brad quickly crossed the lobby, his suit jacket flapping behind him as he moved.

I turned and bumped into CJ. "Busy place," I said. I pointed to the elevators. "I just saw Brad."

"What are you doing here?" CJ asked.

"I was thinking the exact same thing about you." I smiled.

"Ladies first."

"I stopped to check in on Mrs. Spencer. You?"

"The same," he said. "I've been trying to reach you all day."

I slipped my phone out of my purse. I'd put it on silent at some point and forgotten to set it back. Five missed calls. "Yes, you did. Anything important?"

"I heard about the break-in and wanted to make sure you're okay."

I sagged a little. The break-in. It seemed like days

ago and reminded me I needed to find Luke. CJ gathered me into his arms.

"You've had a rough few days."

"Indeed."

"I'll take you out to dinner."

Saying no presented too many problems. "Okay."

"I'll pick you up around six-thirty if it works for you."

"Perfect." It gave me a few hours to track down Luke. But how?

Chapter 7

Luke wasn't as hard to find as I'd thought he would be. He was sitting on my couch when I got home and almost gave me a heart attack.

"How did you get in?" I asked, as I set the bags full of cheese and the cannolis on the kitchen counter. He followed me into the kitchen, reached around me, and plucked a chocolate mousse cannoli out of the box.

"You need better locks. Any kid could pick that thing."

"Weren't you worried someone would see you coming up?"

"There weren't any cars in your parking lot. I figured it was safe." He polished off the cannoli in three bites and started on another one. I slapped at his hand, but it was too late.

"Sorry about this morning," we said to each other at the same time. Then we both smiled because we'd done that a lot as kids.

"We're going to have to find somewhere else for you to stay."

"Can't I crash here tonight?"

"No. I'm not hiding you anymore. Someone is going to see you. And CJ's taking me to dinner tonight. He usually stays over. I can pay for a room for you somewhere." While CJ and I might be slowly getting our lives intertwined again, our finances remained completely separate. Fortunately, he had no way of tracking my spending. He'd never know if I paid for Luke's room.

"Contrary to how it may look, I do have money. You don't have to pay for a room for me. It's nice spending some time with you." He polished off his second cannoli.

I felt all warm and smushy inside. "It's good to spend time with you too. But I can't keep moving you around. Someone will see you. Unless you changed your mind about wanting to be seen?"

"Not for a few more days. Until I'm done investigating this story."

It took all my willpower not to question him. *Don't scare him off. You are just rebuilding your relationship.* "Okay. There are a couple of motels in Ellington and some in Bedford."

"I'll let you know where I land."

"Do you want me to make sure the coast is clear?"

"Naw. If I run in to anyone, I'll pretend I heard about the apartment being for rent."

* * *

"Can you meet me at the house this evening?" Tim called at four, not long after Luke left.

I really didn't want to. "Could it wait until tomorrow?"

"Mom had a relapse this afternoon."

"I'm sorry." Why in the heck did he want to meet me then?

"I'm going nuts sitting here when there's nothing I can do. I'd like to go over, and I really don't want to go alone."

That was understandable. "Okay. What time?"

"Does five-thirty work for you?"

"It's perfect." It would give me time to help Tim and be back to meet CJ for dinner. "I'll see you there."

I parked in front of the house right before five-thirty. The neighborhood was quiet. The crime scene tape was gone, but I wasn't anxious to get out of the car. Going back into the garage sounded like about as much fun as cleaning scum out of a clogged garbage disposal.

In the rearview mirror, I saw a small car swing around the corner. I hoped it was Tim. It slowed as it headed toward me, then came to a complete stop in the middle of the street. After a second, the car reversed, did a U-turn, and sped off. How odd. I craned my neck to watch it drive off as I ticked off reasons someone would do that. They were lost or forgot something or got a call to do something else.

Perfectly reasonable. But what if they'd seen my car and didn't want me to see them? It gave me the creeps.

I started my Suburban, deciding to follow them. But as I did, another car pulled into the drive. Tim climbed out. At least I thought it was Tim—he looked different. I got out of the car and greeted him, but part of my mind was still on the car that had U-turned in the middle of the street. "You shaved," I said.

"My mom hates beards. I figured if she woke up, when she wakes up, she'd be happy to see me clean shaven for the first time in five years."

Without the beard, I could see the round shape of his face and how he did look like his dad. I took an envelope out of my bag and handed it to him. "Before I forget, here's the money from the garage sale."

He looked in the envelope full of money. "Did you deduct whatever it is my parents were supposed to pay you?"

"I didn't. It wouldn't feel right under the circumstances." We headed up to the house. "So what do you want me to do?" I asked.

"The police must have had you do this already, but would you walk through the house with me to see if you notice anything different than the last time you were here?"

The police hadn't had me look around. I decided not to share that information. It was an excellent idea. Even better, maybe I'd find something that would help me figure out who had attacked the Spencers and why.

"Sure. Garage first or last?" I asked. We both turned to look at the garage.

"Last," Tim said, shoulders slumping. He unlocked the front door and held it open for me. He flipped on a light as we stepped in. We stood in the living room since the Cape-style house didn't have a foyer. He looked around and sighed. Even with the moving sale, there was a lot left in the house. A big, overstuffed leather couch filled one wall. An end table next to a leather recliner was to our left. Tim picked up a Hummel figurine, a little boy with rosy cheeks.

"My mom loves these things."

"She wouldn't sell that one. She said it reminded her of you." I glanced at him. "This must be hard for you."

"It's not like I ever lived in this house. My parents moved here long after I was gone." He put the figurine back on the table, scanning the room, looking down the hall toward the dining room and kitchen. "I didn't get here as often as I should. Too busy with my career and family."

"It's hard. My parents are out in Pacific Grove, California, near Monterey. I understand how difficult it can be to get away." Since my divorce, my parents had pressured me to move back. But now that CJ and I were trying again, I was especially grateful I'd stayed in Massachusetts. We walked through the dining room, kitchen, and enclosed porch. Nothing looked like it was out of place since I'd last been here on Saturday morning.

Tim opened the door to his father's office.

"Oh, wow," I said.

"What? Is something different?"

I walked into the room. The desk was covered with files sitting next to a cardboard book box. "The few times I was in here, it was pristine." A drawer on the file cabinet was open and a stack of moving boxes in the corner had been jostled around. "I wasn't in here on Saturday. I can't say if this was your father packing things. Or . . ."

"If someone else was in here going through things."

I nodded. Tim had completed my thought. I walked over to the wall and straightened a picture of Mr. Spencer when he was young, arms thrown around a couple of guys in fatigues who must have been part of the platoon he'd loved to talk about. "Your dad was sure proud of his service. Did you move around a lot as a kid?" CJ and I had moved on average every couple of years when he was still active duty.

"He was out before I was born. I was one of those miracle babies born to my parents late in life. I don't think my mom loved being a military wife. She didn't like to talk about it."

"Not everyone takes to it," I said. "Some people aren't cut out for all the moves and being far away from family. I loved it most of the time."

"Would you look at the files on his desk and see if anything stands out?" Tim asked.

"Yes. Although I'm not sure I'll be helpful. Like I said, the office was always neat." I went around to the back of the desk and plopped into Mr. Spencer's chair. It hit me again that he was dead. Such a cheerful man, it was hard to believe anyone would hurt him. It made me wonder if he'd died defending his wife. Because as mean as it sounded, someone wanting to kill her didn't seem unlikely.

"I'm going to look in the file drawers for the powers of attorney and wills," Tim said. "My dad liked to be prepared. I guess it's a good thing."

I started leafing through the files on the desk. "It looks like taxes, health insurance, medical records. This one seems out of place—it's a folder of places to visit in Florida."

Tim came and looked over my shoulder as I thumbed through the files in the box.

"It's more of the same in this box, plus a folder of assisted-living places," I said.

"I didn't know they were looking at assisted-living places. I thought they planned to buy a house," Tim said.

"Maybe a better term is 'retirement communities.'" I set the folder aside but hesitated before pulling out the next file. "This one is labeled 'Life Insurance.'"

I handed Tim the folder. "Do you want me to leave? A lot of this is really personal and none of my business."

Tim shook his head. "It's okay. Another set of eyes, having someone else here, is a huge comfort.

My family has nothing to hide. I'm fine with you staying, unless you don't want to."

"I'll do what I can to help." I was relieved. I felt compelled to stay, to figure out what had happened and why. Since the crime had been committed at my garage sale, it made me feel responsible.

Tim flipped open the life insurance folder. He frowned as he read through the papers, and then his eyes widened. "Unbelievable," he muttered.

Chapter 8

I stood next to him, not wanting to intrude but dying of curiosity. Tim showed me a sheet of paper and pointed to a figure.

"A million-dollar policy?" I was astounded.

"I had no idea. I guess he wanted to make sure Mom was taken care of."

"Again, it's none of my business, but when did he take the policy out?"

Tim flipped through the policy. "Ten years ago. What are you thinking?"

"I'm not sure. Maybe, if it was recent, your dad had some concerns about health or something else." Something that had nothing to do with me or my garage sale. "Since it's ten years old, it doesn't seem likely."

We put the files back in the box, looked through the open file cabinet drawer, and straightened the stack of boxes in the corner.

"I'm sorry I couldn't be more help in here," I said to Tim as we left the office.

"No worries. Let's go upstairs and take a look around."

Ten minutes later, we were back downstairs and headed to the garage. We stopped at the door and looked at each other. Tim opened the door, flipped on a light, and stepped in. I followed. It was cool and the single bulb didn't light the corners. The sheets I'd used to divide the garage sale from the things that weren't for sale still hung, dividing the garage in half. Tears burned in my eyes, and I inched backwards.

"Are you okay?" Tim asked.

I swallowed and nodded. "Let's take the sheets down and see what it is we're dealing with." We took them down. Someone from the police department had haphazardly piled the unsold items from the garage sale near the big garage door. Fingerprint powder covered some of the surfaces, but other than that, it would have been hard to tell anything out of the ordinary had happened in here. The money, Purple Heart, and lobster buoy that had been on the floor were all gone. A dark stain that must be blood from Mr. Spencer's head remained.

He looked around with his hands on his hips. "Can you tell me what you saw? Anything you heard?"

I moved around the garage as I explained what I'd seen. He even wanted to know where his mom had been, and his dad. I told him everything I could remember.

"My dad always wanted me to be handy. To work with wood like he did." Tim looked around the garage. He spotted an old birdhouse and lifted it off the hook it hung on. "My dad and I made this when I was in first grade. I can't believe he still has it." Tim turned it around in his hands. Bright splotches of red, green, and yellow covered the sides and roof. "I was quite the painter back then."

I laughed. "Do you still build things?" It was a skill I'd long admired.

"Not often. I loved to draw and spent way too much of my time with a sketchbook and pencil."

"Do you still draw?"

"Not in a long time. I'd have gone to art school if I could, but my mom said I needed to do something practical. So I'm an engineer." He shrugged. "The pay's a heck of a lot better."

"Maybe you can get back to it someday."

"Maybe, but not while I have a family to feed and college tuition looming in the future."

After we finished, Tim locked the house and walked me to my car. "Here's an extra key to the house. I'd really like to try to get the rest of this stuff sold as soon as possible. Can you finish the garage sale on Saturday?"

The key weighed heavy in my hand. "I can't this weekend. I could do it next weekend."

Tim nodded. "I'll try to gather some more things for the sale. Mom will be mad as heck, but better to do it now."

"Okay. If you think that's best." I wasn't sure this was the right course of action, but since Tim was in charge, I'd leave it to him.

* * *

I was fifteen minutes late getting home, but CJ wasn't there yet. My stomach was growling so I started nibbling on the cheese Mike had given me. When I hadn't heard from CJ by seven, I tried calling him, first on his cell phone and then at the station. All I got was voice mail. At seven-fifteen, I grabbed my keys, one part of me worried while the other assured the worried side this was a normal part of being involved with someone in law enforcement. I'd had this conversation with myself hundreds of times when we were married. I decided driving by his house and stopping at the station wouldn't hurt anything.

As I reached for my coat, my cell phone rang. CJ.

"We've had a break in the Spencer case."

"Oh, good," I said.

"It is, but . . ." Silence stretched across the phone line.

"But what, CJ?" My stomach started to flutter.

"I hate to tell you this on the phone, but I don't want you to hear it when you're out and about."

I gripped my phone tighter. "Hear what?" I barely managed to get the words out.

"We got a hit on some of the fingerprints from the Spencers' garage."

"That's good news, isn't it?" I asked.

"Yes, but . . ."

I waited, but CJ didn't say anything and I was starting to get scared. "Spit it out, CJ."

I heard a big deep breath.

"The fingerprints belonged to Luke Winston. Your brother."

Chapter 9

I dropped my keys and sank to the floor, clutching the phone to my ear. CJ yakked away, but only part of what he said registered. Since Luke had been in the military, his fingerprints were on record, which meant the results came back fast. CJ couldn't come over. He said he was mystified, that he was sorry, that I shouldn't tell my parents, and he'd call soon. Then he hung up before I could say, "Wait. Luke was here." I'm not sure how long I sat there trying to figure out what to do. I knew I should call CJ back and tell him I'd seen Luke. That he couldn't have killed someone and then headed over here and acted so casually.

I pondered his appearance at my door. He had been tense, not casual. I'd chalked it up to us not having seen each other for such a long time. Luke had reacted when he'd seen CJ's jacket on my kitchen chair. He didn't want anyone to know he was in town. Because he was investigating something, not because he'd murdered someone.

There'd be no reason to come here if he'd killed someone and certainly no reason to stay in town. I pushed myself off the floor but only managed to walk over to the couch before collapsing on it. I could make all the assumptions I wanted, but how well did I really know my brother?

I looked at the phone gripped in my hand. I had to call CJ back and tell him I'd seen Luke. But I didn't dial, damn it. I couldn't. I sat for a few more minutes, my mind a kaleidoscope of images, one swirling to the next before I could focus. But I finally punched in CJ's number, doubting what I should do with every digit.

"CJ," I said.

"Sarah, I can't talk right now unless someone's bleeding."

My heart was bleeding. "No one's bleeding." I started again, "CJ."

"I have to go." And he did.

Maybe it was a sign. A sign to help Luke, or maybe it's what I wanted to do. I shot off a text telling CJ to call me as soon as possible. Then I sent him an email saying the same, emphasizing that it was important. I forced myself up, grabbed my light spring jacket. I'd find Luke and contact Vincenzo DiNapoli to defend him. Vincenzo had helped not only Mike Titone but my friend Carol out of jams. Once I had those two things in place, we'd all go to CJ together. Luke was here investigating a story. It may have led him to the Spencers' house at some point for some unknown reason. But I knew Luke was no killer and I had to prove it.

My first stop was DiNapoli's for food and hopefully to find out if word about Luke was out yet. I stood in line waiting for my turn. A woman I'd never seen before took orders. She was tall, with short blond hair. She moved with an efficient energy and talked with a loud Boston accent. I heard every order she repeated back as the line got shorter, a large sausage pizza, pronounced *pizzer*, with double cheese, an eggplant *pahm* sandwich, a chopped salad with a side of fries. None of it sounded it good.

"What can I get you?" she asked.

The person in front of me had moved off to the side to wait for their food. Options continued to stream through my head. I looked at the menu written on boards hanging from the ceiling as someone sighed and shuffled behind me. It had been a stupid idea to come here.

"Try the shrimp sandwich, Sarah. It's new." Rosalie came over and stood next to the cashier, little worry lines more pronounced around her eyes as she studied me.

I nodded, wondering if her worry was because she'd heard about my brother or because she knew someone had died at my garage sale.

"You're Sarah?" the cashier asked. "I've heard lots about you. I love, love, love tag sales."

I tried to smile. "Me too. The shrimp sandwich sounds good."

She stuck out her hand. "I'm Gale. G-A-L-E." She gave my hand a vigorous shake. "My mom said I came into the world like a strong gust of wind. And I haven't slowed down yet."

I could use a good strong wind to blow me in the right direction. I found a table against the wall. One of many lining the right side of the restaurant. Angelo was cooking at a frantic pace and shouting out orders as he finished them up. There was only a low wall between the tables and kitchen. I think originally the purpose was so he could watch over the restaurant, but on nights like this, he was fun to watch. He chopped, he stirred, he tossed pizza crust into the air. I figured he felt the crowd watching him and enjoyed putting on a show. I knew it after he tossed one crust into the air, executed a full circle, and caught the pizza. The crowd clapped and he bowed.

Gale brought my shrimp sandwich. Large breaded shrimp sat on a New England–style hot dog bun, which was sliced across the top instead of on the side. I took a bite. The breading had a slight spice but wasn't so thick you couldn't taste the shrimp. A light tartar sauce complimented the shrimp but didn't overpower it. If it weren't for the shocking news about Luke, this sandwich would be heaven.

Sadly, Rosalie and Angelo were too busy to join me. And after listening in on a few conversations and not hearing a word about the murder or my brother, I realized the Ellington High School baseball team was there celebrating a win with their families. It explained the crowd.

I tried to relax and focus on my food until a bit of a soft conversation going on behind me drifted over.

"If she's such a hero, how come she didn't stop that murder? At her very own tag sale," a woman said.

Oh, for goodness' sake, would the people in the town just get over the hero thing? Being called a hero wasn't as fun as it might sound. When I'd saved a life last February, the whole town had rallied around me to the point where it had become embarrassing. There'd been talk of a parade, but it had been quickly squelched by me and town budget constraints. However, I'd been chosen to be the grand dame of the Ellington Days parade next fall. No amount of squelching could get me out of it. I was going to be forced to ride in someone's swanky convertible and wave to kids along the parade route like I was some kind of homecoming queen.

"Give her a break. She's not Superwoman," a man whispered.

I kept trying to fold my superhero cape and tuck it back in the drawer. But the more I tried, the more I found myself in situations where people called me a hero. Last March, I'd saved some kittens from a storm drain. I hadn't made a big deal of it, but some passerby had taken a video of me lying in the mud, pulling out the kittens one by one. It had gone viral—I hoped because of the adorable kittens and not the way my muddy shirt had clung to me. But it had cemented the idea I was some sort of hero.

A couple of weeks later, I'd stopped a baby from being kidnapped at the mall. It had been dumb luck. The kidnapper had sprinted by me. I'd stuck out my foot instinctively and managed to catch the baby when she'd squirted out of his arms like a football. Then, last month, I'd happened upon a car wreck and badgered a group of people into helping me lift the vehicle off the person trapped underneath. It had been a Mini Cooper, not a Humvee. I'd done what anyone would have done. I was no hero.

"Well, some people around here act like she is."

"She's sitting right there. She'll hear you," the man said.

"I don't care. I'd say it to her face."

What people didn't realize was I was a fraud and a fake. I'd had help the night I'd saved a life back in February, when this whole stupid hero thing had started. Mike Titone's help that I'd sworn never to talk about. Help that haunted me. Help that kept me up at night when I watched CJ's back rise and fall as he slept or when he pulled me to him with a contented sigh.

I took my napkin from my lap and wadded it into a ball. I wanted to turn and say something to the woman, but what good would it do? Instead, I slipped out of the restaurant and figured out what I needed to do next.

Ellington had only three motels, two seedy and one a nice inn. I couldn't imagine Luke staying at an inn in a historic Colonial home. I'd heard the place was pricey and that they provided an authentic Colonial experience. Bed warmers to warm the sheets, a fireplace in every room, and they served authentic Colonial meals based on recipes passed down from generation to generation. I drove by it anyway, in case Luke was sitting outside on one of the rockers on the porch, whiling away time. The cars in the lot were all luxury models. I didn't know what kind of car Luke had or if he had one at all, but he didn't seem like a luxury-car kind of guy. He'd driven an old Jeep when we were in high school.

Next, I tried the Hotel de Ellington, a grand name for the boxy three-story building on Great Road. About a year ago, the state had started placing homeless families there. It had created a lot of controversy, as those things always did. Some claimed it would strain the school system, others that it would create more crime.

I drove around the building once. A group of men hung out behind the building. I pressed the accelerator and headed back to the front. I found a parking spot across the street and went into the lobby. A TV blared in one corner. The tile hadn't seen a mop in some time, and it smelled like burnt popcorn.

A lone man sat on an uncomfortable-looking stool behind a counter. I gathered my thoughts as I waited for the man to acknowledge my presence. I didn't even know how to ask about Luke. I didn't want to say his name or show even a very old picture in case the police came around or already had been around.

"You need something, or do you just like the view?" the man said. He turned to the side and flexed his arms over his potbelly, like he was a weight lifter. Then he chuckled. "I'm guessing it's not the view."

"I'm looking for someone."

"I'll need a little more to go on, missy."

"It's my . . . friend." Oh dear, I'd almost said brother. "He's a man. A head taller than me with brown hair. And a brown beard."

The man narrowed his eyes, assessing me. "You get left at the altar?" It came out *altah* with his accent. "You pregnant?" He opened a drawer and thrust some pamphlets at me.

"No. No, nothing like that. He's a friend."

He nodded like he'd heard it all before. "Listen, unless you can do a better job of describing your . . . friend, I can't help." He sighed. "Even if you could describe him, I couldn't tell you if he was here or not. Privacy and all that. You're welcome to have a seat and wait to see if he comes through. But it's the best I can do."

I looked over at the stained couch. Was the man trying to tell me Luke was here without coming out

and saying it? I looked at him hopefully. But I
didn't see any secret message in his eyes.

"Honey, look," he said. "Maybe move on with
your life. Find a better man."

I flushed, nodded, and slunk out.

Chapter 10

My next stop was the Ellington Motel on the west edge of town. It was one of those long, stretched-out places with a couple of little cabins at one end. This place looked more plausible. The cars were older, and a few of the lights above the doors were missing bulbs. The A-framed office sat in the middle. The NO on the VACANCY sign blinked on and off erratically. I'd practiced my spiel on the way over. This time, when I walked up to the desk, I was ready.

"Hi, my friend checked in earlier today. He forgot to tell me his room number. I was supposed to meet him at eight." I kept my voice light and friendly.

"You pregnant?" The woman glanced at my belly, and I followed her look. Did I look pregnant? The man at the other hotel had said the same thing. Yeesh. CJ and I had tried often enough when we were married without success. My stomach looked smooth and flat. I'd actually lost five pounds over the past few months, but I sucked in a little anyway.

I'd bought this flowy, blue top at a yard sale for fifty cents, but it wasn't worth it if it made me look pregnant.

"*No.* It's a friend." Geez, didn't people understand friends around here?

"Whatever. I'll need a little more than when he checked in. Does he have a name?"

"Of course." But what name? He wouldn't check in as Luke Winston if he was undercover or in trouble. I smiled. "Bartholomew Winst." It was the name he'd always used when we were little and played a spy game.

She tapped on a keyboard. "Yeah."

My heart leaped.

"But he checked out this morning. I'm guessing because of this." She slapped a flyer on the counter in front of me. It was a picture of Luke taken when he was in the Marines—all high cheekbones and stern look.

"Where did you get this?"

"The police brought it by a while ago."

"They know Bartholomew was here?"

The woman snorted. "'Course they do. You think I'd lie to the police over some man staying here?"

"No." I leaned in closer and dropped my voice. "What'd they want him for? The scumbag owes me money."

"No idea. But you got to find yourself a better man."

Yeesh, enough with the man advice. "Did you see what kind of car he was driving?"

"He wrote a Buick down on his form, but it's not what I saw him driving."

We looked at each other, both waiting for something. "What did you see him driving?" I finally asked.

"A blue Prius."

"Do the police know?"

"They didn't ask."

Sloppy police work and a woman with an interesting take on ethics. But I knew more than I had an hour ago.

I went home at nine-thirty when I couldn't figure out anything else to do. When I was really stressed, I cleaned. I scrubbed the plates in the sink, dried them, and put them away. In my bedroom, I stripped the bed and changed the sheets, and then moved on to dusting. I quit when every surface in the house sparkled.

It was times like this I wished I had a bigger apartment because cleaning this place hardly took any time. As I plumped the throw pillows on the couch, I spotted a small spiral notebook wedged between the couch cushion and arm. I pulled it out and flipped it open, recognizing Luke's handwriting, even after all of these years. I must have knocked it out of his backpack the first night he was here.

Under other circumstances, I might not have read his notes. But something was horribly wrong, and this might be my only chance to help him. I flipped through the pages and found a list of cities next to a list of names. Most of the names meant nothing to me but some did. *Verne, CJ, James, Brad, and Seth.* My heart twisted at the sight of their names. Why would Luke have written them in his notebook?

If I was patient, maybe Luke would come back for his notebook. But I wasn't patient. I grabbed my car keys and purse again. Even though it was already ten, I'd try to talk to some of the people on the list. I hid the notebook under some sweaters in my chest of drawers just in case Luke came back to look for it while I was out.

I parked across the street from Seth's house and turned the car off. I listened to the *tick, tick, tick* of the engine as I studied his place. Lights were on; no cars were parked in front of his house. It didn't mean he was alone, but I hoped he was. Seth had been named Massachusetts's Most Eligible Bachelor for the past two years in a row. He had plenty of women throwing themselves at him. His picture was always in the society pages of the Boston newspapers with some model-like woman by his side.

Lights flickered through the curtains covering the small basement windows, like a TV was on. I'd decorated the room for him and he'd loved how it had turned out. I'd worked on the rest of the house too, but hadn't ever finished his living room or his bedroom.

I hated unfinished business. Like his house, like our relationship. It had ended when I'd promised CJ I wouldn't let him die a lonely old man. He'd been in the hospital, injured, fragile, and all the love I'd ever felt for him had come rushing back over me. Seth had come to CJ's room that night as I'd sat by CJ's hospital bed. He had been involved in something I hadn't understood, something I hadn't been sure I wanted to understand. But none of it mattered right now. What mattered was finding Luke. I needed to sort out why Luke's fingerprints had been at the crime scene.

I forced myself out of the car, hustled to the door, and rang the bell before I chickened out. I wouldn't normally stop by someone's house this late, and especially not Seth's. When nothing happened, I held the bell down. If I was interrupting something, I was going to die of embarrassment. The porch light came on and the door was yanked open. Seth stood on the other side of his storm door in a pristine white dress shirt, untucked over faded jeans, bare feet, and mussed hair. He stared at me with such shock, I might as well have been the yeti Flossie Callahan thought she'd seen coming out of her apartment. A look of hope crossed his face, but it was fleeting.

"Are you alone?" I asked, trying to discreetly look around him.

"Sarah," he said, shaking his head.

Did he mean he wasn't alone? This might be humiliating, but I'd do it for Luke. "I need to ask you something." Seth opened the storm door.

"Come in."

"I shouldn't. Really." I didn't want to see whomever he was dating. Talking on the porch worked for me.

"No one's here." The words came out sharp. I must have hurt him more than I'd realized. "I was downstairs watching the Red Sox game. I heard about your brother." His voice softened a little bit.

I followed him into the living room. It looked almost like the last time I'd seen it, furnished with things I'd found for him at garage sales. The chair I'd had reupholstered in brown leather looked great, but was in the wrong place. It had been delivered after CJ and I got back together. I walked over to it and shoved it until it was just right. Then realized what I'd done. "I'm sorry," I said.

Seth had a bemused expression on his face.

"I'll put it back."

"No. It looks better there. Leave it."

He sat on the arm of the sofa and gestured for me to sit. I perched on the edge of the chair.

"What do you want?" Seth asked.

I detected a note of something in his voice. A bit of hope.

"I wanted to talk to you about my brother."

"Ah." Seth rubbed his hand over his stubbled jaw. He was one of those men who could pull off a five-o'clock shadow and look even better than he did clean-shaven. "I didn't even know you had a brother."

"He's been estranged from our family for a long time. I haven't seen him in almost twenty years and only talked to him a couple of times." I stopped myself from blurting out, "until two days ago." That would have been a disaster because I needed to find Luke and talk to CJ first. I almost shuddered at the thought.

"What do you think he was doing here?" Seth asked.

Investigating a story. Please let it be the truth. "I don't know." That was the truth, right? But I wanted to be the one asking the questions. The lawyer side of Seth just naturally kicked in.

I leaned forward. "CJ told me Luke's fingerprints were in the Spencers' garage. Couldn't it be some kind of horrible mix-up? Someone whose fingerprints are a near match? Or a clerical error?"

Seth was shaking his head no before I'd even finished speaking.

"Everything's digital. The chances of an error are next to zero. Unless he can prove he wasn't in the area." Seth gave me a direct look. One that must wilt witnesses. "Do you know where he is?"

"No. I wish I did." Boy, did I. "But no."

After an awkward silence I thanked Seth and left. I sat back in my car and burst into tears. All the pent-up emotions surrounding the death of Mr. Spencer, my brother's arrival, and even seeing Seth flowed out of me. I leaned on the steering wheel and sobbed.

A knock on the window shocked me straight up.

Chapter 11

Mike Titone stood there. I glanced from Mike to Seth's house. What the heck?

"Are you okay?"

I rolled the window down, swiping at the tears. "I'll be fine." The words came out terse.

"What are you doing here?" he asked.

"I could ask you the same." How odd to see him twice in one day.

"I'm just driving by. On my way home."

"You're just driving by Seth Anderson's house? The DA? On your way home to the North End?"

"Anderson lives around here?" He looked around, surprised. "Interesting."

I didn't buy his very convincing act for a minute. They were involved with each other in some way that worried me. Not my problem, at least for the moment.

"What are you doing out here crying?"

I swiped at the tears rolling down my face. Not

his problem. He'd made that clear earlier today. "A bad day."

Mike studied me for a minute, then shrugged. "Okay."

I watched as he strolled back to a black SUV I hadn't even noticed idling behind me. Luke's appearance in my life had thrown me completely off my game. Mike opened the passenger door, but paused. He looked at me for a minute before clambering into the SUV. It took off around me. I gave a slight wave as it passed, but the dark tint of its windows prevented me from seeing if anyone waved back.

I started my car, ready to head off in search of Luke, when it hit me. I'd asked Mike Titone to hide someone for me this morning. If he heard about my brother, if he told Seth . . . it was almost too awful to think about. I rammed the car into drive. I had to find Luke fast. I called James as I left Seth's house since there had been a James on Luke's list. I didn't know if it was the James I knew but I'd better find out. He had worked for CJ when CJ had been the commander of the security forces on Fitch. I'd hoped he was home so we could talk at his apartment, which wasn't far from mine. But he was on patrol duty on base. When CJ and I were still married, we'd call his troops "our kids." Those feelings didn't go away, although I never felt like a mother figure around James.

It was almost eleven by the time I parked behind the Shoppette, where James had told me to meet him.

The Shoppette, which was kind of like a 7-Eleven in the civilian world, was already closed. Across the parking lot, a few people went in and out of the gym. The bowling alley next to it was also closed. All and all, it was a quiet night. I yawned as I waited.

James pulled in beside me a few minutes later and motioned for me to get in his patrol car. "Mind if we talk and drive?" he asked once I closed the door. "I'm still on duty."

"Sure." Although it would be more difficult to watch his reactions. I'd been worried about James since he returned from a deployment in Afghanistan last October. He had a harder edge to him than before the deployment, and I'd yet to get to the bottom of why. Stella thought James liked me in a romantic way, but I wasn't sure. I had seen him around town and on base with other women.

He took off, turned onto Travis Road which took us past the library and the thrift shop. This time of night, though, everything was closed. James turned left and we drove to a quiet section of base where the old thrift shop had been. A young enlisted officer had been killed here, and soon after, the thrift shop had moved to its new location on Travis, the main street that cut from one side of base to the other.

"There's been some complaints of kids partying out here," James said. "They've climbed the fence a couple of times onto the runway." Fitch Field was right behind the trees. It was a facility shared by

Fitch and the Massachusetts Port Authority. "A pilot had to abort his landing the other night because of kids on the runway."

"That's awful," I said.

"It could have been a disaster in the hands of someone less skilled." He slowed down as we passed the thrift shop and shined his light in a wooded area. A blur of movement caused James to slam on the brakes. He swung the light back around, and a coyote paused to stare at us for a moment before trotting off. James continued on, past a back entrance to Fitch Field on our left and a tower the base's fire department used for practice on our right. We got to the end of the road. James turned the car around and then cut the engine.

He leaned his head back against the seat. "What did you want to talk about?" His eyes closed.

I knew shift changes were hard on the body. But I was worried James was this tired while he was on duty.

"Are you okay?" I asked.

James nodded but kept his eyes closed. "Talk to me."

"Do you know Bartholomew Winst?" I figured if my brother was doing some kind of undercover investigation he might have used his alias for more than just hotels.

James's eyes snapped open and he turned toward me. "Bart? Yes. But how do you?"

"I've known him for years." I didn't want to add anything else, didn't want to betray our real relationship until I absolutely had to. "Where'd you meet him?"

"At Gillganins."

Gillganins was a popular Irish bar right off base. They had everything from karaoke nights to wakes. I loved going there. What if I had run into Luke there? It would have been more shocking than finding him at my door. "When?"

James studied me for a minute. I didn't think he was going to answer without asking me a lot of questions first. It was one of the problems with trying to get information from someone in law enforcement.

"About a week ago."

Luke had been in town a whole week? Why hadn't he contacted me sooner? Maybe he hadn't planned to at all, but then something had happened at the Spencers' and he'd needed a place to lie low. I still didn't want to believe he would murder anyone, or use me to hide. But since he hadn't called me all day I was beginning to have doubts.

"Have you talked to him since?"

"Not for a couple of days."

"What did you talk about? Did he say why he was here?"

"You're starting to worry me, Sarah." James looked alert now, like he'd gotten a second wind. "If you want me to answer your questions, then you're going to have to answer mine."

"I might not be able to. Not tonight anyway."

James didn't say anything.

"Can you please just trust me?" I asked.

He nodded. "Okay. We struck up a casual conversation at the bar."

"Who was there first, you or Bart?" I had a bad feeling there was nothing casual about Luke starting a conversation with James since James had been on Luke's list of names.

James frowned. "I guess I was. Bart sat on the stool next to me. It wasn't any deep conversation. Just chitchat."

"Did he tell you what he was doing here?"

"Said he was a marine. Not active duty. He was walking the Appalachian Trail in segments. Working out some issues."

That didn't sound like the brother I knew. But I guess I didn't really know him at all. Because the brother I knew would have gone surfing to work out his problems and mocked hikers as people who just walked.

"What issues?"

James closed his eyes again. He was quiet and his breath so even I thought he'd gone to sleep.

He opened his eye and rubbed a hand over his face. "We swapped war stories. He's seen some terrible things. I felt bad for him."

Luke had seen terrible things? Things he could talk about with a total stranger but not his own family. It made my heart hurt for him. Perhaps what he'd seen had driven him away from us. "But you could understand because you saw terrible things too." I was guessing, or maybe it really wasn't a guess but a fact of war.

James started the car and gripped the steering wheel. "I did."

It was what I'd suspected for some time now. "Are you getting help for it?" I had wondered if James had PTSD.

"This is off the record."

I didn't think any of this conversation was on the record. "It's just you and me talking, James."

"Unless you tell me something I have to report," he said.

Or vice versa. I nodded. "I wouldn't ask you to compromise your position here on base."

"I've been seeing someone off base, a shrink. I don't want it on my record."

He started driving back down the road. I hated that there was still a stigma about getting psychological help in the military. "I'm glad, James. But seeing someone off base without anyone knowing could land you in trouble." I didn't know the exact regulation that covered that, but I knew there was one.

James nodded. As we passed the fire tower, I yelled, "Stop."

James slammed on the brakes. "What is it?"

I pointed toward the base of the tower. "Over there. It looks like someone is slumped over by the base of the tower."

James flipped on his searchlight. He rotated the light in the direction I pointed. The light crossed the blacktop, the rusted leg of the tower, and then the figure of a man. I was out of the car and sprinting toward the figure, ignoring James's shouts for me to stop and get back in the car. Next to the figure was a backpack. It was Luke's.

Chapter 12

The crumpled figure wasn't Luke. Thank heavens. It was my main thought as I kneeled in front of the man. I almost cried with relief. But I recognized him. Ethan, a homeless vet who roamed the streets of Ellington. He refused offers to stay in shelters or at the VA hospital. Although, he always accepted a cup of coffee and donut from Dunkin' with a crooked smile and a thank-you.

James shoved me aside. I stumbled over the back-pack, upending it. James checked Ethan for a pulse, yelling into his shoulder mike as he did. But Ethan was dead. Blood caked the back of his head. I clapped my hand over my mouth at the terrible sight and gagged. This looked all too similar to what had happened to Mr. Spencer. *Luke.* He'd been at the Spencers' house and now his backpack was here.

James was busy with the business of death and policing, so I looked through what had spilled out of the backpack. Luke's things had been replaced with Ethan's—a grubby shirt; a worn copy of *Walden*, by Thoreau; a pack of gum; a scrap of paper with a phone number, which I palmed; a dented tin canteen, diabetes medication and needles; and most startling of all, a stack of cash.

"Stop. What are you doing?" James' voice came out low and commanding.

"I knocked this over when you shoved me." I gestured to the backpack.

"Don't touch anything. Do you know him?" James asked. "You bolted out of the car like you recognized him."

I still shook from the panic of thinking it was Luke. "It looks like Ethan."

"Last name?"

"I don't know." I filled him in on what I did know.

"Has he been around long? I don't remember seeing him."

I concentrated on James, his serious face, trying to recall any details I could about Ethan. "I've seen him at yard sales and auctions."

"Auctions. That sounds highfalutin for a homeless guy."

"I'm not talking Sotheby's. These are ones held in someone's front yard or in a barn. Where swatting at a fly at the wrong moment has you bidding on something whether you meant to or not."

"Did he bid on anything?"

James sounded so incredulous I almost laughed. I closed my eyes for a moment trying to remember. "Clothes, military memorabilia, books, camping equipment. Stuff like that. Nothing I was ever interested in. I don't think we ever bid against each other on anything."

James squinted his eyes. "That backpack. I've seen it before."

Oh no.

"Bart Winst carried one just like it," he said.

I heard sirens heading toward us and knew I'd better come clean with James now before finger-prints on the backpack told him what I already knew. "I have to tell you something about Bart." I stood. "Bart's real name is Luke Winston."

James stared at me. "Your brother. The one wanted for questioning in the Spencer murder. You lied to me about a murderer?"

Before I could answer, squad cars arrived, brakes screeching and doors slamming. James stalked off.

I lingered off to one side, getting a headache from the flashing lights of the growing number of police cars and first responders. The bright blue lights cut through the dark night. I alternated be-tween worrying about Luke and wanting to smack him. A squad car from Ellington showed up. The base and towns surrounding it had signed memo-randums of agreement allowing them to help each other with investigations. Awesome climbed out. He jabbered something into his shoulder mike as soon as he saw me.

I was sure CJ would come as soon as he heard about the backpack and my presence. I hoped he'd seen my email and text or listened to my message before he arrived. What if CJ hadn't read my email yet? And he must not have since he hadn't called me. I pulled my phone out of my jacket pocket. No calls. I dialed his number again, but it went to voice mail.

James ignored me. If only it was because he was busy instead of mad. I worried he'd be in trouble because I'd been with him in the patrol car. But it wasn't only James who ignored me—so far, other than a couple of glances, everyone had avoided me. Someone should be coming over to take my statement. I wrapped my arms around my waist, trying to stay warm.

Where was Luke? Why had Ethan had his backpack? And the cash. Mr. Spencer had cash too. It seemed like neither of these deaths had been robberies or maybe they had been failed robberies.

I edged around the crowd, staying out of the way, but heading toward James. I finally caught his eye and he came over. "We have to come up with a story," I said. "I don't want you to get in trouble."

"I already have a story."

I was relieved. "What is it?"

"The truth. I'm not going to make this any worse than it already is by concocting a story and then getting caught when one of us flubs it."

My stomach suddenly tightened like it was cinched in a corset. "Okay. Put the blame on me. I'm the one who called you, who asked you to meet."

James nodded.

"Are you going to mention our conversation?" I asked.

"Yes. My commander is going to want to know why I had a civilian in the car on patrol."

"Can you say this was a ride along?"

"If it was anyone but you, she might believe it, but you've been on a million of them. I don't think that will fly with her."

I hadn't met the new commander, but had heard she was tough. "Tell her whatever you need to." The corset around my stomach cinched in tighter. I didn't care if she was mad at me. She was the least of my problems. I checked my phone again—no calls from CJ.

Maybe I hadn't really wanted to tell CJ before I found Luke. I could have driven to the station. I could have told him I was bleeding and made him listen. Finding Luke and getting hold of Vincenzo had been my priority. I'd thought if Luke turned himself in it would be better than Luke being hunted down. I was still trying to protect him after all of these years.

"Look, Sarah, I won't mention what you wanted to see me about unless I have to," James said, his voice weary.

"No. I don't want you to do that. Tell her what you know, what I said."

James had worry lines sprouting around his eyes.

"I'm not going to say anything about what you told me." I touched his arm briefly. "It's not important to what happened here tonight."

James nodded. "Thanks."

* * *

I remembered the phone number on the piece of paper. I walked as far away as I could from everyone else and dialed the number. It rang and rang, but no one answered. There was no cheery voice saying who the phone belonged to or telling me to leave a message. I tried again. This time, it was answered, and as I'd feared, or hoped, it was Luke.

"How the hell did you get this number?" he asked.

"A man, Ethan, had your backpack. I recognized it."

"How do you know Ethan?" he asked.

"Everyone in town knows him. How come he has your backpack?"

"I saw him the other day. The paper bag he hauled his stuff around in had split open. I emptied my stuff out of my backpack and gave it to him. I left him my phone number, told him I could help him out. Get him off the street."

"Where did you see him?" Did Luke somehow have access to base? He was a veteran, but he hadn't served twenty years so he didn't have a retiree ID.

I heard another car driving down the road. It was CJ in his official police business SUV. I turned away like he couldn't see me with my back to him. "I have to tell CJ I saw you."

"What? Don't. Give me a couple of more days to get this story finished."

"Call Vincenzo DiNapoli." I recited the number to him.

"Why?"

He must know. His fingerprints were at the Spencers' house. I felt a rush of tears in my eyes. I didn't think I'd ever been around this many people and yet felt so isolated. "Trust me. Call Vincenzo and turn yourself in."

"Sarah," CJ called to me.

I kept my back to him. "Do it now, Luke, because all hell is about to break loose."

Chapter 13

I hung up seconds before CJ wrapped his arms around me. I turned and rested my head on his chest.

"Are you all right?" CJ asked.

"Yes." *No.* "Did you get the email I sent you? Or my texts?"

"I haven't had time to even look."

"Chuck," someone called. It sounded like Awesome.

CJ dropped his arms. "I've got to see what they want. I'll be back in a minute. Love you."

"No. Wait . . ." But it was too late. He'd already loped off. *"CJ."* I yelled it as loud as I could. He hesitated for a second but went on. I watched as he stood by Awesome, who'd yet to even glance in my direction. James and the security forces commander joined them. James did a lot of talking. I saw CJ's posture stiffen. Then they all turned and looked in my direction. James shrugged like he was trying to apologize from afar. But CJ had a terrible look on his face and he shook his head. I wanted to run, but knew I had to stay and face whatever came next.

I walked over to the group, my chin a little higher than normal, my teeth clenched together. Awesome finally looked at me. If someone could express disappointment with just their eyes, he was doing it. He headed over to his squad car. James and the commander walked off too.

"CJ—"

"I can't believe you didn't tell me you'd seen your brother. Where is he?"

"I don't know. I've been trying to find him."

CJ folded his arms over his chest.

"I tried to tell you, but you hung up."

"You told James but not me?"

"I told James right after we found the body. I texted you, called you, left multiple messages, and emailed you. Check your phone."

"I look like a fool. My own wife knows where the suspect is."

"I'm not your wife."

"You should be." He started to turn away.

"Stop. After all these years, don't you think you should listen to my side of the story? You are always in such an all-fired hurry. You won't even listen to me. The job comes first, the job's more important. I'm supposed to understand, be there when you want me to be, be happy if you're there or not. Did you ever once stop to think how it felt from my side?"

We stared at each other. I'm not sure where all of it came from. I don't think I'd ever consciously thought all those things. We both were breathing hard, like we'd been running a long time and we'd finally, suddenly stopped without a cool-down.

"I didn't know you felt that way."

I didn't know either. I was shaking, not from the cold, or the death, but from emotion. Was this it? Was this the end of our relationship? Could we get beyond this moment?

"Let's sit in my car. I'll listen."

The car was warm and smelled like CJ, woodsy, lemony, clean. Nothing was out of place. Not a speck of dust to be seen. "Like I said, I don't know where Luke is. I haven't since you told me Luke's fingerprints were at the scene at the Spencers' house." As mad as I was, I had to tell CJ about calling Luke. I took Luke's phone number out of my pocket.

"But I do have Luke's phone number."

CJ's jaw tightened. "You had his number all this time and didn't tell me?"

"No, I got it tonight. I called him and told him to turn himself in."

"How long ago?"

"Right when you pulled up."

"James said you went through the backpack. Is that how you got the number?"

"Yes."

"Please try calling him again."

I dialed, but it went straight to voice mail. I tried again, but it did it a second time. CJ called the police station to see if they could track down where the cell phone was. He listened for a long time before hanging up.

"It looks like he took the battery out. It pinged off a cell tower in Bedford, near the VA hospital. Does he know anyone there?"

"I'm not sure."

"How about the Spencers? Ethan?"

"I don't know what kind of connection he has to the Spencers." I explained how Luke had met Ethan. "Luke showed up at my house two days ago."

"Two days? Are you kidding me?" CJ clenched his hands on the steering wheel.

"You said you were going to listen."

CJ loosened his grip. "You're right. Go on."

"He said he was investigating a story. He was undercover and asked me not to tell anyone he was in town."

"What story and for who?"

"I don't know."

"None of it seemed odd to you?"

Put that way, it did, but in the moment, I'd been so happy to see him I would have accepted almost any story. "I haven't seen him in almost twenty years and barely talked to him. I didn't want to scare him off."

CJ scowled but motioned with his hand for me to continue.

"When he found out you were around most of the time, I worried he'd take off again. I let him stay in the empty apartment by mine for a night." This next part wasn't going to go over well. I really wished someone would need something from CJ right now. For once, I'd be grateful if someone hollered, "Chuck" or lightning struck. But there was no divine intervention or interruption of any sort. I went on. "The next night, I let him stay at the Callahans'."

"Wasn't there a break-in at their apartment?"

Oh boy. This was going to go over like broken crystal at a garage sale. Maybe it was time to make a run for it. But instead I laced my fingers together. "Not exactly." I explained what had happened. Then I listened as CJ ranted about wasting police resources. I got it. I'd been wrong, even if, at the time, it had seemed like for the right reasons. I'd have to come clean to Stella and the Callahans too. I sighed at the thought.

"Are you even listening to me?" CJ asked.

"I quit sometime after the second round of wasting police resources and what was I thinking."

CJ's lips twitched and then he laughed. "You drive me crazy."

"It's a gift. I found a notebook of Luke's in my apartment. It had a list of names. It's why I came to see James. Your name was on it and Seth's, among others. Ethan and Mr. Spencer's names were on the list too."

CJ frowned. "Do you have it with you?"

"No. It's back at my apartment. When I get home, I can take a photo of it and text it to you."

"Okay. How did you leave things with Luke?"

"I told him to call Vincenzo and turn himself in."

"Do you think he will?"

"I don't know."

"For his sake, I hope so." CJ sounded ominous.

"I could try calling Vincenzo, but if he did talk to Luke, he wouldn't tell me anything anyway."

"So that's it."

"Wait. Luke said he needed another forty-eight hours to finish his story."

"What happens in forty-eight hours?"

"I don't know. Maybe it's his deadline for submitting the story." But if I knew for sure, maybe I could figure out what Luke's story was about and find him. "Luke's not a murderer, CJ. He wouldn't murder someone and then come to my house."

"You don't know him anymore. His fingerprints were at the crime scene."

"Then there's some explanation for why," I said. An explanation I wanted to hear. "Will you give me a ride to my car?"

"Where is it?"

"Behind the Shoppette. That reminds me. The desk clerk at the Ellington Motel told me Luke's driving a blue Prius."

"Why would someone from there tell you that?"

"I've been out searching for him."

"Sarah!"

"It's one of the places I stopped. I couldn't sit around and wait for you to call me back."

"Okay. Hang on. I'll call it in."

I watched as people continued to move around Ethan's body. Poor Ethan, he'd had a rough life.

CJ clicked off his radio. "How much trouble is James going to be in?" I asked.

"Maybe you should have considered that before you tried to get information out of him," CJ said as he drove back to the Shoppette. He paused. "James will be fine. I talked to the commander and explained how persuasive you are. Stubborn might be the better word." CJ parked next to my Suburban. "Now that I know you've seen Luke, would you stop by the station tomorrow and listen to some of the 911 calls from the day of the garage sale?"

"There was more than one?"

"Yes, about nine. Lots of people at the garage sale must have whipped their phones out and called."

"Why do you want me to listen to them?"

CJ just looked at me. I realized if one of the callers was Luke, it connected him further to the crime scene. I wanted to say no, that I wouldn't do it, that I couldn't betray my brother that way, but I knew I had to help CJ.

He stared out the windshield. "Because I have a murder to solve. You want to help me, don't you?"

"Of course I do. How will it help?" Maybe I was wrong and he wanted me to listen to them for some other reason.

"We're trying to sort out who was there."

"Did you listen and recognize Luke's voice?"

"I haven't talked to Luke in years. I can't be sure."

In other words, he suspected one of the callers was Luke.

"You have to face reality here, Sarah." CJ rubbed the stubble on his jaw. "Two men are dead. Both with similarities. Both with some tie to Luke."

"Luke wouldn't do this."

"The boy you knew growing up wouldn't, but Luke's a man. A veteran. You don't know him anymore. War changes people. Maybe it changed him."

There was no point in arguing. I opened the door, exhausted from all that had gone on. CJ grabbed my hand.

"Are we okay?" he asked.

"Yes." I hoped it was true, but my fence mending wasn't over by a long shot.

Chapter 14

I had to go home before I continued my search for Luke. I had to find him. I was surprised CJ hadn't told me to stay out of it. Was he too tired or overwhelmed to remember? Or maybe he thought I really did know where Luke was and had lied to him. I glanced in my rearview mirror. No one was following me, unless they were really, really adept at their job. I shook my head, knowing I was too tired to think straight. But I drove a circuitous route through town instead of taking a direct route home.

It was one-thirty in the morning by the time I got back to my apartment. I quickly took shots of the lists from Luke's notebook and sent them to CJ. He texted back a thanks. I reread the list. Ethan's name was on it too. It hadn't meant anything to me when I'd seen it earlier. *Oh, Luke what have you done?* After studying the other names on the list I changed into black yoga pants and my black Celtics sweatshirt, made a big pot of coffee, and when it finished brewing, I poured the coffee into a thermos after downing a quick cup. I crept down the stairs as quietly as I could. I figured Awesome was still working, but just in case he was with Stella, I didn't want him to hear me leave.

Stella. I wondered how mad she was going to be when I told her the truth about Luke staying in the extra apartment and at the Callahans'. I'd have to face that problem tomorrow. Make that later today.

I drove through a very quiet Bedford. Not unusual in and of itself because most nights were quiet in the little towns around here. This area wasn't renowned for its nightlife. Still, it was quieter than I'd expect for a night when the police knew a potential murderer was on the loose. I followed a road that took me near the VA. Near the cell tower that the ping from Luke's phone had come from. It yielded me nothing.

I pulled onto the VA grounds, looking left and right as if Luke would suddenly materialize. *Beam him down, Scotty.* I passed by the big brick houses where some of the staff lived. A couple houses had porch lights on, but other than that, they were dark. I tried to puzzle out if there was any connection between Mr. Spencer and Ethan other than they were both veterans. One lived on the streets, one happily married. Well, married anyway. Both had had large amounts of cash with them at the time of their death. Neither of those things answered any of my questions.

The hospital buildings were on my right. More lights were on there. I doubted Brad would be working at this hour or that he'd answer any of my questions if he was. I continued on the road and took a left, driving by a construction site. Last October, there had been a fire here, burning down creepy, old chicken coops. Now, low-income housing was going up. Behind the chain-link fence, the buildings were taking shape with walls and roofs but not windows or doors. Fog formed, dimming the light from the sparsely spaced streetlights. I slowed down, wishing I had a searchlight like James did on his patrol car.

The road dead-ended. I did a five-point turn to get the Suburban back around. My cell phone rang as I headed back down the road. I grabbed it, hoping it wasn't CJ outside of my apartment door wondering where the heck I was.

"Hello," I said.

"What are you doing out here?"

Luke. I slammed on my brakes and craned my head in all directions but didn't see him. "Where are you?" I asked. "The police are tracking your phone."

"Not this one."

I shook my head, wondering how many phones he had.

"Can we talk for a few minutes before you call CJ? I know you have to tell him I'm here," he said.

"Okay. We talk, then we find Vincenzo, and then go to CJ. Promise?"

"Yes."

"Yes, what?" I asked, remembering all too well

the times he'd tricked me with his logic when we were kids.

"Yes, I promise we'll talk, find Vincenzo, and then CJ. I'm in the last unit. There's a hole in the fence just down from you."

"You want me to come there? Come here. My car's warm."

"I need your help. I sprained my ankle. It puffed out so much I took my boot off and I can't get it back on."

"How the heck did that happen?"

"I slipped on a board hurrying down the stairs of this place."

"Oh for pity's sake," I grumbled. "I'll come." Luke and I had gotten each other out of so many scrapes when we were kids. What was one more?

I used the flashlight on my phone to find the gap in the fence. I ignored the NO TRESPASSING signs as I crawled through the hole. My sweatshirt snagged on the chain link as if it were warning me to stop what I was doing. I worked free and walked down to the last unit. At least I managed not to trip on the rutted ground or step on one of the nails that littered the place.

I stepped inside. It smelled of freshly sawed wood, and cool spring air.

"Over here," Luke called.

He sat on the steps leading upstairs. For a moment, I stared down at him. Part of me wanted to yell at him and part of me wanted to protect him. It wasn't unlike how I'd felt most of the time I was growing up. I plopped down next to him. In the dim light, I could tell he looked as tired as I felt. He hugged me tight and I almost couldn't breathe. It was then I realized he was shaking.

"I found your notebook with the list of names and cities. Some of them were crossed off. CJ's name was on there and Seths, the DA's. Why?"

"I always study who's in charge when I'm in the middle of an investigation. Usually to make sure I can turn over evidence when I have it. But sometimes it's to make sure they aren't involved in something they shouldn't be."

"And which is it here?"

"They're both clean."

That was a relief. "Let me see your ankle."

Luke stuck out his foot and rolled up his pant leg. I shined my light on the puffy, red skin.

"Something else to add to your troubles," I muttered.

"What troubles?"

"They found your fingerprints in the Spencers' garage."

Luke picked up his boot and tried to put it back on, but winced with pain. He didn't deny being there.

"And Ethan's dead." I wanted to see his reaction. He stared at me.

"No. How?" he asked. The vein that always popped out on his forehead when he was angry throbbed madly.

"I'm not sure." Tears swarmed my eyes. "When I first saw him, I was sure it was you."

Luke slung an arm over my shoulders. "I'm sorry.

I keep screwing up. Ethan was supposed to meet me here tonight."

"What? Why this place?"

"He's been camping out here at night. The walls provide a bit of shelter. But he insisted it had to be here."

This was a dark, creepy place. "I don't like that. Let me help you stand and let's go." I held out my arm. Luke gripped it and stood, but he couldn't put any weight on his foot. I picked up his boot and had him sling his arm over my shoulder.

A creak from the back of the house interrupted us. Luke shoved me behind him. We both held our breath and heard another creak. Someone was back there.

Luke whirled around and shoved me out in one motion. "Run," he yelled.

I did, stumbling over the uneven ground until I came to the hole in the fence. This time, I slithered right through. A bright light blinded me.

"Stop," a man's voice shouted.

A sudden image of Luke and I playing red light, green light in our driveway with the neighborhood kids flashed through my mind. Only this was no game and I couldn't see who was on the other end of the light.

"What are you doing here, miss?" the man asked.

Oh, thank heavens it was security instead of a bad guy. My knees almost gave out. I put my hand in front of my face, trying to block the light and see whom I was dealing with.

"You're trespassing."

"Would you lower the light please?" I realized I didn't really know it was security. It dropped a bit, and I could make out a man in a uniform with a VA security car behind him. "Could you call Brad Carson or CJ Hooker? Please?" I added when I saw the man shake his head. "They can vouch for me."

"Stay right there. I'll make a call." He climbed in the car and got on a cell phone. His thick beard and mustache made it hard to read his expression, especially with a ball cap pulled low over his forehead. What if whomever he was talking to said to turn me over to the police? I couldn't hear what he was saying, but he watched me the whole time and shrugged a couple of times.

I strained to listen for sounds of Luke, but heard only the whisper of wind gusting around the construction site. Should I tell the security guard Luke was still in the house? If someone else from security had found him, why weren't they dragging him over to us? Even worse, what if whomever Luke was investigating had found him? I was lucky to have run into security.

After he hung up, he came back to me. "I'll take you to Mr. Carson's office. He and Chief Hooker will meet us there."

"Can I follow you there?" I gestured toward the Suburban.

He gave me a stern look. "You're lucky I'm not taking you to the Bedford Police. The car will be fine for now, or if you give me your keys, I can have someone drive it over to the admin building."

I dug around for my keys and handed them to him. "Thanks." He held the front passenger door open for me, shutting it gently after I hopped in.

As he started the car, I heard a noise from the backseat. Something soft looped around my neck. It tightened and my brain couldn't catch up with what was happening. The pressure increased and I struggled to breathe. I tried to wedge my fingers between the soft material and my throat but they wouldn't cooperate and my hands fell weakly to my lap. CJ would be so mad at me for getting into the car with a stranger.

Chapter 15

Bright sunlight streaming through my bedroom curtains woke me. I grabbed my phone. 10 a.m. I swallowed. My throat hurt as if someone had taken a rake to it. Memories of last night shoved to the surface. I tossed off my covers. A quick glance down told me I was dressed in the same clothes as last night. I leaped out of bed and ran to the mirror over my dresser. I yanked the black sweatshirt over my head. A large bruise ringed my throat. I gripped my dresser and stared. The last thing I remembered was sitting in the security man's car with dots in front of my eyes thinking about CJ. How had I ended up back here in my bed?

I dialed 911 before I crept out into the hall. I peeked into my bathroom. Clear. And then peered around the corner into the living room. What if someone was still here? The room was empty. As was the kitchen. I hustled over to the window. My Suburban was parked in its spot in the driveway. My purse and car keys sat on top of the trunk I used for an end table. My stomach twisted, and for a minute, I felt like I was going to be sick. Someone had knocked me out, driven me back here, and tucked me into my bed. Who? I finally realized a tinny voice was emitting from my phone.

"Where's your emergency?" a woman asked sharply. I heard her say to someone, "Get a car over to 111 Oak Street. It's the chief's wife. Something's wrong." My phone number was registered with the police department. Then to me, "What's your emergency?"

"This is . . ." My voice rasped. It hurt to talk. "Sarah Winston. I need to speak to CJ." I filled her in as best I could.

"I've got a car dispatched and will send the chief."

I opened my front door and slumped onto the couch waiting, remembering the events of last night. I drew my knees to my chest and clasped my arms around them. Oh, Luke. What had they done to him? Why had they let me go? Sirens blared, car doors slammed, and footsteps pounded up the stairs. Pellner arrived first, followed by CJ. Stella ran in after them.

CJ looked at her. "Not now, Stella."

Stella looked at me.

"Stay," I managed to say. CJ frowned but didn't argue.

CJ turned his full attention to me. He spotted the ring of bruises around my neck and his face went white. He froze. Stella paled too when she saw the damage done to my neck. Pellner stepped around them, kneeled down, and moved my head gently up. "I'll call an ambulance."

"No," I said.

CJ lifted me into his arms, hugging me. The stubble on his face scratched my cheek but was somehow reassuring. I slid out of his arms and sat on the couch.

"What happened?" CJ asked.

Stella headed toward my kitchen. "I'll make some tea. It will be good for your throat."

CJ sat next to me on the couch. He held himself rigidly like if he let loose he might smash something. Pellner paced. A few minutes later, Stella hustled back in with a cup of tea. I took a sip. She'd added lemon and honey, and it felt soothing on the back of my throat. After a few more sips, I put the cup down and told them what had happened in a voice scratchier than an old record. After I finished, I noticed a pulse in CJ's neck beating a wild tattoo. Pellner was already on his radio telling someone to check out the construction site at the VA in Bedford.

"Where's Luke?" CJ asked.

"I don't know. I'm afraid for him. What if he was captured or killed?" I grabbed CJ's hand and gripped it in mine. "Why didn't Luke run too?"

No one answered.

"I don't understand why they let me go. How I ended up in my own bed." I repressed an outward shudder. Inwardly, I was a shuddery mess. Who had carried me up the stairs and tucked me into my bed? "Did you hear anything, Stella?" I drank more of the tea.

"Not a thing. I'm sorry."

"It's not your fault," I told her.

"I have to get ready for class. I'll be home later if you need anything," Stella said as she left.

"I'm going to call Brad," CJ said. He walked into the kitchen. I could hear the murmur of his voice. Pellner talked quietly into his radio. When CJ came back in, he rubbed his hand over the back of his neck. "They found a security guard hog-tied in the trunk of his car this morning. All he had on was his underwear."

"So someone used his clothes and his car to get to me." I paused for a moment. "To get to Luke. They didn't know I'd be there." I stopped again. "I was a complication for them."

"We'll get a forensic team here to go over your car. Maybe they left some fingerprints behind," CJ said. "They can dust doorknobs in here."

"The fake security guard I talked to last night knew who Brad was. He said he was taking me to Mr. Carson's office and Chief Hooker would meet us there. It's why I went with him. He acted like he knew both of you."

"They are clever, whoever they are." CJ frowned. "You were supposed to come to the station and listen to the 911 calls today. If it's too much, we can hold off until tomorrow."

"I'll do it today." I might as well get it over with. Maybe it would help Luke instead of making things worse for him. "Anything new on Ethan?"

"We don't know. We're investigating." CJ glanced at his watch. "I have meetings I have to be at," CJ said. "Pellner can take you to the station and then stay here with you until I get back."

"That's crazy. The department can't afford to assign me a personal bodyguard. Besides, I have an appointment at one this afternoon. I won't even be here."

Pellner drifted out into the hall, which meant he wasn't expecting CJ to react well to my news. I held up a hand before CJ could speak.

"I'll be with Gennie Elder. I'll be as safe with her as anyone." Gennie was not only Stella's aunt, but a recently retired mixed martial arts expert and cage fighter. In those circles she was called Gennie "The Jawbreaker." "I'll go nuts if I just sit around here."

CJ frowned again. "Okay."

"I'll need my car though."

CJ shook his head. "Your car won't be done by then." He dug in his pocket and handed me a set of keys. "Pellner can drive you over to my place and you can take my car." He pulled me to him. "I'm begging you to stay out of this. Quit putting yourself at risk. Luke is obviously in some kind of serious trouble. I don't want to lose you because of it."

By twelve-thirty, I sat in one of the interrogation rooms at the police station. Pellner had set up the equipment for me, then left me alone in the stark room. The calls were all variations on the same theme. Someone's hurt, someone's dead, there's an emergency. Some of the calls were frantic, some calm. I could have quit listening halfway through because I'd recognized Luke's voice right away. His call was the fifth one.

I'd listened to all the others, hoping to hear something that would point the finger at someone other than Luke. Nothing came to me so I played Luke's over and over, my heart breaking a little more each time I heard it.

"Two people are injured," he said.

He didn't know Mr. Spencer was dead.

"Where's the emergency?"

Luke rattled off the address way too easily. I hit pause. It didn't help me pin suspicion on someone else. Did I even want to? He'd brought up the incident at the Spencers like he knew nothing about it the day we had lunch in the Callahans' kitchen. I'd told him everything I'd seen, heard, and felt. I restarted the tape.

"What's the emergency?"

"Like I said, two people are injured." His voice panted a little.

Was he running or stressed?

"What kind of injuries?"

"I'm not sure. Two down." Luke's breathing was even more strained. He was running. And the police would think he was running away because he'd done something horrible to the Spencers.

"I've dispatched response units. Please stay with me on the line."

I heard a click.

"Sir? Sir? Are you there?"

But there wasn't an answer, and the next call clicked on. I closed my eyes and pictured that day. It dawned on me then. The person I'd seen running toward the woods behind the Spencers' house. It had been Luke.

Chapter 16

At one o'clock, I stood in the foyer of Gennie's Colonial house. She was in the process of opening an art studio in Dorchester, which she planned to live above. Last fall, she'd hired me to sell her incredible collection of antique and vintage furnishings. Each room had been decorated with pieces from different eras. I'd realized selling everything at once would be complicated and would lower prices. Last October, I'd sold her knickknacks, lamps, and *objet d'art*. Over the winter, we'd done the artwork. Now, in our last phase, it was time to sell her furniture.

I slipped off my jacket and unwound the scarf around my neck. When I saw Gennie staring gape-mouthed at the bruises, I remembered I'd planned to leave the scarf on.

"What happened to you?" Gennie asked. She planted her muscular arms on her hips, Her feet slightly apart as if she was ready to go into fighting mode at any minute.

I quickly explained in my new soft, whispery voice. Although I left out the bits about Luke being at the scene, about his asking me about what had happened at the Spencers' like he didn't already know. The 911 call proved Luke had betrayed me in ways I couldn't imagine or understand. If the sale wasn't this weekend, I would have gone home and climbed into bed. Gennie shook her head the whole time I was talking. Her long brown braid flipped back and forth as she did.

"Do you have any kind of self-defense training?" she asked.

"No."

Gennie blew out a puff of air. "That's it. I'm going to start self-defense classes. It's crazy women run around not knowing how to protect themselves."

"Art studio and martial arts? Sounds, um, unique."

"Unique maybe, but practical. You will be my first client and we start right now."

My eyebrows shot up. "Now?"

"You want to wait until someone attacks you again?"

"But the sale."

"It can wait. Safety can't."

Forty-five minutes later, I dripped sweat on the mat in Gennie's basement. She'd loaned me workout clothes. I'd wanted to quit thirty minutes ago, but Gennie wouldn't let me.

"One more kick," she said. "Make this one count." She held a punching bag for me to kick.

Not one of my kicks had been strong enough to even make her move. This one was going to be different.

I side kicked my leg out, slipped in my own sweat, flew into the air, and smacked down hard on my rear end. I lay there, panting. Gennie stared down at me with a grin.

"Get up."

"Can't," I panted. Gennie reached down, grabbed my arm, and hauled me to my feet before I could blink.

"Getting you in shape is going to be fun. Let's go to the kitchen and get some water."

Gennie trotted up the stairs and was out of sight as I hit the bottom step. I clung to the rail and dragged myself up one step at a time. Gennie watched me as I slid onto a stool with a little moan and gulped down some water.

"You have good upper-body strength," she said. "I need to teach you how to use it to your advantage. That's what we'll work on tomorrow."

Tomorrow? No way. "I'm booked all week." *Thank heavens.*

Gennie snorted. "Yeah, you're booked with me every afternoon. We'll use part of the time for your training."

I opened my mouth, but shut it. I had no good excuse not to come.

CJ was waiting outside my apartment door at five-thirty with a pizza box from DiNapoli's in his hand.

Maybe it was time to give him a key. I didn't climb the steps quite as quickly as normal. I groaned a little as I moved up them.

"Are you okay?" he asked. "Did something happen?"

It looked like he was ready to go into full cop mode. I waved my hand around. "I'll be fine." My voice now sounded more throaty smoker than breathy Marilyn Monroe. I gave him a kiss and inhaled the smell of the pizza. After I unlocked the door, CJ followed me into the kitchen. I grabbed a bottle of wine, rummaged in a drawer for the corkscrew, and started the process of opening the bottle. CJ took out plates and napkins.

I moaned again as I tried to pull the very stubborn cork out of the wine bottle. CJ took the bottle from me and easily slid the cork out.

"What's wrong? Do I need to force you to go to the doctor?"

I sat down at my small kitchen table. It was covered with a vintage tablecloth with red roosters decorating the corners. I opened the pizza box. Oh, yum, a Greek pizza, with feta cheese, olives, artichokes, red onion, and chicken. I took a bite before I even set it on my plate. Getting kidnapped and working out made me really hungry. CJ stared at me.

"Gennie decided I needed some self-defense training. We started this afternoon. I'm a little sore."

CJ burst out laughing. "Good for Gennie."

"Did the team find any fingerprints?"

"Nothing yet. They eliminated yours, but are still running the others. It will take a while."

"How long is a while?"

"It could be weeks. I brought the Suburban back."

"Great." I never felt safe in CJ's small Sonic. "Any word on Luke?"

CJ shook his head. "You?"

"Nothing." We ate silently after that. Me worrying about where Luke could be and CJ worrying about . . . who knew? I hoped he wasn't worrying about me. He had enough going on without me adding to it. I vowed to be a better partner. One who would make his life easier, not harder.

I barely budged Wednesday morning when CJ kissed me as he headed out to go to the gym over on Fitch. It was a rare day when he missed his morning workout. *Workout.* I ran through the reasons I shouldn't go over to Gennie's this afternoon, but couldn't come up with one. Her sale was this Saturday, and I had to have everything ready.

When I woke again at eight, I hopped out of bed. *Woo-hoo.* I wasn't as sore as I'd expected. Running yard sales had made me stronger than I'd realized. After showering, I slipped on a black turtleneck. That way, I didn't have to look at the ring of bruises and neither did anyone else. Jeans, makeup, and a blow-dry for my shoulder-length blond hair, and I was almost as good as new. Until I thought of Luke.

I grabbed my phone, hoping Luke had called. I did a quick check. Nothing, no numbers I didn't recognize, no calls at all. The workout and good night's sleep had made me realize Luke hadn't betrayed me. He was protecting me while he gathered information. Luke must have a good reason for having been at the Spencers' and for leaving. At least I hoped that was true.

I made a Fluffernutter and opened my computer to my virtual garage sale site. Things were humming along swimmingly since I'd added another administrator to help out during yard sale season. It was the easy part of my day—now for the hard stuff.

Two men were dead and Luke was missing. Surely he would have called me if he was okay. I found the photos I'd taken of the list of names Luke had in his notebook. CJ had taken the actual notebook when he'd left this morning. I studied the list. Nothing popped out at me. I still didn't recognize any of the other names. It seemed like a dead end.

I looked at the list of cities and started Googling them one at a time. The only thing I could find was most of the cities had a VA hospital. Luke had been on VA hospital grounds the last time I'd seen him.

There'd been a lot of scandals surrounding the VA hospitals and vets getting the services they needed. Maybe Luke was here investigating them, but I had thought it had been investigated and reported. Which left me with no answers at all.

I heard Stella singing an aria below, something I didn't recognize. Most days listening to her sing made me happy. Today, it meant she was home.

Time to go confess I'd used the empty apartment and tell her what had really happened at the Callahans'.

Twenty minutes later, Stella sat staring at me with a slight frown on her face. "Why didn't you just tell me?" she asked, after I told her the whole sorry story of hiding Luke in the building. Tux was curled on the couch between us. Stella stroked his back and he purred with contentment. At least one of us was happy.

"Luke asked me not to tell anyone he was here."

"But you could have asked to use the apartment for a couple of days. I would have said yes."

"I didn't want CJ or Awesome to know."

"Then you could have told me that too."

Stella had been wonderful to me and I'd been a complete idiot. "I'm sorry. I screwed up," I said.

"And?"

I looked at her, trying to figure out what I was supposed to say next.

"And you won't let it happen again, right?" Stella said.

"I promise it won't happen again. I'm sorry."

Stella stood. "Enough with the 'I'm sorries.' Want some coffee?"

Oh, whew. She forgave me. "Yes. I'd love some. How's Awesome?"

"Awesome."

I opened my mouth. Did she mean he was awesome, or was she asking me if I meant Awesome?

"He's great. As in awesome," Stella said with a laugh as she poured the coffee. The smell of the rich, roasted beans wafted up. "My mom invited him over for a family dinner this Thursday night. Meeting Mom and my aunts ought to be really interesting."

My eyes popped wide open. Besides Gennie, her other aunt was our town manager. As a group, they could be terrifying. "Do they know about his, well, fatal flaw?"

Stella laughed. "Which one? That he knows nothing about music?"

"No, the other one. The more important one."

"That he's a Yankees fan?" She shook her head. "Not yet they don't."

"But it's bound to come up. They're playing each other at Fenway for the next three days." Stella's family had had tickets at Fenway since the beginning of time. They were passed in wills from one generation to the next. And the Yankees were their sworn enemies.

"How bad can it be?" A small line formed between Stella's eyebrows. She handed me one of the two mugs of coffee. "What else is bothering you?"

I held the mug of coffee in both hands trying to warm them. "Luke made a list of cities and names. I'm trying to figure out what it all means. Most of the cities has a VA hospital. But the names aren't complete. They're only first names, or in some cases just a last name." I drank some of my

coffee. "I haven't heard from Luke. I'm worried."
Very worried.

The line between Stella's brows deepened. "I'm
sorry you don't know where Luke is. Want me to
take a look at the list?"

I whipped out my phone and found the picture.
Stella took the phone and we huddled over it.

Stella studied the list closely before handing the
phone back to me. "If only one of these names was
more unique. Then we'd have something to work
with."

"Thanks for trying." I finished my coffee. "Ugh.
I've got to go talk to the Callahans now. They are
going to think I'm crazy."

"You're in luck. They left for Vermont this
morning to spend the week watching their grandchildren."

"I'd almost rather get it over with. Hey, want to
meet me at Gennie's house this afternoon? She's
teaching me some self-defense moves."

"Thankfully, I have to teach a class this afternoon. But I'd pay good money to watch."

I gave her arm a light smack as I stood to leave.

"Someone's coming by to look at the apartment
this evening. If you want a say on our next tenant,
be here by five."

At ten, I walked into Mrs. Spencer's room. I was
flummoxed to find Brad Carson sitting on a chair
next to Mrs. Spencer's bed. "Brad?"

"Sarah, I'm surprised to see you."

"No more surprised than I am to see you sitting here," I said. I moved into the room and to the foot of the bed. Mrs. Spencer's condition seemed unchanged since the last time I'd been here. Tim had told me she was improving, but it didn't look like it to me. She was still hooked to all kinds of machines. Her skin was as pale as the blanket tucked under her armpits. She lay very still. Soft swooshing noises came from all the equipment.

"I knew Mr. Spencer from the VA hospital." Brad looked distressed as he watched Mrs. Spencer. "This is a bad deal."

Had he mentioned that when I ran into him in the lobby on Monday? I don't think so. "I came to see how Tim and Mrs. Spencer were doing. Where's Tim?"

"I sent Tim off to get something to eat. He looked like he could use a break."

"That was nice of you. I'm here for the same reason. I still feel guilty all of this happened during their garage sale."

"You can't blame yourself, Sarah." Brad studied Mrs. Spencer and then looked at me jerking his head to the door. I stepped outside with him. The bustling hallway felt jarring after the quiet of Mrs. Spencer's room.

"How are you doing?" Brad asked. "I can't believe you were attacked."

"I'm okay," I tried to say it with confidence.

"Can you tell me what happened the night you were kidnapped?"

"I figured you knew."

"I heard from the police, but would like to hear exactly what happened."

I filled him in, wishing as I did that telling this story would make it less scary, but it didn't. "What did the security guard who was stuffed in the trunk have to say?"

"He was patrolling by the construction site when someone flagged him down. He doesn't remember anything until he woke up in the trunk," Brad said.

"Is there any chance he's lying? Maybe he could be in on it?" This was what my world had come to. Not believing anyone I didn't know.

"No way. The man's solid. He's worked at the VA for ten years without as much as a complaint against him."

"What's his name?"

Brad shook his head. "Uh-uh. CJ would kill me if I told you."

"He doesn't have to know."

"Nice try." He glanced at his watch. "I'd better get to my meeting. Tell CJ I'll try and meet him at the gym in the morning."

I watched him leave and then turned back to Mrs. Spencer. Something felt off about Brad being here.

Chapter 17

I parked my car in front of the Spencers' house. I'd promised Tim I'd have things ready for the sale next week, but I'd been putting off coming back here. I unlocked the front door. I'd run into Tim at the hospital as I was leaving. He'd asked me to be brutal about getting rid of stuff. Mrs. Spencer would be mad as heck if she knew. Now I had to walk a delicate balance of Tim's needs, which I sympathized with, and Mrs. Spencer's needs, which I did have a modicum of empathy for.

I decided to go through room by room and throw away things Mrs. Spencer clung to that had no value except as recyclables. As I did, I'd set aside things Tim might want to get rid of but his mother might want to keep.

First, I needed a box to put stuff in. I had large black plastic bags I could use to haul the recycling to the garage and for actual garbage. I went to Mr. Spencer's study because I remembered seeing some flat boxes and tape there. As I reached for a box in a group leaning against the wall, I knocked a picture off. Fortunately I grabbed it before it hit the floor and shattered the glass.

It was the photo I liked of Mr. Spencer with men from his unit when he served in Vietnam. Boys really, not men. The picture was in black and white and kind of blurry. The three of them struck a jaunty pose like they didn't have a care in the world. Behind them was a jungle. I stared down at the picture of young Mr. Spencer. *Who killed you?* Sadly, I wasn't going to get any answers staring at this picture.

Mr. Spencer had shown it to me one day as he told me about his experiences in Vietnam. He'd laugh them off like it was a big adventure instead of the most frightening period of his life.

It made me think of James. While I was relieved he was getting help, I wished he could be more upfront about it. I was sure his unit would support him. It had been a great group when CJ was commander. And James could get in trouble by not reporting that he was seeing someone off base and off the record. I needed to talk to him again. I set the picture on Mr. Spencer's desk and snapped a picture of it with my phone. It was one of the last times I'd ever see it and it was a nice memory of my time spent with Mr. Spencer.

An hour later, I took two large bags full of stuff and emptied it into the recycling. I had another bag full of trash and a box full of things set aside for Tim. I sent him a quick text telling him I'd left a box in the living room for him to look through.

Tim could decide what he wanted to keep and what he wanted to sell.

He sent a text back. I can't get away right now. Mom had a seizure of some kind today. Things aren't good.

Poor Tim. Mrs. Spencer hadn't looked well this morning. I sent another text. Anything I can do?

Pray.

I checked the time on my phone. If I hurried, I could grab a sandwich at home and then head over to Gennie's house. Maybe if I told her I was full, I'd be able to get out of my training.

Being full only bought me an hour and a half reprieve. Gennie had informed me it would be plenty of time to digest and be ready for a workout. I glanced at the time on my phone. I only had another fifteen minutes to finish a minor repair on a lovely Victorian settee. I had it upside down with the legs sticking up in the air. I fisted my hands on my hips as I stared down at it.

"You are not going to win this battle," I told the piece. The legs were pegged to the frame of the bench. When I got one peg in correctly, another popped out on a different side. "Come on, pretty please? I don't want to use wood glue on you." Maybe talking nice to the darn thing would work better. It had heard some words I didn't normally use as I'd struggled with it. I got two of the pegged pieces in on one side. I set the bench on that side and leaned on it hoping the pressure would keep those two in place. After some wrangling, I got the other two pegs in. Voilà, the piece was sturdy. I set it back on its four legs.

"Stay," I said, pointing a finger like it was a dog and would listen. I could have asked Gennie for help, but I didn't want her to find me any sooner than necessary.

On Friday, an appraiser who was a friend of mine from Acton, Massachusetts, was meeting me here to price the last of the pieces. There were a few I wanted to make sure I was in the right ballpark with. Hmmm. Maybe it would get me out of a workout. I grabbed my hair dryer and plugged it in. I double-checked to make sure it was on the cool setting. The settee had a lot of intricate carving along the bottom and on the legs. I'd use the dryer to get dust out of crevices. It usually worked, but if it didn't I'd use a soft paintbrush. Then I'd do a quick polish with lemon oil.

I worried about Luke as I polished and checked my phone for calls. Worrying about Luke made me think of the Spencers. Which made me think of Ethan. Three men, all vets, connected or not. My mind swirled with the motion of my cloth as I worked the polish into the carving.

"Playtime's over. Let's get to work," Gennie said.

I jerked my head up and gasped. Gennie stood in the doorway. "Be still my heart," I said, looking up at her. "This is hardly playtime. It's my job and affects you if it isn't done well."

Gennie nodded. "I scared the crap out of you. If I'd been an assailant, you reacted too slowly."

"But I feel safe here so I let my guard down. I

can't be worried about getting attacked every second of the day." After one last swirl with the polishing cloth, I pushed off the floor. "I don't think I have time to get everything ready for Saturday's sale." That was a complete fabrication. My sales were always organized by the date of the event.

"You can work in the mornings."

"I can't. I have another sale to get ready for." Why wasn't I saying no? It was a two-letter word I normally had no trouble using.

Gennie jerked her head toward the basement. "Come on. What is more important than your safety?"

My hand went to my throat. Almost being strangled had scared me more than I realized.

She was right so I followed her to the basement. "Shouldn't we be listening to 'Eye of the Tiger' or something?" I asked.

"At this point, I don't think you need the distractions."

Fifteen minutes later, I was a sweaty beast. I'd been on my butt on the mat more times than I'd ever admit to anyone. "Face it, Gennie, I have terrible balance."

She laughed. "We'll work on it. Come on, let's try a bit of boxing." She grabbed a pair of boxing gloves. "I'll let you try these to get the hang of things, but in the real world, you won't have them."

I slipped my hands into them and Gennie tightened them for me. I immediately started jabbing the air and moving my feet around in what I thought was a pretty good imitation of a boxer. As

I was getting into it, I heard a half-snort, half-hiccup noise from Gennie. I stopped. Her eyes were watery and she made the funny noise again.

"That's what you think boxers do?" she asked.

I put my hands up in what I thought of as a classic boxer's move, one a bit higher than the other with my elbows bent at ninety-degree angles, holding them far from my body. "How's this?"

"It's great," Gennie said. I beamed at her. Maybe I was a natural. "If you want to get coldcocked."

She smacked my arms apart like they were spaghetti strands and had her fist grazing my jaw before I could blink. She didn't actually hit me, but she could have. So much for being a natural. Gennie taught me to put my arms and fists close to my body to protect my core.

"This is going to sound counterintuitive, but if you have to fight, you want to go in close to your opponent."

"I thought I should run and scream."

"If you can, absolutely do it. But if you can't, move toward your opponent."

"Toward him? That doesn't sound smart."

"If they can pull their arm back, then extend it fully, their hit is going to have a lot more force behind it. And do a lot more damage." She demonstrated both on the punching bag. "Now try to hit me."

I tried more than once. My arms were starting to tire and all I was hitting was air. *Yeesh*.

"Have you ever actually hit anyone or anything?" Gennie asked.

Had I? "I slapped my brother once when he shaved the head of my Barbie doll."

"How'd it feel?"

"Not good. Especially after a week of hand washing all the dishes and going to bed a half an hour early."

Gennie laughed again. "But in the moment. Can you remember how you felt?"

"I was furious. It was my favorite Barbie. She had long blond hair and she looked like me."

"You have to tap into that fury. Unless you have a better moment of fury."

I nodded. "Someone tried to kill me."

Gennie got very still. "Were you mad or scared?"

"Scared first. Then mad." I thought back to the incident last spring, one I usually tried to forget. "I think both emotions worked to let me save myself."

"Excellent. Now I'm going to hold the bag and you punch it."

We walked over to the long, cylindrical bag in the corner of her basement. It's cheery red color did nothing to make me feel better.

"I've got to warn you, it's not like punching a pillow. It doesn't have much give."

I nodded and put my hands up the way Gennie had shown me. I shuffled my feet a little and then hit the bag.

"You call that a punch? I bet you slapped your brother harder."

I tried again.

"Come on. You didn't even make me feel it."

Gennie was making me pretty angry with her mocking tone. I struck out with a fast jab. The jolt zapped through my hand, up my wrist, and right to my shoulder. "Owwwwww."

Gennie grinned at me from the back of the bag. "Do it again." I'm pretty sure she murmured, "Wuss," under her breath.

I felt like one of those cartoon bulls who swiped their feet in the dirt, head down, before they charged. That bag was going to get everything I had.

Chapter 18

I struck out, but Gennie moved the bag a bit to the left. My trajectory took me past the bag toward the mat-lined wall. Gennie snatched the back of my shirt. It allowed me just enough time to twist so my shoulder smacked the padded wall instead of my face. But a shock wave of pain surged through my body.

I rubbed my shoulder. "What did you move the bag for?"

"You think your attacker is going to just stand there?" She started loosening the boxing gloves. "Good work. Let's get you some ibuprofen and water."

We settled in her kitchen at stools by the massive granite-topped island. "How are things going at your new place?" I asked.

"My contractor's mad because I'm changing the space in Dorchester from our original design." It came out *Dorchestah* with her accent. "But I have to so I can teach the self-defense classes."

I rubbed my shoulder, then took the ibuprofen with great gulps of water. "Yeah, that's a great idea because you're so good at it."

Gennie laughed. "Okay, maybe I've been a little bit hard on you."

"A little bit?" I asked.

"I'm trying to prepare you for real-world situations."

"You might have to tone it down a little if you do offer classes. But it is a great idea."

I checked the time on my phone. I wanted to be back home by five to meet the potential new renter. Luke's list popped up again and I stared at it.

"What's that?" Gennie asked, looking over my shoulder.

Gennie was a local. Maybe some of these names would mean something to her. I showed her the list. I didn't like to talk about Luke and what was going on, but if Gennie knew someone, maybe it would give me some answers.

"Have you heard the police are looking for my brother, Luke? They are calling him a person of interest in Mr. Spencer's death."

Gennie ducked her head for a moment. "It's around town," she admitted.

Of course it was. Maybe that was why I'd unconsciously been avoiding places I usually went. I'd seen the DiNapolis two days ago and hadn't seen Carol at all. We'd talked once, last Friday, and made plans to attend an estate sale later this week. I was surprised she hadn't called me. Brad had to have told her what happened to me at the VA. I hoped everything was okay with her. With Brad.

"Sarah?" Gennie asked.

"Oh, sorry. Luke left a notebook in my apartment that contained a list of names. Some of the names are crossed off." I sat for a minute trying to compose myself. "I recognized some of the names." I took a drink of my water. "I talked to James and he had met my brother who was using an alias." I made a note to myself to call James and apologize again. It wasn't my only reason though. Maybe Luke had said something that hadn't seemed important at the time but may now have some significance. I handed Gennie my phone. "Do you recognize any of the names?"

Gennie frowned as she read through the names.

"And look at the list next to the names. It's of towns. Some of them have VA hospitals in them, but not all of them."

"Can I see the list?"

I took my phone back, flicked to the list, and handed the phone back to Gennie.

She flipped back and forth between the two lists. Her eyebrows popped up.

"What?" I asked her.

"I may be wrong, but if you put some of the town names behind some of the names on the list, you have names of people who live in Ellington."

"Show me."

"I may be way off base."

"It's okay. It's more than I've had to go on."

"Charlie and Davenport fits together, and so

does Susan and Fairfax. Then this one, Herb and Fitchberg. Could that be Herb Fitch?" Gennie asked.

Herb Fitch was a retired police officer and a veteran, descended from the Fitch family who'd fought in the Revolutionary War. The base was named after their family. I hadn't seen him since last October. He lived across the alley from Carol's shop, Paint and Wine. Herb had once called the police to report me as a suspicious person.

"I know Herb," I said. "But he'll be hard to talk to without arousing his suspicion. He's a wily one."

"He is. Susan passed away a few years back."

"So she's a dead end." I thunked my hand to my head. "Poor choice of words."

Gennie laughed and shook her head.

"Would Charlie talk to us?"

"Absolutely. Shall we go see Charlie?" Gennie sounded excited.

I'd rather go alone, but maybe having Gennie along was a good idea. New Englanders didn't always take to people they considered outsiders. And as much as I loved my adopted home state of Massachusetts, no one here would consider me a local. "Right now?"

Gennie was already standing up. "Yes. Let's go. I'll drive."

Ten minutes later, we stood on the porch of a rambling Victorian house not too far from where I lived. The bright pink, purple, and green paint peeled in spots. Gennie *bam, bam, bammed* on the screen door.

"You're going to knock the screen door off its hinges," I said.

"Charlie's a little hard of hearing," Gennie said. She yanked open the screen and beat on the deep purple six-panel door.

I found a doorbell in the shape of a dragonfly. I pushed on it and we both heard a deep gong from inside. Gennie raised her fist to knock again when the door opened abruptly.

"You tryin' to raise the dead?" Charlie asked with a scowl.

"You don't look dead yet," Gennie said with a grin.

"Too ornery for heaven or the devil, I guess," Charlie said.

I was surprised—Charlie was a woman about an inch taller than my five-six with a large Afro and a commanding presence.

"Come on in. You two must need somethin' important making all that racket," Charlie said. I watched her well-developed hips swish down a hall until Gennie gave me a poke and I followed.

"You could have told me Charlie was a woman," I said over my shoulder to Gennie.

She grinned at me. "The element of surprise is important in any fight."

"What are you? Yoda now?" I asked. She laughed and motioned me forward.

We settled in what the Victorians would have called a parlor, but it was now part office space and part family room. As Gennie introduced us, I looked at the pictures on her walls and realized Charlie must be older than she appeared. Her brown face was unlined, but some of the photos were of her serving in the Vietnam War. Gennie and I had decided on the way over it wouldn't be prudent to tell Charlie she was on a list written by a murder suspect. It troubled me even to think that way about Luke. Instead, we'd decided to ask if she knew Mr. Spencer or went to the VA herself.

I picked up a framed photograph on the end table next to the couch where Gennie and I sat. It wasn't much different from the one Mr. Spencer had in his office, only this one was of three women. Their arms were around each other; the blonde on the right had a cigarette in her hand. They looked so young.

"I lost them both on the same day. Blown to bits by a sniper," Charlie said, pointing to the photo. "I keep it out to remind me to be grateful for every day I have." Charlie straightened her shoulders. "Now, why are you here?"

I guessed her grateful philosophy on life extended to not wasting time. I glanced at Gennie, but knew she was waiting for me to ask the questions. "Did you know Mr. Spencer?"

"The man who was killed in his home?" Charlie asked.

I nodded. "He was a veteran."

"Yeah, I read it in the paper, but I didn't really know him."

Darn it.

"Why do you care?" Charlie asked.

I didn't want to mention my brother to Charlie. "I feel like he died on my watch. I was running the garage sale at his house. I'd gotten to know him and his wife." I shrugged. "I have a misplaced sense of responsibility."

Charlie pursed her lips and studied me. Then she glanced at Gennie. Charlie nodded at the picture of her and her friends. "I get that. Why don't you come with me to the American Legion tonight? We can see if anyone there knows him."

The American Legion was an organization for veterans. There was a large retiree population who stayed in Ellington because they could use the services on Fitch, such as medical care, the pharmacy, and shopping at the commissary or BX, base exchange. It saved them money.

"Okay, what time?" I felt like I'd won Charlie's approval.

"Let's say seven-thirty. It can get pretty crowded and we'll want a good table. How's your singing voice?" Charlie asked.

Oh boy. "Why do you ask?" I tried to sound casual.

"It's karaoke night." Charlie grinned.

Rats. I looked over at Gennie. "Want to join us?"

"No way. You two have fun."

A few minutes after five, Stella and I stared at each other from behind Mrs. Thatcher's back while she looked around the empty apartment. Her breath came out in wheezes. She wasn't smoking a cigarette, although it seemed like a cloud of smoke hung over her like the dust did over Pigpen in the *Peanuts* comics. She was a stocky woman with more wrinkles than a Shar-Pei puppy.

"I thought it would be bigger," she said.

"The ad did say it was a one-bedroom, one-bath," Stella said.

"I didn't realize there'd be so many stairs," Mrs. Thatcher said.

"The ad did say it was on the second floor." Stella raised her eyebrows at me.

Mrs. Thatcher dug through her purse and pulled out a pack of cigarettes. Then she dug some more and pulled out a lighter with a Patriots logo on it.

"There's no smoking in this building," Stella said. She'd instituted the rule after a problem last winter.

"The ad didn't say that." Mrs. Thatcher looked at Stella with a raised eyebrow. It started a coughing fit. "It's too small anyway."

We walked down the stairs with Mrs. Thatcher, one in front, one in back, in case she collapsed, which seemed all too possible. Mrs. Thatcher lit a cigarette as soon as she was out on the porch and inhaled deeply.

Stella closed the door behind her and leaned against it. "Am I ever going to find a renter?"

"Well, they can't all be like me."

"Thank God," Stella said.

"Hey. You should be so lucky."

"I know. I'm kidding." But Stella looked a bit down. I hoped it wasn't man trouble with Awesome.

"I'm going to karaoke at the American Legion tonight. Want to come along?" I asked. I knew how much Stella loved karaoke.

"Sure." She studied me for a moment. "Why are you really going? I usually have to drag you with a promise of reduced rent to get you to go."

"It's uncanny how you can read me."

"Unless it comes to hiding your brother in my building."

I guessed she wasn't quite over it yet. "I'm sorry. It was wrong."

Stella waved a hand and waited for me to go on.

"I'm trying to find out more about Mr. Spencer. If I find out more about his background, maybe I can figure out what Luke was doing and find him." Every time I thought about Luke, my stomach twisted. I realized if I could find out who killed Mr. Spencer then Luke would be free.

"I'm in," Stella said.

Chapter 19

Stella had her choice of spaces as she parked in the big lot behind the American Legion at seven-thirty. She locked her car and then yanked on the handle to make sure it was locked.

"Everything okay?" I asked her.

"Two murders and your missing brother warrant extra caution. Have you heard from him?"

"No. Have you been here before?" I asked Stella. The warm spring day was turning into a cool spring evening.

Stella tightened a purple silk shawl around her as we headed toward the door. "A few times. We go in through the door over there." She pointed to one on the right side of the building. "The bar's beyond a meeting room toward the front of the building."

We walked into the bar. About half the tables were occupied. Charlie waved us over to the bar, where she sat drinking a Sam Adams lager, and introduced us to Lesley Rife, the bartender.

"She makes the best drinks in all of New England," Charlie said.

"What can I get you?" Lesley asked. A lock of bright turquoise hair fell across Lesley's forehead. It contrasted with the rest of her hair, which was pale blond and spiky.

"I'll have a Cape Cod," I said. A cranberry and vodka sounded perfect. Stella ordered the same. Lesley had on a sleeveless orange shirt and snug white jeans. Colorful tattoos covered her muscular arms, which seemed to come to life as Lesley whipped up our drinks. She added a couple of fresh cranberries to each drink before setting them in front of us.

I bought the round and left a good tip. Then Charlie took me around the room, introducing me to people. I asked each of them if they knew Mr. Spencer. Most said no, a few said only from the newspaper articles about his death, and a couple said yes but had never seen him here.

Stella and I settled in with Charlie at a small round table in a corner near the stage. Stella and Charlie's families went way back. I half listened to them chat and watched as people came in. The crowd was a mix of old and older. A few must be Korean War vets, but the majority of the people looked to be from the Vietnam era. Some were around my folks' age. The room filled quickly—it always surprised me how popular karaoke was. A harried waitress brought us three more Cape Cods. I could see Lesley making drink after drink. She moved in a brisk but smooth way; the growing crowd didn't seem to faze her at all.

James slipped in with a few airmen from base. This was a great time to talk to him. I excused myself and went over to where James and his friends leaned against the wall. They all had beers in their hands.

"Hi, guys," I said. James and two of the men stood straighter while the third looked at them and then followed suit. "Yeesh, at ease," I said. "I'm not in the military." The action was a show of respect for CJ when he had been their commander. Some things were hard to shake off, especially when you were associated with the military. We chatted for a few minutes.

"James, could I borrow you for a minute?" I asked. He looked wary but nodded. His buddies exchanged looks, and I hoped this wouldn't cause any gossip on base. We stepped a few feet away.

"I wanted to apologize again for putting you on the spot the other night," I said.

He folded his arms across his chest. "I wasn't very happy. You could have been truthful with me."

Ouch. James's comment zinged me like an arrow. I nodded. "I'm sorry. It won't happen again." It seemed like I didn't trust anyone anymore.

James stood there like he was waiting for me to ask something else, but I couldn't.

James took a drink of his beer. "I've been thinking over my conversation with your brother."

"Did he say where he'd been?"

"All over."

"Or what he did for a living?"

"He was vague. I didn't push."

"Oh."

"He did mention being estranged from his family. That he had a sister he loved very much and hoped that someday soon they would patch things up."

I felt tears starting to well up and blinked furiously. I didn't want to cry here. "Thank you, James." I had to hold on to that and figure out what had happened to the Spencers so when I did find Luke we could work things out. "Are you going to sing?"

James relaxed. "No. I came to watch."

"Have fun then," I said. I patted his arm. I noticed a table of four men watching James and me like we were specimens in a Petri dish. Well, three of them watched and one was focused on his phone. I didn't recognize any of them and wondered why the heck they found James and me so interesting. But as soon as they realized I'd noticed them they all looked away. A couple of them leaned forward and talked. Another whipped out his phone. I shook my head and made my way back to my table. I wished I could hear what they were saying because they had my antennas up and rotating.

"Charlie, see that group of men over there? The guys in the plaid flannel shirts?" I asked when I arrived back at our table.

Charlie and Stella turned in their seats to take a look. "Are they locals? I don't remember seeing them around before." But I hadn't lived here that long.

"I don't recognize them," Charlie said.

"Me either," Stella said.

"I haven't seen them in here before," Charlie said. "Why?"

"They were staring at me. In a creepy way."

"Well, honey, I'm not surprised they were staring. Have you seen yourself tonight? You look pretty cute."

We all laughed. The noise index rose as the room filled. Music blared from the speakers. The beat pounded into my temples. My chair was wedged between the table and the wall. Getting out wouldn't be easy and I felt a little claustrophobic, which I usually wasn't.

Seth walked in. What the heck was he doing here? He wasn't a vet. Then I noticed someone holding his arm. Instead of his usual model type, it was Herb Fitch. He stood as erect as he could with a cane and Seth's help. It looked like the arthritis Herb battled was taking its toll. I wondered how they knew each other. Maybe because Herb used to be a police officer and Seth had worked in the DA's office a long time before he'd become the DA.

Seth glanced around for a table and spotted me. We looked at each other for a long moment before someone called his name. He smiled and helped Herb to a table, which, thankfully, was across the room. But once he sat in one of the two available chairs, I realized we'd be facing each other all night. I could ask Stella to switch spots with me, but that in itself seemed awkward.

"Sarah? What are you staring at?" Stella asked. She swiveled around in her chair and spotted Seth. "What's Seth doing here?"

I shrugged. "I don't know."

Charlie glanced back at them. "Seth often brings Herb. It's getting harder for Herb to get around."

I wanted to talk to Herb, but it would be hard to do with Seth sitting there. Impossible to do with Seth sitting there. Not because I had any feelings for Seth, but because he'd know I was snooping.

"Good evening, American Legion," a man said from the stage. He drew the word *evening* out in an imitation of Robin Williams from the movie *Good Morning, Vietnam*. The crowd cheered in return. "I'll kick this thing off with the one, the only, Elvis." He launched into a rousing version of "You Ain't Nothing But a Hound Dog." Everyone joined in on the chorus, and I relaxed and enjoyed myself.

I saw Herb stand up several songs later. Seth started to rise, but Herb put a gnarled hand on his shoulder and said something that made Seth sit back down. This was as a good a time as any to go to the bathroom. I yelled into Stella's ear that I needed to get out and slipped away as everyone sang the chorus to "Mustang Sally."

I pushed out the door from the bar into the hall. The music quieted out here. Herb went into the men's restroom. I hurried into the women's, did my thing, and hustled back out as Herb left the men's room.

"Herb, it's great to see you." I took his hand and gave it a gentle squeeze. He sized me up and then gestured to a couple of wingback chairs upholstered in a dark tapestry fabric.

"Looks like you got something on your mind," he said as we sat.

"A girl can't powder her nose?"

"Maybe other girls, but your timing is suspect."

I grinned, glad to see even if his body had slowed since last fall, his brain certainly hadn't.

"Go on then," he said, "I'm guessing this is about the trouble your brother is in."

Herb certainly knew more about the police investigation than I did and likely wouldn't share anything he did know.

"I wondered if you knew Mr. Spencer. Did he come here?"

Herb was shaking his head before I finished. "Not everyone who served wants to belong to the American Legion. Some people aren't joiners, some don't want memories dredged up."

"Mr. Spencer was really friendly. And he told me lots of stories about his service."

Herb studied his hands, placed one on top of the other on the wooden cane. "There's stories, then the truth, the bits you don't share with most folks. The bits that keep a person awake at night."

The door from the bar pushed open and music followed Seth out. His face was creased with concern but smoothed slightly when he saw Herb and I sitting together. We stood.

"I was worried, Herb," Seth said. Then he gestured

to us. "But maybe the two of you talking should worry me more."

"Not at all, son," Herb said with a wink at me. "You worry too much."

I patted Herb's hand. "I can't pull anything over on Herb." I turned to Seth. "It's nice to see you."

Seth nodded. "Herb, we're next. Come on."

I watched as Seth and Herb went into the bar, disappointed I didn't have more time to talk to Herb. Maybe I could track him down later. I hurried after them and squeezed back into my chair. Seth and Herb singing? This I had to see.

Chapter 20

Seth and Herb stood on stage. Herb rolled his eyes at something Seth said and then shrugged. Seth grinned. The music started and I almost popped off my chair. They sang "You've Lost That Lovin' Feeling" by the Righteous Brothers. Stella twisted to look at me, eyebrows raised. I lifted my hands in a go-figure gesture. They sang it a la Tom Cruise in *Top Gun*, clasping their hands over their hearts and gesturing to women in the audience. Everyone got into it and stood singing and swaying. Seth didn't look at me once until the very last line as the music faded.

The waitress set another Cape Cod in front of me. Stella leaned over. "I figured you'd need another after Seth's song." Thankfully, Stella had driven us over here.

I took a healthy swig.

"Besides," Stella said, "we're next. And I already picked out the song."

I almost spit my drink out but managed to swallow,

then choked. Stella pulled me out of my chair and onto the stage. Charlie came with us. I'd have to remember not to leave them alone together in the future.

The announcer kept the mike. "Next, we have American Legion member Charlie, singing instructor Stella, and our very own local hero, Sarah Winston."

People cheered and whistled. I grabbed a mike and flicked it on. If only these people knew the truth. I glanced at Seth because I was sure he did. "I'm not the hero here, but all of you who served and are serving are. Thank you for giving much and getting little in return."

When the song came up on the screen of the karaoke machine, I glared at Stella, but I was trapped between her and Charlie.

"I'm going to kill you," I whispered to her.

Stella laughed. The music started, and she belted out the opening line to Garth Brooks's song, "Friends in Low Places." The crowd stamped their feet, hooting and hollering, before joining in. It was a breakup song about someone who preferred the beer-drinking bar crowd to the champagne-sipping, black-tie crowd. It was all too true for my life and Seth's. Although we both had managed straddling the two worlds well enough. I'd met him at a dive bar in Lowell, not knowing he came from a family with a house on Beacon Hill and a compound on Nantucket. I hoped to heck Seth didn't think I'd picked this. I didn't dare look his way.

Charlie had a strong voice. One that made me

think she sang in a church choir. We held our own against Stella, but only because she toned it down for us. When the song ended, we took a bow. I heard a loud whistle among the cheers and calls for more drinks. I looked around and spotted CJ lounging by the door. He wore jeans and a Henley shirt so he wasn't here on official business. My heart pattered a little. It felt like days since I'd seen him. But his arrival meant an end to my mission. There'd be no more questioning people about Mr. Spencer tonight.

He found a chair, pulled it up to our table, and introduced himself to Charlie. "You all were great," he said. CJ was originally from Fort Walton Beach, Florida, aka Lower Alabama or the Redneck Riviera, and had a drawl that crept into his speech every once in a while. He threw an arm around me and pulled me close. I winced as he hit what must be a giant bruise on my shoulder from my training session with Gennie.

"What?" he asked.

"It's nothing. Just a bit sore from my workout with Gennie." I couldn't help myself. I glanced over to Seth's table. He and Herb were standing and looked like they were saying their good-byes. CJ must have realized they were here. He might have looked like he was casually watching me from the door when I first spotted him, but he would have checked out the crowd and assessed its risk for threats at the same time.

"What brings you here?" I asked CJ, leaning close to him and breathing in his scent.

"I was off duty and looking for you since you didn't answer my calls or texts."

I dug in my purse and found my phone. Sure enough, three texts and one voice mail. While I had my phone out, I checked for calls from Luke, but there weren't any. "And you said to yourself, I'll bet she's at the American Legion?" It's not like I'd ever been here before.

"I have my sources."

Stella snorted. "Yeah, and his 'sources' are Awesome."

"As in great?" I asked.

"No, as in Nathan. I told him we were coming."

CJ put his hand to his heart. "Stella, you're ruining my man-of-mystery persona. I'm hurt."

We all laughed. Awesome came in a few minutes later. The night ended with everyone singing patriotic songs. As CJ drove me home, the weight and worry about Luke settled over me again.

At 8 AM on Thursday, Carol and I were parked in my old Suburban outside a two-story Colonial home on Great Road in Bedford. From this distance, I couldn't read the plaque on it that would say who'd originally built the house and how old it was. From the looks of the white clapboard, it was an original. Some of the houses in this area dated back to the 1600s. I clasped my hands around my cup of Dunkin' coffee to keep from reaching for another of the homemade cinnamon rolls Carol had brought along.

"Remind me again why we are sitting here two hours before the sale even opens," I said.

"Because this estate sale is going to be huge and I saw a game table I want on the company's website. It's one of those really old ones where the top folds over. When it's closed, it's a semicircle. The flat back part can sit right against the wall so it takes up less room." Carol, as usual, looked like an ad in a fashion magazine. High-heeled boots, sweater with a wide belt slung around her hips, and leggings. "Plus there was some china that would help me replace pieces in the set I got from my grandmother. Lots of dealers will show up, and I want to be the first one in the door."

I shook my head and laughed. "My, what a difference a year makes." Last spring, I had taken a reluctant Carol to her first yard sale.

"Yeah, you created a monster all right, and I'm not too proud to admit it."

"You know what they say about early birds," I said.

"They get the worm, or in this case, the table."

"And they pay the highest prices. Especially at an estate sale." I didn't like estate sales as much as I liked garage sales or going to thrift shops. The prices were usually higher, and they were less likely to negotiate, especially on the first day. But I was happy to spend time with Carol.

We'd seen each other more often now that CJ and I were back together, since CJ and Brad were also friends. We'd done dinner and theater nights in Boston and family game nights with Carol's twin boys and daughter. The kids called us Aunt Sarah and Uncle Chuck. For some reason, the kids thought the name "Chuck" was hilarious. They loved to yell, "Up Chuck" to him as they held their arms out to be picked up and swung around.

All of us had gone ice-skating on the rink on the town common before spring hit and the ice melted. I was a terrible ice skater. Long ago, someone had told me I had weak ankles, which I think was a nice way of saying I was a klutz. We had picnics planned at Walden Pond in Concord and there'd been talk of camping and fishing. Carol and I planned to let the guys take on that one, and we would have a fun girls' weekend somewhere. But since I'd seen more of Carol in a couples setting, we'd had less times like this when it was just the two of us.

On the way over, we had talked about my crazy week. I turned to Carol. "So what's going on with you this week? How is Paint and Wine?"

"The shop's been really busy, and Olivia hasn't been able to help as much." Carol frowned. "I need to find someone more reliable." She raised her eyebrows at me.

I laughed. "Not me. My garage sale business is booming. How are the kids?"

"They're all in some type of spring sport, then there's field trips, and class parties multiplied by three." Carol smiled. "Getting away this morning is a treat."

"I ran into Brad a couple of times recently."

"He's up to his eyeballs in meetings, and then

with you and the security guard getting kidnapped. He's hardly been home."

"Do you know the security guard? He must have been terrified." I thought back to the night at the VA. The seconds between the time the noose had slipped around my neck and when I'd passed out had been the scariest of my life. "I heard he was locked in the trunk for hours."

"Poor Frank. I'm not sure he'll continue working there."

"What's Frank's last name? Do I know him?"

Carol bit her lip. "I'm not supposed to tell you. I've had strict instructions from both Brad and CJ."

"You're going to listen to them?"

"They're afraid you'll get in more trouble."

"I get it, but it's me you're talking to."

Carol threw up her hands. "Frank Thomas. He's a vet. Older man who was bored after retiring from corporate work."

"Guess he's not bored anymore." My brain was ticking away. *Another vet. Was he really kidnapped, or was he in on the whole thing? Brad vouched for him vehemently, but Brad has been acting kind of weird himself.*

I noticed Carol was staring at me. "How's Brad doing with all of this? His job is stressful enough as it is." The VA hospital system had been a mess, and not everything had been resolved. Fortunately, the VA where Brad worked had been scandal free. I wondered again if that was why Luke was here.

"It keeps him incredibly busy trying to stay on top of everything, new regulations, more inspections. But he's been amazing and seems to be taking it all in stride. Plus, he's in a new organization for hospital administrators. They asked him to be the president. It's lovely for him, but another thing on his plate."

That was a relief to hear. Maybe he wasn't acting strangely at all and he was just overworked. "I ran into him a couple of times when I went to see Mrs. Spencer."

"He's taking this one personally." Carol paused. "If you go see Frank and it gets back to CJ or Brad, I'm in big trouble."

I nodded, not making any promises, and wisely changed the subject. We yakked away until another car pulled in behind us forty-five minutes before the sale. I grabbed some giant canvas totes I always kept in the Suburban. We hustled out of the car and onto the front stoop of the house to start a line.

Chapter 21

"Did you measure the space in your house so you know the table will fit?" I asked Carol, handing her three of the totes. I only kept one for myself because I wasn't planning on buying anything, but I'd told myself that plenty of times before.

"Oh, darn. I completely forgot." She got a determined look on her face. "I want the card table. I'll make it fit."

To tell the truth, I wasn't much of a measurer either. I always advised other people to do it, but when I found something I loved, I made it work somehow, much to CJ's chagrin. I searched my purse. "Here's a tape measure just in case," I said, as I handed it to Carol.

By the time we finished filling each other in on what had been going on in our lives, it was almost time for the sale.

Carol looked around. "Good heavens, there's a lot of people here."

I looked behind me. The line snaked down the

front walkway, to the drive, and out to the sidewalk in front of the house. I recognized a few dealers who regularly attended the garage sales I organized. I had developed a bit of a following and a reputation for being fair.

I turned back to Carol. "A couple of the dealers in line are aggressive about getting what they want. It's a good thing we got here early."

"I'm never going to get everything on my list." Carol frowned, but then her eyes crinkled and she grinned at me. "Sarah?"

I knew from our long friendship that tone of voice meant trouble and most likely for me. "What?"

"I'm going to be the first one in, and if I had a few extra minutes in there by myself, I could grab everything I wanted. Did I mention the necklace I saw? It reminded me of one my dear old gram had." She batted her eyelashes at me.

I groaned. "And what would this few extra minutes involve?"

"I don't know. You're going to be the second one in. Be creative."

If it was anyone but Carol, I wouldn't even try to think of a way to delay the crowd. But she'd always been around when I'd needed her, especially when CJ and I had been separated. I sighed. "I'll do my best."

The door opened and a smiling woman gestured Carol in. Carol darted past her. Before the woman could turn, I fake tripped and grabbed the woman, pulling her toward me. We both ended up outside the door. "Oh my gosh," I said, still holding on to her so we blocked the door.

"Are you all right?" Someone tried to edge in around me, but I moved slightly so they couldn't make it.

"I'm sure I'll be okay." But I winced as I pretended to put weight on my ankle.

The woman tried to pull away. "I need to get back in there," she said.

I clung to her. "Give me one second while I check my ankle. I twisted it. Could you hold my arm for me?"

"Oh dear. Of course." She turned to the crowd. "Hold on for a minute, people. We need to make sure this woman isn't injured." A few people grumbled.

I bent over slowly, lifted the leg of my yoga pants, and studied my ankle. It looked fine, and I was running out of ideas to milk the situation. I stood back up. "I think I'm fine, but could you hold everyone back until I take a couple to steps just to make sure I can get out of their way?" Carol had better appreciate this. I tried to look nervous. "I don't want to be reinjured trying to get out of the way of the crowd."

"Absolutely."

I felt like a jerk. I knew the woman didn't want to have a liability issue for her company. I grabbed the doorframe like I'd seen Herb do, hauled the rest of my body in, and then took a couple of slow limping steps. I turned back to the woman and gave a nod. "Thanks so much. I'm sure I'll be fine." I fake limped down a hall to the farthest back bedroom of the house so I wouldn't have to face anyone for a while.

The small bedroom had faded cabbage rose wallpaper, white lace curtains, and a chenille bedspread on the double bed. I checked out the tag on the bedspread. Overpriced. I opened a closet door since anything goes at an estate sale like this. *Wow, quilts.* They were stacked on the top shelf. I stood on my tippy-toes to pull them down and laid them on the bed. My heart beat a little bit faster. The top one was a double wedding ring, hand stitched. One underneath had blocks with women's names embroidered on them—Chloe, Ursula, Rowena. I wondered who they were, how long ago they'd stitched this quilt together.

Sometimes estate sales made me sad. Why didn't some family member want these quilts? They were beautiful. But I cheered myself by realizing a sale like this allowed other people the opportunity to love and treasure these things. Maybe someone like me.

I tucked the name quilt into my tote to keep with me as I walked around the sale. It didn't have a price on it, but I wouldn't ask until I was at the checkout. Hopefully, there'd be a long line of buyers behind me and whoever manned the register wouldn't want to leave it to find the real price. A few people asked me if I was okay as I roamed. It was so embarrassing.

I slipped into a study lined with bookcases full of books and a few objets d'art. There was a beautiful brown leather desk chair behind a large mahogany desk. A lamp with a green glass lampshade and an old leather blotter were the only things on it. I trailed a hand across the wood, then went over to the bookshelves and started perusing. I found a book by Marc Cameron, one of CJ's favorite authors, so I put the quilt next to my feet and flipped the book open to read the cover copy. Maybe CJ hadn't read this one yet.

"Nice job out there."

I turned. A man stood there looking down at me. His deep green eyes, wavy jet-black hair, and cleft chin didn't impress me much. He looked like he thought he was the bomb with his one shoulder resting against the bookcase, feet crossed.

I straightened to my full five-six and lifted my chin. "I have no idea what you're talking about." But heat crept up my face. Darn it.

"The ankle seems fine." He smelled of expensive aftershave and his sweater looked like cashmere, but his jeans were worn and his boots scuffed.

"I've always healed quickly." I realized one hand was on my hip and I was leaning toward him. I straightened, but in my head, I was going over the moves Gennie had taught me the past few days. Man, would I like to use one on this guy.

"You can't con a con," he said. Then he winked at me as he headed back to the door of the study.

I stared after him, my hand back on my hip.

"Sarah?" Carol came in carrying totes that looked

full. "Excuse me," she said to the winker. She noticed my red face and turned to look at the very fine backside of the man exiting the room. "What's going on?"

I pointed at the man. "I guess I won't be getting any Academy Awards for my performance at the front door. That guy called me out."

"Do you know him?"

"I've never seen him before."

"What did you do?" Carol laughed as I explained, then she held up her totes. "It was worth it. I got everything I wanted, plus some. Thank you very much."

"What about the table?"

"They are holding it for me until I'm ready to pay for everything."

"Are you ready to go?" I asked. While I loved spending time with Carol, Luke was like a shadow following me around.

"I checked. Olivia actually showed up and is covering at the shop this morning. I'm good. I haven't been down to the basement yet."

We wandered through the rest of the house and poked in corners of the basement.

"What's that?" Carol asked.

I peered behind the cedar chest she was pointing at. "Ooooh. It's an old rag rug. Let's pull it out."

We hefted the rug over the chest and unrolled it on the floor. It was a cotton, oval rug. "Wow, someone put a lot of work into this."

"Someone made it?" Carol asked. She wasn't a huge fan of antiques.

"Yes, out of old clothes, sheets, or leftover material cut into strips." This one was soft blues, reds, and whites. "I wish I had a place to put this."

"What about your bedroom?"

"It would look nice in there." I found the price and sighed. "It's too much. At most they'll come down ten percent and probably not that with the crowd that's here." Since it wasn't Carol's style, we left it behind.

When I got home, I dropped the book by Marc Cameron on the trunk that served as my coffee table. I realized CJ might have already read it in the year we were apart. If so, I'd donate it to the library after I read it myself. I hadn't bought the quilt because the cashier had found someone who knew the price. I hadn't wanted to pay three hundred dollars for it, even though it was worth every penny and more.

I checked in on the virtual garage sale site. I approved a couple of posts, but everything looked great. One less thing to worry about. I shot off a quick note to the other admin, thanking her. Now that I was home, I started thinking about Luke again. I'd had fun with Carol, but the whole time I was gone, part of me had been worrying about him. He should have gotten hold of me by now. He'd been missing for two days with no word.

And granted, we'd been out of touch for much longer than two days, but after how we'd parted at the VA, I knew he'd at least call to make sure I was okay if he could. Wouldn't he? When I wasn't keeping busy, fear crawled around inside me. I couldn't think of anything else to do that might help me find him. Or could I?

Chapter 22

Fifteen minutes later, I knocked on the door of a neat Cape-style house off Great Road in Bedford. A man with a ruddy complexion and a slight paunch opened the door.

"I'm Sarah Winston."

Frank Thomas's eyes widened. "Yeah, Brad and Chief Hooker told me you'd show up and not to talk to you."

Darn. CJ and Brad were now upping their game. First, they'd told Carol not to talk to me, and now Frank. I turned to go.

"But to tell you the truth, since I left the army I haven't been good about following orders. Come on in and let's swap stories." He stepped back.

I hesitated for a moment because what if this jovial man was involved in my kidnapping? But I didn't sense any threat so I entered his living room. It had shiny wood floors, a blue upholstered couch, and two large leather recliners positioned toward a large-screen TV.

"Who's here?" a woman's voice called. She appeared, wiping her hands on a dishcloth.

"This is Sarah Winston, Ruth."

"The woman you aren't supposed to talk to?" The woman's dark eyes snapped with energy. Her gray hair was cropped short and she moved like a woman who was used to being in charge.

I looked back and forth between them, knowing I was going to get tossed out.

"We've been so anxious to meet you," Ruth said. "Let me make us some tea, and then we can hear all about you."

If jaws could actually drop, I'm pretty sure mine did. She hustled out of the room and reappeared a few minutes later with a china tea set and a plate of homemade gingersnap cookies on a tray. Ruth poured me a cup of tea with milk and sugar, not checking to see whether that's how I liked it. She poured two more cups, passed the cookies, and settled in one recliner while Frank sat in the other. They swiveled to face me with the precision of a drill team.

I took a sip of the tea to gather my thoughts. It was delicious. I set the cup back in its saucer and put it on an end table next to the couch. A framed picture of a group of young men and women dressed in white T-shirts and jeans at a beach was next to the cup. "Your family?" I asked.

"Yes," Ruth said. "But I'm guessing it's not why you came."

"Or why they told us not to talk to you," Frank added. "You look pretty harmless considering the stern warning."

I couldn't help but smile. "Can you tell me what happened to you that night?"

Frank leaned forward. "I was out on patrol like any other night and spotted a car over by the construction site."

"What kind of car?" I asked.

"A blue Prius."

I nodded. "It's what my brother was driving."

"I got out to see if anyone was in it, and next thing I remember was waking up hog-tied in the trunk of my very own patrol car." He shook his head with disgust. "Can't believe they got the jump on me."

I was disappointed. I'd hoped he'd seen or heard something that might tell me where Luke was. "I'm glad you're okay."

"You don't want to know the rest?"

I perked back up. "There's more?"

"Sure is. I could have told you that much at the door."

"Doesn't seem like the police would care if you heard that," Ruth added.

"What else happened?" I asked.

Frank leaned forward. Carol and Brad might have thought Frank was traumatized by the whole experience, but to me, he seemed energized.

"I heard a couple of men talking about someone named Ethan. How things hadn't gone well with him. 'Course, at the time, it didn't mean a thing to me. Until I heard later in the day about Ethan being killed over on the base."

"Was it only two men talking?"

Frank sat back and was silent for a moment. "I believe so."

"Did they say anything else?"

"Something about Ethan had been cooperating until a problem with a cart. But they'd figured out a way to deal with that."

"It doesn't make any sense," I said. I tried to think if I'd ever seen Ethan pushing a cart around Ellington, but usually he only carried a paper bag. Maybe he'd hidden something in some cart that would lead to whoever was behind all of this.

"Well, everything was kind of muffled with me being in the trunk."

Then it hit me. "Could they have said Bart instead of cart?"

"It's possible. And it might make more sense of what I heard next."

"Which was?"

"As soon as they got their hands on the cart, their problems would be over."

Chapter 23

I sat back, stunned. This was what CJ and Brad hadn't wanted me to find out.

"Drink some of your tea, dear. It will help with whatever ails you," Ruth said.

I took a sip and then another. It didn't mean whoever had Luke had killed him. I had to hold on to the belief these people weren't killers. They'd taken me home more or less unharmed. I had to hold it together because I had more questions.

"You know Brad Carson fairly well?" I asked.

"Yes. Why do you ask?"

"It seems like he's been under a lot of stress. His wife is one of my best friends, and I've been worried about them."

"Brad reminds me of me when I first got out of the service and worked as a civilian."

"How so?" I asked.

"You think you have to prove yourself and quickly. A man like Brad finds it hard to say no to any project. I've told him to slow down or he'd burn out faster than a dud firecracker."

I hoped he was right. That Brad was just over-working and there wasn't something more sinister going on. "Did you know Velma and Verne Spencer?" I asked.

"Of course," Ruth said. "Well, I knew Velma. We were in the garden club together."

"I heard her behavior changed about six months ago."

Ruth nodded. "It's true."

Sometimes talking to New Englanders was like pulling ticks off a dog, slow and painful. "Do you have any idea why? Her son said he noticed it too."

"Piffle," Ruth said. "He's the cause of it."

I scooted to the edge of my chair. "Really? How so?"

"I'm not sure. Velma's a very private woman. One day, we were out planting pansies on the town common. She mentioned Tim being up to his old tricks and she wasn't sure moving close to him was the best idea."

"Did she say why?"

"When I asked her, she clammed up."

I stood. "Thank you for your time and the tea."

Ruth and Frank stood too. They glanced at each other, then focused on me.

"Is there any chance you could come with us to our breakfast club some Wednesday morning?"

I looked at them.

"They are going to be jealous when they heard we met you," Frank said.

"They are?" I asked.

"Oh, and especially when we tell them we might have helped the town hero solve the latest Ellington mystery."

I wanted to smack my head. "I'll try."

As I left Ruth and Frank, Laura sent me a text asking me to meet her for lunch at the bowling alley on base. I did my usual getting-onto-base rigmarole, which included stopping at the visitors' center; showing my driver's license, registration, proof of insurance; and getting a pass to display on my dashboard. The two security airmen working the desk were too busy to chat, but both waved to me.

I drove sedately down Travis, the main thoroughfare, maintaining a precise twenty-five miles per hour to avoid getting pulled over. Base cops were sticklers about speeding. Lots of people were using their lunch breaks to stroll on this lovely spring day. Birds chirped, clouds were few, and the scent of warming earth filled the air. Spring in Massachusetts was hard to beat.

Laura was standing at the counter ordering when I walked into the restaurant at the bowling alley. She was slender and athletic. Her usual close-cropped dark hair had grown out a little. Laura was often mistaken for Halle Berry, which she pooh-poohed, but she did resemble her. We both ordered greasy burgers and fries, which were always better than the anemic salads they offered.

We settled at a rickety metal table for two by a window overlooking the parking lot. The sounds of pins crashing, bowling balls hitting wood, and people laughing provided background noise as we ate.

"We got our orders," Laura said.

"Oh no." Getting orders meant Laura's husband had a new assignment and they would be moving. "Where? When? I don't want you to go."

"The report date is fifteen July. Joint Base Lewis-McChord near Tacoma, Washington."

"At least it's not the Pentagon." Lots of military members wanted to avoid what they called the Puzzle Palace. As a colonel or lieutenant colonel on a base, they might be in charge of a huge program and have lots of responsibility—like Laura's husband, as the wing commander of Fitch. An assignment at the Pentagon meant long hours, long commutes so the family was in a good neighborhood with good schools, and a job that could end up being kowtowing to a three-star general's whims.

"We're both grateful for that, but our families are all on the East Coast."

"How are the boys taking it?" Middle school and high school moves were hardest for kids.

"As soon as they found out there were good hockey teams out there, they were fine. Well, at least okay. They're used to moving and knew it was going to happen."

I was grateful I didn't have someone telling me when and where to move anymore. Ellington felt like home now, and thinking of leaving it behind along with all my friends here was awful. I tried not to look smug. "I have a friend in Seattle. Her husband was Air Force too."

"Who is it? Maybe we've crossed paths."

"Emily Diamond. She's a gemologist."

"I don't think I know her."

"I'll send you each other's email addresses. At least you'll know someone in the area then." I would miss Laura. She was always ready for an adventure and always knew what was going on. "I hate being the one left behind."

"I know what you mean. It's always hard to leave, but then you get caught up in the packing, moving, driving across country, and unpacking and it keeps you busy. I'll miss you, and I'd love Emily's contact information."

We chatted about the base thrift shop and how it had thrived under Laura's leadership. It wasn't an official duty of the wife of the wing commander, but it was expected.

"Have you heard who the new wing commander is?"

"Not officially." Laura stopped and stared out the window at a teenage boy walking across the parking lot to the Shoppette.

"Who is he?" I asked.

"Phil Crawford."

I looked out at Phil. He had shaggy blond hair and a husky build. "The name's familiar."

"He got kicked off base last year for dealing drugs."

"Ah, that kid." I'd heard some girls talking about him last year in one of my not-so-finest moments.

"Why's he back on base?" I watched him walk into the Shoppette.

"He got kicked off for a year. His family is still stationed here so he's back."

"He lived with his aunt in Bedford, right?"

"Yes. And he should be in school. Excuse me." Laura threw down her napkin and left.

I watched her hustle across the parking lot and enter the Shoppette. I finished my fries while she was gone.

She came back a few minutes later. "He said he's sick and he was getting some Sprite." Laura rolled her eyes. "He didn't look sick or sound sick."

"James told me there'd been some problems with kids getting in trouble by the old thrift shop. Is Phil part of it?"

"I'm not sure. As far as I know, everyone's been trying to keep a close eye on him. No one wants those kind of problems on base."

Phil came back out of the Shoppette with a plastic bag in his hand and headed toward the base housing area. He had the kind of swagger girls loved. It made me think of Lindsay, my helper at the garage sales. I tried to think if she'd mentioned any boys lately and hoped she was staying far away from him.

"Any news on your brother?" Laura asked. "I heard he might be involved in Ethan's death."

I shook my head. "I don't believe it. But I haven't heard from him and I'm worried." I filled Laura in on what had happened the other night.

"And you woke up in your bedroom." Laura

shivered. "I'm not sure which is scarier. But I'm really sorry Luke is missing." We both ate a few bites of our burgers. "So aren't you going to ask me about the investigation into Ethan's death?" Laura asked.

"I wasn't, actually." Okay, I was hoping Laura would bring it up. "But if you know something, I wouldn't mind hearing it." After my incident with James, I didn't want to put any of my other friends in an awkward position.

"There's a rumor Ethan was a heroin addict."

"Did you hear it through the wives' network?" I asked.

Laura shook her head. "No. This time it was the two teenage boys' network."

"They might be wrong. Ethan had type-one diabetes. There were syringes and insulin with his things."

"It wouldn't be the first time the boys were wrong."

"Have you talked to Carol or Brad lately?"

"No. Why?" Laura leaned forward.

"He's seemed really stressed lately. It worries me."

"Have you heard anything?"

I balled up my napkin. "Just that his job is stressful and he's taking on too many other things."

Laura studied me. "You've got a lot going on. Maybe you're so used to looking deeply at something that you can't accept. In this instance, it is what it is. There's nothing else."

"You're right. If it looks like a duck and quacks like a duck." A little stress seeped out of me. I'd been worried about so many things lately. I was borrowing trouble, as my grandma used to say.

"Do you have time to stop by the thrift shop?"

I glanced at my phone. "No. I have to go over to Gennie 'The Jawbreaker's' house. We have a big sale on Saturday." Ugh. Another workout.

"What? You moaned. Isn't it going well?"

"The sale is going fine. Gennie decided she needed to teach me to fight. I have more bruises and sore spots than I can count."

Laura finished her burger. "Ha. Good luck."

"I'll need it."

"Can you still help out on Friday night?" Laura asked.

"I live to spend my Friday nights at the thrift shop. That's how exciting my life is." After a quick hug I headed over to Gennie's house.

Chapter 24

There was a note on Gennie's door saying she was in Dorchester working with her contractor on the building she was renovating. *Woo-hoo!* That was good luck, and tomorrow my friend the antique dealer was coming over to appraise some items, which meant no workout then either. My body might survive this week after all. Fortunately, I had a key to Gennie's house. I spent two hours at Gennie's house and then drove over to the Spencers'.

I called CJ as I headed over but only got his voice mail. I wanted someone to know where I was because being alone at the Spencers' still gave me the chills. He wouldn't be too happy about it, but it was work and I needed it.

When we'd first decided to get back together, I'd told CJ I wanted to take things slow. I think I wanted to be wooed again and do some wooing myself. But maybe once you'd been married for almost twenty years, it was impossible. We'd soon fallen into a routine of CJ spending most nights in my apartment. I liked it, usually, but I think a bit more wooing—cards, flowers, an unexpected gift or date—would have been good for both of us.

It was after four when I stood in the Spencers' kitchen with Tim.

"I can't stay long. It seems like Mom's coming around." He looked down at the old linoleum floor. "Of course, that last time, I thought that she had a seizure."

"Please don't feel like you have to stay. I'm used to working alone."

"I wanted to ask you about someone."

"Sure."

"It's just, he's a friend of yours."

I was mystified. "Ask away."

"Brad Carson. How well do you know him?"

"Really well. I've known him for almost twenty years. Why?"

"It's just . . . he's been hanging around my mom's room a lot. It just seems odd to me."

It seemed odd to me too.

"And he was there both days that she had seizures."

"What are you trying to say?" Did he think Brad had something to do with Mrs. Spencer's seizures or what had happened at their house? That was impossible.

"He said he was at the garage sale the day my

dad died, and then he keeps showing up at the hospital."

"I know he was at the garage sale and I also talked to him in your mom's room the other day." I wasn't sure what Tim was insinuating. But it bothered me that I was concered about Brad's behavior too.

"Have you reported this to anyone?" I asked.

"No. I mean, it's probably just a coincidence. I know he works at the VA. He probably knew my parents. And maybe he's just one of those guys that goes above and beyond his normal duties."

"He told me that's where he knew them from." But Brad didn't work with patients so I wondered again about their connection. I worked up a smile. "You're right. It must be a coincidence. Brad wouldn't hurt anyone."

"Thanks. That makes me feel better. I'll head back to the hospital." He stopped at the door. "And thanks for all of your support."

After Tim left I went back to work and tried to ignore all the little thoughts pricking at my brain about Brad and his recent behavior. I found two sets of china pushed back on a top shelf of a cupboard, one Lenox and one Noritake. The Noritake looked like a pattern from the early seventies and would be hard even to give away. The Lenox was an older pattern, but even it would be difficult to sell at a fair value. So many baby boomers were downsizing, there was a glut of china and silver available, which meant people were only getting pennies on the dollar. And the sites that bought china for replacements didn't pay any better. To make matters worse, millennials didn't seem interested in china.

I hadn't seen either of these sets when I'd gone through the house with the Spencers. Mrs. Spencer must have shoved other, more useless things in front of the china to hide them. Both might have more sentimental meaning to Mrs. Spencer than I was aware of. I put the Lenox back in the cupboard and made a note to ask Tim about the Noritake. For now, my best bet was to get rid of things I knew had no value. It wasn't really my job, but I felt like Tim needed the help. Thinking about Tim made me wonder about Ruth mentioning that he'd been in some kind of trouble. I'd have to do some research later.

When CJ called at five, I was knee deep in a pile of plastic grocery bags I'd found stuffed under the sink.

"What's for dinner?" he asked.

This proved my whole point about the wooing. He now expected me to feed him, even though I'd had a long day of work too and I had a couple hours still ahead of me. I stuffed some of the plastic bags into another one. What was with these things? They multiplied like those Tribbles in a *Star Trek* episode. You have a couple because you might need them, then *boom*, they're everywhere.

"Sarah? Are you there?"

"Yes." I was chanting, *If you can't say anything nice, don't say anything at all,* to myself.

"Soooo," he said.

"We can either stay in and argue or go out." It was my way of giving him a chance to make the right decision.

"I was kidding. I planned to take you out."

I wasn't sure he had been, but maybe we could hash through some of what was bothering me. "Great."

"Where do you want to go?"

I looked down at my outfit, jeans and a long-sleeved T-shirt. "How about DiNapoli's?"

"Okay." CJ didn't sound enthused because the DiNapolis were definitely on my side when it came to CJ and me. I wasn't even sure they were happy we were back together.

"I'll meet you there at seven," I said. With luck, I might have time to shower and change.

"Great. Love you."

"Love you too," I said as I hung up. Maybe he'd finally tell me what was going on with the investigations into the Mr. Spencer's and Ethan's deaths.

As I locked the front door of the Spencers' house, I heard a shout. I turned and an Asian woman in scrubs marched over to me.

"What do you think you're doing?" She had a bob of jet-black hair; strands of silver sparkled in the late afternoon sun.

I introduced myself. "I'm helping Tim go through things. He hopes to move his mom to Florida as soon as she's well enough."

The woman snorted. "Behind her back? Velma would have a fit."

I'd been worrying about it myself. "I'm following her son's wishes. Have you known the Spencers long?"

"We've lived next door for the past five years. Velma's a saint putting up with Verne."

My eyebrows popped up. That had been the exact opposite of what I'd experienced.

"Oh, I know she can be difficult too. But she's moved with him so many times, her head was spinning. And now he wants to move again. Every time she starts to settle someplace, they have to go."

Since military people moved a lot, it didn't seem too surprising, plus they'd been settled here for a while. "Did Mr. Spencer have any problems with anyone else?"

"Who do you think you are? The police?" she asked.

"Not at all. I liked Mr. Spencer. He was lovely to work with."

"And Mrs. Spencer wasn't?"

It wasn't advisable to talk poorly of a client so I didn't answer.

She threw her hands up. "I'm a nurse. I know Velma's changed over the past few months."

"Maybe from the stress of moving again?" Some people really couldn't handle change.

"I think it was more than that."

"Any idea what?" I asked.

"None whatsoever."

"Are you one of her nurses now?" I hadn't seen her the couple of times I'd been up there.

"Yes. Why?"

"I know she's had a couple of relapses. Any idea of the cause?"

"I'm not about to discuss her medical condition with you."

Fair enough. "Could her seizures have been caused by someone, or was it natural?" Ever since Tim had mentioned Brad was at the hospital on the day of his mom's seizures this thought had been rolling around in my head.

Her eyebrows shot up. "Again, I'm not going to tell you anything. Why would you even suggest that?"

"Maybe whoever killed Mr. Spencer doesn't want her to wake up." I clapped my hands to my mouth, stunned I just said that out loud.

The woman paled.

"Did they have any problems with other neighbors?" I asked. She might not answer medical questions, but there was no reason for her not to answer this.

The woman glanced over her shoulder toward her house. I thought she was going to bolt.

"Verne got pretty upset when the Blacks' kids ran through Velma's garden. Words were exchanged." She pointed over to a ramshackle house with a drooping awning over the front door and a yard littered with toys and bikes. "But that was last summer."

"Any other problems?" I asked.

She half turned away but looked back over her shoulder. "The man over on the other side of them. They hated each other, but I don't know why. And he's been gone since the morning of your yard sale."

Chapter 25

When I got home, I sat on my couch. I would ask CJ about the missing neighbor at dinner. I opened my computer to do a little research on Tim before I had to get ready. I plugged in his name. Lots of information came up, too much to sort through, so I typed in Tim's name, followed by **arrest records**. Ruth said he'd been up to his old tricks so I wanted to see just how bad it was. A mug shot popped up. I clicked on the site and a new window popped up that said, **Shocking news about Tim Spencer—view now.** I closed the window and scrolled down. I finally ended up paying to find information on a site that looked somewhat legitimate. I found a copy of a restraining order taken out by Tim's wife ten years ago. And then a document for court-ordered rehab six years ago. Wow. When Frank's wife, Ruth, had mentioned Tim had been in some kind of trouble, I hadn't realized I'd find anything like this. He seemed so nice and genuinely concerned for his mother. Was it all an act? At dinner, I'd make sure

CJ knew all of this. *Dinner.* I glanced at the time and shot off the couch. Time to primp.

I arrived at DiNapoli's at five past seven, freshly showered, mascaraed, and clothed. As I'd showered, I'd realized if I wanted to be wooed I had to put some effort into it too. I put on my sexiest bra and panties, a lacy black set CJ hadn't seen yet, and a low V-neck shirt, tight black skirt, and red heels. It had been warm enough out and the distance short enough that I'd walked over. Maybe I could convince CJ to go for a drive after dinner and we could find some secluded spot to make out at like we had when we were young. Cops always knew a town's best secluded spots.

Rosalie stood at the counter but hurried around to me and pulled me into a big hug. I waved over her shoulder to Angelo, who stirred a big pot of something.

"You look beautiful tonight," Rosalie said when she let go of me.

Maybe I should get dressed up more often. "I'm waiting for CJ," I said.

"I know," she said. She pointed to the seating area. There was a table with a red and white checked tablecloth and a RESERVED sign on it. A silver candlestick held a white unlit candle, and a bouquet of white roses in a crystal vase sat against the wall. DiNapoli's didn't normally have tablecloths, candles, or roses, or take reservations.

"That's for me?" I asked. I melted a little. Maybe CJ understood me more than I realized.

Rosalie nodded. "I'll bring you something to nibble on while you wait."

I headed over to the table a little self-consciously as people turned to see who was getting the special treatment. Most of the tables were full, and I waved to a couple of people I knew. Four men sat at a table behind mine sharing a large meat-covered pizza. The same four men I'd seen at the American Legion. *Yeesh*. If I noticed strangers in town, I really had made this town my home. They all leaned forward, talking in hushed tones. Interesting. I sat with my back to them, hoping I'd learn something about them. I almost laughed at myself. They didn't call Di-Napoli's the town hub of gossip for no reason. But all I heard them chatting about was baseball and how good the pizza was.

A few minutes later, Rosalie brought over a glass of red wine in a stemmed glass and an antipasto platter. I looked around. "Aren't you supposed to put the wine in a kiddie cup?" It was how they usually served wine on the sly to their friends since they didn't have a license to serve alcohol.

"Good news. We now have a license to sell wine and beer." Rosalie beamed. "Someone finally forgave Angelo for being a pain in the patootie and approved the license."

"Finally." I raised my glass to her, then took a drink. "Ummm, my favorite Chianti."

"When is CJ supposed to be here?" Rosalie asked.

I looked at my phone, not only to check the time

but to see if he'd sent a text or called. Nada. "Any minute."

Rosalie looked like she wanted to say something but instead patted my hand and lit the candle. She stopped at the table full of men behind me and asked if they wanted anything. Two of them asked for a Sam Adams lager. The other two wanted water. I hoped this meant they'd start talking again. I tried to remain as quiet as possible. The bits of conversation that drifted over to me were about hunting, who could lift the most, being veterans, which I'd already known since they were at the American Legion, so not helpful, and who'd caught the biggest fish on their last trip. Typical guy stuff. Darn.

I picked at the antipasto plate while I waited for CJ. I hoped he'd have some news about Luke, Ethan, or Mr. Spencer. News he would share. The men had moved on to talking about their families. I went to my virtual garage sale site on my phone to see if there was anything interesting for sale. It was often full of kids' toys and clothes. As I flicked through, I saw a couple of old end tables. They needed a lot of work but the woman was only asking ten dollars for them. I really didn't have room and had a fairly busy few weeks of sales ahead of me. I started to scroll by, hoping I wouldn't regret my decision later.

I flicked back to the end tables and typed interested sending PM under the listing. The old teardrop drawer pulls made me think these were true antiques. Unless, of course, someone had switched them out or ordered realistic-looking replacements. I fired off a message saying I wanted the tables. A reply came seconds later, saying they were mine if I could pick them up tomorrow morning between ten and noon. I told her I'd be there.

I felt someone standing next to me and looked up, smiling. But it was Seth, not CJ.

"Hi," I said. *Brilliant, Sarah.* My phone buzzed. It was a text from CJ saying he had to cancel. It wasn't as if I weren't used to it. It was a way of life you adapted to as a military spouse or as a spouse to any first responder. It didn't stop a little sigh from escaping. Way of life or not, I wasn't always happy about it.

"Bad news?" Seth asked, taking in the flowers, candle, and tablecloth.

I smiled, putting on a happy face as one does. "CJ's busy."

Seth frowned for a moment. "I was going to grab some takeout, but how about dinner?"

What was the right answer here? Saying no seemed petty. I'd made my decision, so why couldn't I have dinner with a friend? However, Seth wasn't just any friend. I'd had feelings for him. But I loved CJ. I'd chosen CJ.

"Dinner sounds great." We were in a public place for goodness' sake. It wasn't like we were skulking around behind people's backs. I'd never pick DiNapoli's for a clandestine meeting. Half the town would know we had dinner together before they went to bed tonight. Besides, maybe Seth would have some inkling about what was going on with Luke or the two murders.

Seth took off his suit coat and tossed it over the extra chair. He took off his tie, stuffed it in his suit coat pocket, and popped open the top couple of buttons of his white cotton shirt. I tried not to stare, but he looked at me right as I tried to look away. He grinned.

"Let's order." He stepped back so I could walk to the counter first.

Gale stood at the counter. I ordered baked ziti.

She looked at Seth with a smile. "The usual?"

"Yep. A hot Italian sub with fries, please. And a glass of Chianti."

Rosalie raised an eyebrow at me from the back of the kitchen. I gave my shoulders a little lift. She nudged Angelo, who whipped his head around. Fortunately, Seth was fussing with his wallet and missed the whole thing. I insisted on paying for my own food. Once we settled back at the table, I searched for a neutral topic because I didn't want to talk about relationships and I didn't want to dig for information right off the bat.

"How's the campaign going?" I asked. Seth had been appointed to replace the ailing district attorney last year, but the term would be ending and he'd have to run for reelection.

"It's starting to gear up. I could use someone with your energy on my team. Actually, I could use you."

Oh dear. What did that mean? I knew he worked very hard at what he did. "If there's some way I can help, I will." The candlelight flickered across his handsome face. I wish I could blow the damn thing out because it was surreal sitting here with Seth in a quasi-romantic setting. One CJ had arranged and meant to enjoy with me.

Chapter 26

Gale brought our food over with an appreciative look at Seth. He smiled at her and she blushed. Seth had that effect on women.

"How's your Criminal Procedure class going?" Seth asked her.

"So much better after the help you gave me," Gale said, batting her enviable eyelashes.

I beat down a twinge that felt something like jealously as Gale sashayed away. Darn, if she didn't have a near perfect backside. "So you've been coming here a lot?" I asked.

"Can't beat the food or the prices."

I picked up my fork and dug in.

"You look beautiful, Sarah."

I felt warmth start in my chest and swirl up my face. I must be redder than a Red Sox cap. Seth had a way of paying attention to me that made me feel like I was the only woman he'd ever noticed, which couldn't be further from the truth. Seth focused on my neck. I realized too late I hadn't worn a scarf or a turtleneck. I'd grown kind of used to the bruises and had thought they were fading. I put a hand to my throat. "I'm fine," I said, even though he didn't ask.

"I read the report. It doesn't sound fine."

"It was scary. But the worst part is I haven't heard from Luke since." I swallowed what felt like a base-ball-sized lump. "I'm scared for him." Okay, this was the perfect segue to find out what Seth knew. "Have you heard anything?" My voice wobbled unexpect-edly. There it was again, the vulnerable feeling when I was with Seth. I realized I felt like I'd been holding my breath since the night Luke had disappeared. That I'd thought if I stayed crazy busy I'd be okay. But I wasn't.

Seth studied my face, his forehead wrinkling. "Nothing you probably haven't heard from CJ."

"I know it doesn't look good that his fingerprints were at the Spencers' house."

"And his 911 call puts him there too."

"But what's the motive?"

"It's not always straightforward. I wish it was." Seth leaned in toward me.

"There must have been other fingerprints in the garage." My voice sounded a little too desperate, even to me. I needed to calm down, but under the circumstances, how could I?

"Of course there were other fingerprints. Mr. and Mrs. Spencers', their son, Tim's, some that haven't been identified yet."

"So someone else could have done it."

Seth settled back in his chair. "I shouldn't have

shared that with you. Please don't spread it around. The evidence points to your brother. No one else."

"But the fingerprints you haven't identified."

"Neighbors, delivery people, a friend who borrowed a hammer and returned it. None of it means it wasn't Luke."

My eyes filled with tears.

"I'm sorry, Sarah. I wish I had better news for you. If we could find him and he could explain, it would be better for him."

"He wouldn't just disappear without checking on me."

Seth just looked at me. There was a hint of pity in his eyes. I couldn't stand that everyone was judging Luke. My heart ached even considering the possibility that Seth was right.

"Have you heard anything that would help us find him? Because we have nothing since the two pings off the cell phone he was using the night he disappeared."

Two pings? I'd only heard about the one near the VA. "It's not much to go on. Although, he was actually at the VA," I said. If he'd been spotted near the second ping, I was sure I would have heard. However, maybe not, since this was the first I was hearing about it. I wondered if the ping had been before or after the one in Bedford.

"Yeah, nothing came from the one in west Ellington."

I sucked in a little bit of air. *New information.* What was on the west side of Ellington? The Concord

River, a bit of conservancy land, some farms, and then the town of Carlisle.

"You didn't know about it, did you?" Seth asked.

I shook my head. This was one of the reasons I'd been attracted to Seth. He understood me on a different level than anyone else ever had. But that was all in the past. "No. CJ doesn't tell me much." I sipped my wine. "And it isn't much to go on anyway."

"It's nothing to go on, Sarah. The area's been searched, and there's no sign of Luke." He reached for my hand, but I jerked it back. "I'm sorry."

I wasn't quite sure if he was apologizing for reaching for my hand or for the situation with Luke.

"I have some sources looking for Luke," Seth said. "I want to find him safe and get to the bottom of what happened."

"Thank you." I wondered if he meant Mike "The Big Cheese" Titone when he said sources. Mike had been in Seth's neighborhood the other night. Or maybe he had other, more legal sources available to him as DA.

"And we're going to find whoever did that to you." Seth pointed at my neck. "If I had my way, we'd toss them in jail and lose the key."

I questioned him about Mr. Spencer and Ethan as we ate. He evaded each of my questions and somehow always managed to turn the topic back to me. How was I doing, how was my business. He even managed to make me laugh by telling me a funny campaign story. Eventually, Seth got a call and left.

Angelo called out to me as I was about to leave. "Can you stay for another glass of wine, Sarah?"

I realized it was almost time for the restaurant to close. The men who'd been sitting at the table behind me had left, as had everyone else but one couple at a table by the window. I glanced at my phone. No messages from CJ. "Sure. I'd love to."

Angelo and Rosalie had become family. And Angelo usually had some story to tell me that had a subtle lesson or bit of advice. I felt like I could use some right now. Others in the community didn't always appreciate Angelo's advice and said he was bossy and opinionated. Maybe he was, but I'd always found it came from a place of love and caring. I sat back down, and the DiNapolis joined me with a bottle of Chianti and a plate of Italian cookies Rosalie had made.

Angelo poured three glasses of wine. We toasted one another. Rosalie pushed the cookies in front of me. "Eat. You look like you're getting too thin."

"I do?" I asked. They both nodded. It was especially nice to hear after having two strangers ask me if I was pregnant the other night. "I don't think anyone's ever said that to me before." I took a cookie.

"Tell us how you're doing," Angelo said. "We keep hearing stories, but want to hear your version."

In a small town, stories spread faster than news of antiques at a garage sale. "What have you heard?"

Angelo and Rosalie looked at each other. Angelo shrugged and spread his hands apart. "You know how the town can be. You killed two people. Your brother's a serial killer, and he's kidnapped the Callahans. CJ's protecting you both."

I gritted my teeth. I think I liked it better when people were calling me a hero.

"Those are the crazy ones. We quickly squelched them," Rosalie said. "Angelo threatened to kick a table full of people out when he overheard them."

"What else?" I asked.

"That your brother's lived in this area for years using an alias," Angelo said. "I told them not to talk about a veteran like that." His face grew a little red. He loved our country and had served himself.

Good heavens, was it possible? I shook my head and then filled them in on what I knew.

"Don't worry about the crazy stories," Angelo said. "Most of the people are rooting for you."

Chapter 27

As soon as I got home, I sat at my small kitchen table with another glass of wine. I opened my computer and Googled Bartholomew Winst. What if he really had been living in this area for a long time? We were so out of touch, it could have happened easily enough. The thought made me sad.

One article popped up with Bart Winst's byline. My eyes widened as I scanned the story. It was about stolen valor, the term used for people who pretended to be members of the military. I sat back in my chair. Had Luke been tracking down people who pretended to be in the military all these years? The article was dated a year ago.

There was a lot of controversy about people wearing uniforms who hadn't served. Some said it was their First Amendment right to wear whatever they wanted. Obviously, those who served disagreed. I did some more digging and ended up watching online videos of confrontations between vets and the posers. The confrontations ranged from polite conversations to ridicule to angry shouting matches. Some of them made me uncomfortable—the ones that people got wrong.

Why was there only one article? I tried another search engine, using Bart instead of Bartholomew. No luck. Maybe he used another name I didn't know about. But I didn't have a guess as to what it could be. I needed to call my parents to see if they knew any of this. Without mentioning I'd seen Luke recently and that he was a suspect in a murder. Maybe this was why I avoided going home. Luke's absence always felt more real when the three of us were together without him. The rift had hurt my parents deeply, and my distance, both physically and emotionally, didn't help.

"Hey, Mom. How are you?" I asked a few moments later. It was only six in California. We made small talk for a while before I took the plunge. "I've been missing Luke, Mom." Heck, that was literally true— he was missing. "Have you heard anything from him?"

"We haven't, honey. Why ask now?"

"I found an article by him using the pretend name he used when we were little. I'll send you the link." It was hard to ask things I should have asked long ago.

"Why'd he leave?" I knew he'd come home from Iraq for a few months when he'd gotten out of the service. But CJ and I had been living in England by then. I hadn't paid much attention.

"Do we have to talk about this?"

"Yes. It's time."

Mom was silent for a moment, then sighed. "We tried to get him help."

"Help? What for?"

"The VA wait was impossible. We offered to pay for a psychologist but . . ."

"But what?" I asked.

"He was self-medicating. First with alcohol and then with who knows what. Then he started stealing from us or friends who came by."

"Why didn't you ever tell me any of this?"

"You'd just miscarried for the first time. And you adored Luke. We didn't want to upset you any more than was necessary."

I had withdrawn from the world for a bit after my first miscarriage.

"What happened then?" I asked.

"We told him he had to see someone or leave." Mom was quiet for a moment. "He left."

"And there wasn't any clue to where he went?"

"No. He left most of his things here. Believe me, we went through everything with a fine-toothed comb. He didn't take much. Just a couple pairs of jeans and shirts. He left most of his medals, books, stuff I thought he valued."

"He has medals? Which ones?"

"I'm not sure what they are. Valor or something."

"Do you still have them?"

"As far as I know, we do."

"Can you snap some pictures of them?"

"Sure, honey. Dad might have to help me find them. But we'll look."

"Thanks, Mom. I love you."

"Love you too."

A few minutes later, my phone binged with a message from my mom. I can't find his uniform.

I sent a text back. You don't have any pictures of him in his uniform?

No. But your father found this.

A picture of a certificate popped up. It stated Luke had been awarded a Purple Heart. I sent a quick thanks and then flipped back to the photo of the certificate. A Purple Heart meant he'd been injured. Another thing my family had never talked about. How had we gone from our happy, talk-about-anything family before Luke enlisted to not discussing anything important? My brother was a war hero with substance abuse problems. It hap-pened all too often. Then someplace along the line he'd started chasing down people who pretended they were in the military. Why?

I stared into my wineglass while I thought. Luke had been at the Spencers' house. Was it possible Mr. Spencer had faked he was in the military? There'd been money on the floor beside him in the garage. What if someone else knew and was blackmailing Mr. Spencer? I sipped my wine. It could have been Ethan. Maybe he'd tracked down the Spencers and was shaking them down. It would explain them both having lots of cash. I wondered if the police had checked to see if the two different piles of cash had serial numbers that were similar.

Angelo had said there was a rumor my brother had been living in the area for a long time. What if he had been tracking down military impostors and somehow ended up near here? I looked through the photos on my phone until I found the one I'd snapped of Mr. Spencer and his war buddies. I downloaded it to my computer because it was too hard to see much detail when it was this small. I pulled it up and studied it. As far as I could tell, it was authentic. It was too late right now to go see Charlie and have her take a look at it. There must be something I could do instead of sitting here speculating. Something that would give me some answers and help me find Luke.

I shot off a text to Mike Titone. I'll be at your cheese shop in forty minutes. Then I turned off my phone. I didn't want him to tell me no.

I waited outside the dark, closed cheese shop. The drive had only taken me forty minutes, but it took another fifteen to find parking a few blocks from here. There'd been lots of people on Hanover Street, but there were fewer people here. Occasionally, a couple would walk by. A neon sign for a bar blinked on and off further down the street. And there were lights in apartments above the mostly closed storefronts.

After waiting five minutes, I turned my phone

back on. No messages or calls. I sent another text to Mike, I'm here. Ten minutes later, a black SUV with dark tinted windows pulled up. Mike popped out of the back passenger seat, dressed in a tux. Even in the dark, I could tell his glacier-blue eyes were icier than normal. I had the decency to feel a twinge or two of guilt. I'd never seen him dressed formally and had obviously pulled him from something important. I was a little surprised he'd shown up instead of blowing me off.

Mike straightened his cuff links before acknowledging me. "Well?"

I looked at him. This version of Mike Titone was scarier than the other versions I'd seen of him— helpful Mike, poker-playing Mike, jogging Mike. Now I could see how all those stories I'd read about him might be true. Maybe he really did leave a slice of cheese on people's porches as a warning if they crossed him. I hoped I wouldn't find one on mine.

"Have you been looking for my brother?"

"Who's your brother?"

"Luke Winston, aka Bart or Bartholomew Winst."

There wasn't a flicker of recognition in his eyes, but once again I remembered he was an Oscar-worthy liar.

"Why would I be looking for your brother?"

I shivered a little in a gust of wind. At least I hoped it was the wind that caused the shiver and not fear. Mike hadn't answered my question. "Because Seth Anderson told me he had other sources looking for my brother."

"And you think I'm his other source?"

"You two know each other and have something going on I don't understand or even want to understand." At least I didn't think I wanted to know what was up between them.

"Get in the car."

A man stepped out from the front passenger side and opened the back passenger-side door for me.

"I'm fine." I tried to sound tough, but my voice wavered.

Mike shook his head in disgust. "For cryin' out loud. Get in the car. We can talk while I head back to the gala you pulled me from."

I climbed in. "CJ knows I came to see you." I should have told CJ was I coming to Boston. But I knew if I had, he'd have tried to stop me.

"Whatevah," Mike said as his driver took off. "So when you asked me to hide someone the other day, was it your brother?"

I nodded. "Yes."

"Why?"

I filled him in, even though I had a feeling he already knew most of the story. The driver pulled up in front of the Omni Parker House.

"What are you doing here?" I asked.

"Attending a fundraiser for a no-kill animal shelter."

Well, that was ironic. Mike opened his door, climbed out, and turned back to me. "I'll see what I can do, but don't get your hopes up. Joey," Mike said. The driver turned and looked over his shoulder at Mike. "Take her to her car."

Joey nodded and straightened his massive shoulders before glancing at me in his rearview. "Where's your car?"

I explained where I'd parked. As we pulled away from the curb and the locks on the car doors clicked down, I wished I'd done more training with Gennie. And I hoped "take her to her car" wasn't code for "put her in cement boots and dump her in the harbor."

Chapter 28

At nine Friday morning, I sat next to Charlie in her living room, alive and cement boot-free. Mike's men had been very polite and had stayed until I'd started my car and pulled away from the curb. I tried to push aside the little unwanted doubts that flicked through my head randomly saying, *Maybe Luke did do it.* I answered them with a firm, *Maybe Tim did it, maybe those four men hanging around town did it, maybe some random person I haven't even thought of did it, the one who left the unidentified fingerprints behind. Maybe Brad killed him.*

Ugh. Stop it.

"You wanted me to look at a photo?" Charlie asked. She had a colorful African print turban on this morning. Jeans and a T-shirt completed her outfit.

"It's of Mr. Spencer with some buddies when he was in Vietnam." I'd brought my computer with me, and I opened it and pulled the photo up. The more information I had about the Spencers, the easier it would be to find their killer. We both stared at the photo.

"Can you zoom in?" Charlie asked.

I made it larger and watched Charlie as she studied it. She narrowed her eyes, leaned in, and seemed to absorb every detail. After a long minute, she leaned back.

"Something's not right with this photo," she said.

"What?" I asked. Adrenaline zoomed around my body. And sitting still became difficult. My foot started jiggling in anticipation.

"It might be nothing." Charlie pointed at Mr. Spencer's T-shirt. "It's not a regulation shirt." She scanned the photo again. "But things were crazy back then, supplies were limited. Any clean shirt would do."

She held the photo farther away.

"Is there something else?"

"Other than I need some reading glasses?" Charlie paused. "It's odd all three of them have the same shirt. But like I said, things were different in the jungle." She looked at me.

"There's something else bothering you," I said.

"It's the foliage. It almost looks arranged." Charlie shook her head. "That's silly. I'm trying to read something into this to help you. Sorry."

I concentrated on the picture again. "It does look arranged. But what does it mean?"

Charlie shrugged.

"Thanks for taking a look at it."

"If anything comes to me, I'll give you a call," Charlie said.

* * *

My next stop was to get the end tables I'd found on my virtual garage sale site. The woman lived down the street from Herb Fitch. It was a street lined with older homes that, for the most part, were nicely maintained. Grass was mowed, flowers were planted, and the houses were freshly painted.

I saw a crowd of people in front of Herb's house, and a police car. *Oh no.* I parked and hurried over to join the crowd. Herb stood clutching his cane like he wanted to beat someone with it. Officer Awesome stood next to him talking calmly about what I couldn't hear. Both of them stared at Herb's house. Someone had spray-painted LIAR in big black letters on the shingles of his covered porch.

I turned to the woman next to me and realized she was Herb's next-door neighbor. "Who would do this to Herb?" I asked.

I saw recognition in her eyes. We'd talked last February when Herb was out of town.

"Well, if it isn't our local hero come to save the day."

I sighed inwardly, wondering when the damn hero thing would finally blow over. "Did they catch who did this?" I asked.

"Ain't that whatcha here for?" She looked me over. "Not that I know of. It's a shame. Herb of all people. Couldn't ask for a better neighbor. He's a do-anything-for-ya kind of guy. Even if he can't do as much as he used to."

"Any idea why someone would write 'liar' on his house?"

"None whatsoever." She headed back toward her house.

I walked over to Awesome and Herb.

"What? Do you have a police scanner now?" Awesome didn't seem thrilled to see me. "Are you becoming an ambulance chaser?"

"No. I'm sorry, Herb." I gestured toward the paint.

There was a bit of steel in his eyes as he looked at the words. "Bastards." It came out *Bastdahds* with his accent.

"Any idea who did this?" I asked him.

"I think I just answered that."

I stared at him for a minute, then smiled. "You're right."

"Good thing I needed to re-shingle the roof anyway. I'll move it up on the to-do list."

"Why would someone do this to you?" I asked.

"Excuse me," Awesome said. "Do you want my badge and notebook?" But he had a hint of a smile.

"Sorry." Although we all knew I wasn't. It changed Awesome's hint of a smile to a full grin.

"No idea," Herb said. "We done here? Standing around like this kicks up my arthritis."

"I think I've got everything I need, Herb. I'm really sorry about this," Awesome said. He nodded to me. "Sarah."

Herb and I watched as Awesome walked back to his car. When he climbed in and drove off, I turned back to Herb.

"Okay. Why do you think someone did this?"

Herb squinted at me. "Don't know." He walked to his porch and went into his house without looking back.

I didn't believe him.

I kneeled down on the cement garage floor to examine the end tables. The owner and her three little kids, one in her arms, the other two each clinging to her legs, watched me. The tables were in rough shape. In some places, the stain was worn off. But the wood looked like walnut, not cheap particleboard. I tried to keep my face neutral and not show my delight. Both had two drawers with brass teardrop drawer pulls.

I pulled open a drawer. The wood was dovetailed together and irregular. *Oh, wow.* It must be a hand-made, instead of machine-made, piece. I slid the drawer out all the way. The thinner piece of wood in the bottom had shrunk a bit. The wood around the edge was slightly lighter. Both were signs of age, which would increase the value of these pieces.

I sniffed the wood. There was a faint musty smell, but no visual signs of water damage. Mostly it smelled like wood. I pulled both drawers all of the way out and looked at the backs. One of them had a bit of white chalk on it, possibly a signature. These were the real deal, authentic instead of fakes.

It made me think of Herb, my brother, and the word LIAR being painted on Herb's house. What if Herb wasn't a veteran and someone had found out? I couldn't imagine Luke spray-painting someone's house. Of course, I couldn't imagine him being all right and not calling either. Not making sure I was okay after what had happened the other night. But I also couldn't handle the idea he was in serious trouble or maybe even dead.

"Is something wrong?" the woman asked.

It jarred me back to the end tables. I stood and looked at her. She stared at me like I'd lost my mind. It wasn't the first time someone had done that when I examined a piece of furniture.

"I have great news. These are handmade pieces. I'm guessing pre-eighteen-seventy." I pointed to the white chalk. "See these marks?" The woman nodded. "It could be a signature of the maker or a partial one, even though most American furniture wasn't signed. These could be very rare and valuable." I sighed. "Even without a signature, they are worth way more than ten dollars. I can't take them from you."

The woman's eyes widened. "Are you sure?"

"Ninety percent. I have a friend who's an appraiser. She can give you more information." I started to look up the number.

"Why didn't you pay me the ten and take them?"

I didn't want to tell her it was because her house looked rundown or the three little kids clinging to her worn clothes made me feel guilty. "Half the fun of going to garage sales and flea markets is trying to find something for nothing. But I have to live with myself," I said. I found my friend's phone number and wrote it down.

"Thank you," she said as I left. "You're my hero."

I cringed. There was that word again.

* * *

I drove over to the Spencers' house. I tried telling myself it was to put the finishing touches on the garage sale. But I knew why I was really going. It was to find evidence to support my theory Mr. Spencer had faked his service, and that my brother had somehow found out and had confronted him. It explained why Luke's DNA had been present at their house. But most of all, I believed someone was threatening to expose Mr. Spencer and blackmailing him. Probably his killer.

I went straight to Mr. Spencer's office and started poking around in the old metal file cabinet. Whatever I found, I'd take straight to CJ. He dealt in facts and laws. I'd gone to him in the past with suppositions. This time, I'd go with evidence. First, I looked for military records, but I didn't find any. Suspicious, but not damning. There were a lot of things already packed away in the stack of boxes in the corner. I flipped through a few tax records. Mr. Spencer had been getting disability pay from his time in the service for years. I stared at the page. The disability pay in and of itself wasn't cause for alarm. Even CJ had a certain part of his retirement pay classified as disability, and therefore, taxed differently. But it meant either I was completely wrong and Mr. Spencer had served, which actually would be a good thing. Or, at some point Mr. Spencer had stolen someone's identity and had been using it for years.

I opened another file drawer. A lot of the tabs on these folders referred to California. There was a base in Los Angeles aptly named Los Angeles Air Force Base or, as those stationed there affectionately called it, Hollywood Air Force Base. It was known to have a more relaxed atmosphere than operational bases, the ones with jets and missiles. I pulled a folder with a handwritten label that said *Tropical Tragedy*. It held a script written by a Velma Cooper. What the heck? Was that Velma Spencer?

I read the first few lines, then grabbed my phone and Googled the title. A few references to a low-budget comedy set in Vietnam came up. I found another file with photos from the set. That's why the foliage looked arranged in the picture I'd shown Charlie. It was a movie set, and it also explained why the uniforms didn't look right.

Maybe that's how the Spencers had met. Mr. Spencer had been cast in the movie based on Mrs. Spencer's screenplay. There was one photo that was very similar to the one on the wall. Only this photo had a fourth man in it, Ethan.

"What are you doing in here?"

I whipped around to find a very angry Tim Spencer staring at me.

Chapter 29

"Geez, Tim, you scared me," I said, as my mind sorted through and discarded stories to tell him.

Tim frowned. "What are you doing in here?" He didn't sound any happier this time.

"I was looking for your father's military records for you. You'll need them for his obituary and the funeral."

Tim's face relaxed.

"I haven't found them yet. They must be packed in one of those boxes." I nodded toward the stack against the wall.

"I'm sorry. There's so many things to think about I can barely keep it all straight."

I edged toward the door. Tim must not have heard the scuttlebutt about Luke or he wouldn't be this friendly. "Since CJ was military, I know about these things. How's your mom?"

"She opened her eyes this morning. Just for a minute or two, but her doctor said it was great progress. I wish she'd heal so she could tell us who did this."

"So do I, Tim." Because then my brother would be off the hook.

"I came by to get her a clean robe and gown. Some underthings." He sounded about as enthused as a person facing their last meal.

"Do you want me to pack a few things for her?"

"I can't ask you to do that."

"I'd be happy to. I'll grab a brush for her, too." I scurried down the hall to the master bedroom. I found an old-fashioned rectangular-shaped overnight case, the kind with a mirror in the inside lid and a tray with little divided sections, in the closet. As I gathered things for Mrs. Spencer, I also looked through drawers, lifting stacks of clothes to see if anything was hidden underneath. But I came up empty.

A few minutes later, I found Tim sitting in the living room, holding the figurine Mrs. Spencer said looked like him. He set it on the table when I came in and looked up. Tears covered his face. It yanked at my suspicious mind. He might have been in trouble in the past, but I'd seen nothing but a loving son since he'd arrived. And how could I judge him so harshly when my own brother had problems too?

"What can I do?" I asked him. I sat on a chair across from him.

He pulled a handkerchief out of his jeans pocket. It was the old-fashioned cloth kind. He wiped his face with it. More tears rolled down his face as he looked at it. "This was my dad's." His fingers trembled, as did his voice. "He was my rock. The only person in my life who always had my back. I don't know what I'll do without him." Tim cried quietly.

I didn't want to say anything trite, like *it'll be okay* or *you'll be fine*. I certainly didn't want to blurt out that his father had lied about his service at a time like this. I shifted on my chair.

"I've done some stupid things in the past. Screwed up more than once." Tim took a deep, shuddery breath. "He helped out financially, but it wasn't only that. It was showing up when I was at rehab, making sure my family was okay. He knew how to handle Mom. What am I going to do?"

I didn't think Tim expected me to answer. I'm not sure he even remembered I was there. We sat quietly for a few minutes as Tim pulled himself together.

"Thanks for listening."

"I wish there was something I could do."

Tim nodded. "Look, Sarah, I don't think I can go through with selling my mom's things without her go-ahead."

"I understand completely. It's been weighing on my mind too."

"I'll need the key back then."

Oh no. "How about I find your dad's military paperwork for you and I can drop it and the key off to you at the hospital?"

"It's very generous of you. But no thanks."

Rats. "I'll grab my purse from the office then." Did Tim know his dad hadn't really served?

Tim nodded. I hurried down the hall, snapped

a quick picture of the script with my phone, and shoved the photo with Ethan in my purse. On the front porch, I handed Tim the key to the house.

"How much do I owe you for the work this week and for the work you did on Saturday?"

"Nothing. Don't worry about it." I wanted to get out of there because it felt like the photo in my purse was a big, throbbing tell-tale heart right out of an Edgar Allan Poe story. I waved as I drove off. Tim stood on the porch staring after me.

I went home and made a salad for lunch. I chopped away on carrots and tomatoes, and ripped pieces of lettuce to tiny bits. I realized I was sad and yet angry at Mr. Spencer. He'd lied to me about his service and defrauded the government. I surfed the Web while I ate, trying to find out more about *Tropical Tragedy*. But there really wasn't anything. Maybe it had never actually been made. If the little bit I'd read of the script was an indicator of its quality, the project might have been filmed and shelved.

I was frustrated that Tim had wanted his key back. It meant I'd lost access to any more information. What had caused Tim to change his mind? Although, finding me in his dad's office might have been reason enough.

After washing my dishes, I took the photo I'd swiped out of my purse. Yes, that was definitely a young version of Ethan. I snapped a quick picture of it with my phone. People had assumed Ethan was a Vietnam vet, but Ethan would never accept any help available to veterans. Maybe because he wasn't one and felt guilty when people assumed he was.

Even scarier, maybe he'd known Mr. Spencer wasn't a veteran either. Ethan could be the blackmailer. They obviously went way back. He'd been buying military memorabilia at the sales we'd both attended. I hadn't seen anything like that when I searched his backpack. He might have been passing it off to Mr. Spencer to shore up his story about being a vet. I thought about Mr. Spencer telling me stories about his time in Vietnam. He always made it sound like some big adventure and I bought it believing it was his way of coping with the situation.

I thought about Herb and many of the other veterans I knew. They were stoic. Filming a story about Vietnam probably was a big adventure. I got up and paced my living room. It was a lot of speculation but my heart started to pound. How dare they?

It all seemed perfectly plausible to me but I needed more to get CJ to look at someone other than Luke. There'd been money on the garage floor and money in Ethan's backpack. Hopefully, there would be serial numbers or something connecting those two piles of money. I needed to ask CJ ASAP.

I barreled out, but saw the door to the empty apartment next to mine open. I hurried over, entered, and heard voices coming from the bedroom.

"This looks perfect," a woman said.

I couldn't tell how old she was from her voice, but at least she sounded normal.

"Great," Stella said. "I left the lease in the kitchen. Let's go sign it."

They turned the corner into the living room where I stood. The woman was tall, thin, and casually dressed and stunningly beautiful in a natural, no-makeup way.

"Hi," Stella said. "I'm glad you could stop by, Sarah. You can meet your new neighbor." She turned to the woman beside her. "This is—"

"I know who she is," the woman said. "Sarah Winston."

My face grew warm. I hope she didn't start in on the hero thing.

"She always finds dead people. No way I'm renting a place next to her." The woman hustled out without a backward glance.

I stared at her back, mouth open. I glanced at Stella and she was doing the same.

Stella put her hands on her hips.

"I'm sorry, Stella."

"That's a first."

"Maybe, from now on, I shouldn't meet the potential renters."

Stella burst out laughing. "I had no idea you were so notorious."

"From hero to zero."

"She was a little too perfect anyway."

"We can't have anyone showing us up." I managed a smile. I was an idiot thinking the woman had been about to call me a hero. Maybe I needed a good dose of reality before I became one of those obnoxious people who believed what they read about themselves in the press.

"How did dinner with the family and Awesome go?"

Stella sighed. "It was going along swimmingly. I warned Nathan not to say anything about baseball. As we were leaving, Aunt Gennie turned the game on. Nathan glanced back as the Yankees made a bases-loaded home run to win the game."

"What happened?" I asked, trying to suppress a grin because I had a good guess.

"He cheered."

"What did you do?"

"Grabbed his arm and made a run for it."

"And?"

"And I've been ignoring all their phone calls and texts."

I couldn't help but laugh.

"So how are you doing?" Stella asked.

"I got fired from one job and am almost finished with your Aunt Gennie's sale," I said. "But there are plenty of other projects lined up."

"Who fired you?"

"Tim Spencer. Actually, selling things while his mom was in a coma didn't feel quite right to me anyway."

"But?"

"There's no but."

Stella looked at me.

"Okay, there's a but. I can't share it right now."

Stella nodded. "Okay, then. I'm going to go put the ad for the apartment back up."

I loved Stella. She always knew when to push and when to back off.

Chapter 30

I drove through Dunkin' at two and bought two coffees and then added a couple dozen donuts to my order. I was going to stop at the police station. Even though the whole cops and donuts thing was some kind of myth, I knew these cops, at this station, loved their donuts from Dunkin'.

Pellner was in the parking lot when I arrived. He relieved me of the donuts and took me in the back way so I didn't have to sit in the lobby and wait to be buzzed in. A few minutes later, I sat across from CJ waiting for him to finish a call. When he hung up, he came around his desk and pulled me into a big hug, kicking the door closed with his foot. He turned me and backed me up against the door, kissing me the whole time. I reached up to pull him closer when the phone on his desk rang. He broke off the kiss. "Sorry."

He sat back down and took the call. While he talked, I looked at the framed photographs on the wall next to CJ. A lot of them were of CJ and his dad deep-sea fishing in Florida. The first shot had been taken when he was around two. The last one I hadn't seen before. It must have been taken while we were separated. CJ had hauled in a big fish. He looked happy. His dad grinned and pointed at the fish. In others, he posed with Air Force buddies or town officials. I'm sure the ones with the town officials had been hung for political reasons and not because he really wanted to see them.

CJ hung up again, but this time he stayed put in his chair. "I'm sorry I didn't show up for dinner last night."

"What happened?" Maybe he knew something about Luke and was avoiding telling me.

"Seth Anderson called and gave me a list of things to follow up on."

"Oh." Seth had given CJ a to-do list and then had dinner with me? Had he planned it somehow? Couldn't have. He wouldn't have known CJ and I'd planned to have dinner last night or that we would eat at DiNapoli's. "What kind of things?" I asked.

"The kind of things a chief of police has to do when the DA asks him."

"Thank you for the flowers and candles. It meant a lot to me that you took the time to do that, especially when you're so busy."

"You're welcome. I hope it wasn't too awkward sitting there alone."

If I didn't tell him, he'd hear it from someone

anyway. "I wasn't alone. Seth happened to be there and ate with me."

CJ's lips formed a grim line as he took that in. Time to change the subject.

"There were these four men sitting right behind me. I think they're from out of town. Have you seen them around town?" I gave him a brief description of what they looked like.

"The turkey hunters? They were at karaoke the other night?"

Trust CJ to have noticed them. "Yes. How did you know they were hunters?"

"They stopped by the station to make sure they had the right permits. Why?"

"I don't know. Something about them bugs me."

"They seem fine. If they were up to something, they wouldn't be coming to the police station or hanging at public places."

"Or it's the perfect cover."

"Sarah—"

"Have you checked out the Spencers' neighbor? He's been gone since Saturday morning."

CJ shook his head slowly.

"You haven't heard anything?" I asked. Maybe this was the break Luke needed.

"I have heard something. Not that it's any of your business." He leaned back in his chair. "His brother died unexpectedly and he left on short notice for Ohio."

"Did he tell you? Maybe he was lying."

"Why are you poking around? Do I tell you how to run a garage sale?"

He'd tried to when I'd started my virtual garage sale, but I wouldn't bring that up right now. "No."

"Don't you trust me to do my job?"

I cringed a little. "I'm sorry. It's my brother we're talking about." I paused. "Any word on Luke?"

"Nothing on where he is," CJ said.

"But there's something else?"

CJ steepled his fingers together. "We have his military records. His record isn't good."

"He had an honorable discharge, didn't he?"

"Yes, but barely. There were fights and arguements with superiors."

"Maybe he wasn't cut out to be a Marine."

"We also found arrest records over the years."

"Recent ones?"

"No."

"What was he arrested for?" I was getting mad, but tried to tamp it down. This was CJ's job.

"Vagrancy. Drunk in public."

"So nothing serious or violent." I paused. "Why are you suddenly sharing information with me?"

"There's a pattern of problems. I know you love him, but I want you to be prepared. All the evidence points to Luke."

It's what Seth had said too. "Luke has a good side." I told CJ about Luke's Purple Heart. "Luke tracked down people who faked serving in the military." I told him how to find the link to the article.

CJ read it and then leaned back in his chair. "That's interesting."

"But wait, there's more," I said, imitating the television commercial. Then I started in with my theories about Mr. Spencer not being a vet and his possible connection to Ethan. I pulled out the picture and gave it to him.

CJ studied it. "How did you get this?"

Oh bother. I hadn't thought it through. "I was working at the Spencers' house. Remember, Tim had asked me to go through the house and find more things to sell."

"And you found this picture with things to sell?"

I refrained from squirming in my chair. "No. I was looking for Mr. Spencer's military records. Tim found me going through the files."

"But he said it was okay to take this picture."

"No. I just took it."

CJ tossed the picture on top of his desk. "And then you decided to bring the stolen picture to me."

I stood. "I shouldn't have taken it. But at least now you have some idea what's really going on."

"What *you* think is really going on. I can't use that picture."

"Are you sure?" I scooped the picture off his desk.

"It's complicated, and I don't want you to end up being prosecuted for theft."

Yikes, I didn't want to be prosecuted for anything. "Did you hear about what happened at Herb Fitch's house?"

"I did."

"Anyone have any theories about why someone would spray-paint his house?"

"We're following up on it."

In other words, *Butt out, Sarah.*

CJ frowned. "Awesome said you were on the scene."

"Just by happenstance. I was going to buy some end tables from a woman who lived down the block from him."

"I don't think there's room for anything else in your apartment."

Ah, the age-old minimalist versus the not-at-all-minimalist argument. "I didn't end up buying them."

"Sorry," CJ said. "Buy them if you want them."

I looked down at the picture in my hands. "Hey, what about Mr. Spencer's Purple Heart? It should have his name and rank on the back of it."

"Did you take it too?"

"No. I saw it near his body. It must be in your evidence room or with his personal things. Did Tim pick those up?" If Tim had and looked at the Purple Heart closely, he might know his dad's been lying. What child would want that out in public? It might be why he wanted his key back.

"Good idea, Sarah." He stood. "I'll check on it right now."

Cue the exit music. "One more thing. Have you talked to Brad lately?"

"What, you suspect him too?"

Of something, maybe, but obviously this wasn't the time to mention it. "I was hoping we could all get together soon. He's been really busy lately."

CJ nodded, but in a distracted way, as he looked over at his computer monitor. I leaned over his desk for a quick kiss. I didn't tell him that our conversation had made me more determined to find Luke and clear his name. Or, if it was Luke, to make sure he was caught and paid for what he'd done to the Spencer family.

Chapter 31

I stood in front of Brad Carson's desk, determined to find out what was going on with him. Carol could brush off his behavior as being too busy, but I wasn't so sure. Tim's questions about Brad had continued to bother me. I hoped my next call wouldn't be to Vincenzo to have him help save Brad's neck. Brad waved me to the chair across from him. His office was cramped and filled with overflowing metal file cabinets. The walls were decorated with official-looking plaques interspersed with artwork by his kids. It smelled faintly of burnt coffee.

"What are you doing here, Sarah?" He looked at me suspiciously.

I guessed it was because I'd closed his office door when I came in. "Something's up with you, and I want to know what. Everyone keeps telling me you are too busy, but I'm not buying it." I was worried Carol didn't even realize something was amiss since she'd just said he was busy.

Brad adjusted his tie. "No idea what you are talking about."

I laced my fingers together in my lap. "Both times Mrs. Spencer relapsed, you were at the hospital." It was a lot harder to get out than I'd thought it would be.

"You think I had something to do with it?" Creases deepened on Brad's forehead. "I wasn't the only one there those days. Not by a long shot. You were there, Tim, many other people. I can't believe you'd even accuse me of trying to hurt her."

I had to so I could watch his reaction. It seemed genuine enough. "I don't think you did anything to her, but Tim thinks it's odd you're visiting her. Something's up. You're an administrator here. You don't deal directly with the patients." I waved my hand around. "Your office isn't even close to the patients."

"It doesn't mean I don't know any of them." He started to put his finger in his collar to loosen it, but jerked it away when he noticed me watching. Brad folded his hands together on the desk.

"Tell me what's going on. I don't want to have to involve anyone else." I couldn't believe I was threatening a longtime friend. But I had to for Carol's sake and their kids.

Brad stood, picked up a marble obelisk, walked over to my side of the desk, and then sat in the chair next to mine. The one between me and the door. He weighed it in his hand, staring like it might have some answers. Brad looked at it so long I began to sweat. I should have been more upfront with CJ about my concerns. I gulped.

Brad finally placed it back on the desk. "After Mr. Spencer died, I decided I'd go over their benefits to see what was available to Mrs. Spencer."

"Why? That's not your job, is it?"

"No. But it was such a tragedy, and I've seen how families are affected. I planned to help Tim navigate his way through the process." He jiggled a knee. "I am an administrator, but I like to get out and remind myself there's a human side of the story. With all the problems we've had in the past few years, I was being extra careful with the paperwork."

"And?"

"I found some discrepancies."

"Mr. Spencer didn't ever serve, did he?"

Brad's eyes widened in surprise. "How do you know?"

"It's not important. What have you been doing at the hospital?"

"I wanted to talk to Mrs. Spencer. I hoped she could shed some light on this. I hoped I was wrong."

"Have you told Tim any of this?"

"No. Not yet."

"How could they get away with this?"

"Back when they started their scam, it was easier. Paperwork wasn't digitalized. It was mimeographed and filed by hand."

"Why would they do it?" I knew the answer even as I asked it.

"Money," Brad said. "Between the disability and retirement pay, the medical benefits. It adds up."

"What are you going to do?"

"I still want to wait and talk to Mrs. Spencer. I still hope I'm wrong."

I sat back in my chair. "I don't think you are."

Brad leaned forward. "Let's keep this between us for now, okay?"

"Isn't it fraud?"

"Yes."

"I don't want you to get in trouble."

Brad stood. "I appreciate that. Will you keep my secret until I can figure out what to do?"

Brad was doing something wrong for what sounded like the right reason. I walked to the door, looked back, and nodded. I felt the weight of keeping another secret for someone weigh on me.

I'd finished everything I had to do at Gennie's to prepare for the sale on Saturday. While I worked, I thought through my list of suspects now that I knew Brad was innocent. Tim loved his dad, so killing him made little sense. Although killing someone never made sense. I was still suspicious of the four men who'd shown up in town right when all this happened. I knew CJ was convinced they were just here to hunt turkeys, but I wasn't as sure. There were the fingerprints from the unknowns, as I'd taken to calling them in my head. And then Luke. Each day that passed increased my anxiety about Luke and his involvement in all this.

I realized I was staring blankly at the Victorian settee I'd fixed the other day. It had held together. I'd have to tell whoever bought it the truth about its precarious legs. Everything looked as good as it could. My friend the appraiser had come in and helped with the pieces I didn't feel confident in pricing. Stripped down of all the paintings and knickknacks, the room's elegant Colonial lines showed through. Even with the low ceilings and dark woods, I could envision living here. It was a beautiful home.

"Sarah?" Gennie called.

I found her in the kitchen, although I dragged my feet a little getting there. I wasn't ready for another lesson, but knew it was inevitable and good for me.

Gennie patted the kitchen stool beside her. "You look like you're preparing for the guillotine."

"Maybe that should have been your nickname—Gennie the Guillotine, instead of Gennie the Jawbreaker."

Gennie laughed. "Where were you when I needed you?" She handed me a bottle of water. "Drink up. I want you hydrated before we sweat."

"Is this some kind of trick?"

"My, aren't you suspicious. Which is a good thing when assessing an enemy. Girls are trained to be nice. Today I want to talk some of that training out of you and then teach you a couple of moves."

"Okay." Talking was much better than punching a bag. I rarely injured myself while talking. Well, there was the one time when I was chattering away to a friend and smacked face-first into a parking meter. But it was a long time ago.

"The two most important things are knowing you will do whatever it takes to save yourself or someone else. And assessing your enemy."

I nodded. "Got it."

"Are you willing to gouge eyes, break a nose, see someone else bleed?"

I winced. "Sure."

"You winced and said sure like you were some timid little lamb."

Now she was making me mad. I'd fought once and survived. "I'm sure."

"That's better, because if you give off an aura of confidence, you're less likely to be a victim. It makes you stand taller, gives you a look that makes a bully or career attacker go elsewhere."

I straightened my shoulders.

"Do you know who Ronda Rousey is?" Gennie asked.

"Mixed martial arts fighter. Undefeated for a long time."

"Before her first loss, Ronda said she might lose. It gave her opponent a mental edge."

It's not like we were in the same league, but I got the point. "Okay."

"If you have to fight, know how to. Let's go down and I'll show you a couple of moves. There's only so much you can learn in a few days."

Thirty minutes later, I'd worked up a good sweat.

"So what's today's takeaway?" Gennie asked.

"Attitude is everything. You can attack the eyes,

but the blink reflex often saves them. If someone is coming at you, step to the side and yank them past you if you can."

"And then?"

"Run fast and scream." I pantomimed screaming and pumped my arms like I was running.

"Very funny. It's not much, but it will have to do until I have things set up in Dorchestah. I'll expect to see you down there."

I nodded. As sore as I was, it made sense to know something about defending myself.

I hurried into the apartment, feeling bad I was twenty minutes behind schedule. I'd promised Stella I'd be there at six to meet the latest person who was interested in renting the apartment next to mine. My hair was matted with sweat, and I was pretty sure I smelled really bad. Hopefully, whoever was coming would be late too and I could grab a quick shower.

As I hustled into the foyer, Stella came down the stairs with a man following her. They were both laughing. I skidded to a stop and stared at the man with his jet-black hair, deep green eyes, and cleft chin. The man who'd called me out at the estate sale I'd gone to with Carol.

Chapter 32

"Sarah, perfect timing. This is Ryne O'Rourke," Stella said.

"We meet again," he said.

"You can't rent the apartment to him," I told Stella, gesturing to Ryne.

"Why not?" Stella asked. She glanced back and forth between us.

"He's a con man. He told me himself."

"It was a joke," he said. "You know, like you can't kid a kidder?"

"That's not what you said." I shook my head. "We need to check him out first."

Stella glanced away. "Um, it's too late. Ryne signed a lease."

Stella was a terrible judge of men. Although she and Awesome seemed to be doing okay. I couldn't believe she'd let a stranger rent the place without checking his credentials. I looked at him. "I don't care if he signed or not. She has to run a background check."

Ryne laughed. "Be my guest."

"My ex-husband is a police officer," I said. Maybe that would scare him off.

"Well, I guess we won't be seeing much of him then," Ryne said.

"But you will because we're kind of back together."

"Kind of?" he asked.

Jeez, he was annoying. "We are back together. He's here a lot. And Stella dates a cop."

"Great. Can't wait to meet them. See you later, ladies."

He sauntered out. Stella and I both took in the fine view. Then I shook it off. "Stella."

She held up a hand. "Not a word. It will be fine."

"You don't know that."

"He moved here to help his ailing uncle with his antique business in Concord. He's a nice man."

"Time will tell," I muttered, and headed up the steps to my apartment. Ryne O'Rourke. The name was so Irish it sounded fake. I'd have to have CJ check him out. At the landing, I looked down for Stella, but she'd already gone into her apartment. Probably so she didn't have to hear anything more from me.

A small brown box sat by the door to my apartment. I picked it up, carried it inside, and opened it in the kitchen. I lifted off some packaging material. A wedge of Edam cheese or one of those others with the bright red waxy coating sat at the bottom. My knees felt rickety as I stared down at it and its blood-red coating. Oh no. Maybe the rumors about Mike were true. I should have stayed away from him. That last trip to Boston must have been one too many.

With shaking hands, I dumped the packaging material in the trash. A thick, creamy envelope was mixed in with it. What was in it? Anthrax? Explosives? I held it up to the light, but couldn't see a thing. I held it away from me and ripped the envelope open. Nothing happened. No white powder spilled out. Nothing went boom. It contained a card with a message. *Sorry, I haven't been able to find your brother. Hope the cheese brightens your day. Mike.*

I collapsed on one of the kitchen chairs. I really needed to quit Googling people and believing what I read.

My phone dinged, reminding me to meet Laura at the thrift shop at 7:30 PM. I took a quick shower, fluffed my hair, and swiped on some makeup. Since I still had some time before I needed to leave, I settled on my couch with my computer. The woman who owned the end tables had sent me a nice thank-you message.

I read through a few other messages about the virtual garage sale site and then moved on to my next research project, Herb Fitch. I typed his name into the search engine and, as expected, quite a few articles came up. Herb was well known in the community, had served on the police force, worked with disadvantaged youth, and participated in a lot of events at the American Legion.

I read several articles and found a picture of Herb

in his uniform at a Legion event from a couple of months ago. Charlie stood near him. I zoomed in on the picture and studied it. I was no expert, but everything on his uniform—patches, ribbons, and medals, plenty of the last two—looked real. Then I noticed his belt. I frowned at the photo and zoomed some more. It definitely wasn't a military belt. I snapped a photo of the picture with my cell phone. What if Herb hadn't served and whoever had written LIAR on his house was right? I called Charlie and left a voice mail telling her I needed to talk to her.

Laura and I surveyed the back room of the thrift shop. We hadn't worked here for the past few days so it was a sea of clothing, boxes, and bags. I couldn't sit home waiting for word of Luke or I'd go completely nuts. I'd learned nothing from CJ and Mike hadn't found anything. I wasn't sure how much effort he had put into looking for Luke because he had no real reason to. And until I talked to Charlie, I wasn't sure what my next step would be. But maybe Laura would have information about Ethan.

"Anything new and exciting going on around here?" I asked.

"Mark got his official orders, and the report-no-later-than date said fifteen June instead of July."

"Nooooo," I said. "Don't leave me." I started yanking things out of bags. I made three piles—keep, recycle, and discard.

"Hey, be gentle. You might break something."

"Yeah? Well, too bad." I grinned to soften my words. It was inevitable in the military. Oh, the odd family here and there managed to plant themselves someplace and stay for years. For most of us, it was always onward and upward.

"I talked to your friend Emily. She gave me a lot of great information about the area. She loves it there."

"Maybe I'll figure out a way to come see you next fall." I grabbed a sweatshirt out of a bag, but it felt lumpy. I unfolded it carefully. "Look at this, Laura. It's a Belleek ring holder." I plunged my hand into the bag. "I think there's more in here too."

Laura stopped hanging up clothes and waded through the sea of containers over to me. We dug out three Belleek bowls of varying sizes and a Belleek sugar and creamer. Belleek was made in Ireland, a cream bone china with delicate green shamrocks hand-painted on them.

"How valuable is it?" Laura asked.

"Not thousands of dollars, but depending on the age, it can be pricey." I held a piece up to the light. The china was so delicate I could almost see through it. "It's called Parian china."

"Which is?"

"It's supposed to imitate marble and is named after the Greek island of Paros."

"Why?"

"Because the island is known for its white marble."

"You are such a smarty-pants."

"My grandmother had Belleek. I've always loved it."

"Maybe I can use all of the pieces for the charity auction this month," Laura said.

"When is it?" Every year, the spouses club had a big event with a silent and regular auction. All the money went to scholarships for the dependents of military members. It was usually a fun party, and there was always a happy rivalry among the bidders.

"It's in a couple of weeks. You and CJ should come."

"We haven't been to anything on base in a really long time. Maybe it's time to reappear as a couple."

"We always had a great time when we were all together."

"Maybe I can get Carol and Brad to come too."

"Yes. And let's ask them to join us for a last fling together before we move."

"Oh, come on, there will be more than one fling." There were usually lots of going-away parties when you left a base, some official events like a change of command, and some fun office and neighborhood parties.

Something thunked against the back door. I hurried over and yanked the door open. Lindsay stood there with Phil, the reformed drug dealer. His arm was around her waist, holding her tightly to him. He had a relaxed "everything's cool" look on his face, but Lindsay's hair was messy and her breath came out in short pants, as did his. Laura walked up behind me.

"It's about time you got here, Lindsay," I said. "Are you going to help us sort through stuff too, Phil?" Phil's eyes widened when I used his name. I had no idea what was going on, but wanted to make sure Lindsay was safe. Something about Phil gave me the shivers. I stepped toward Lindsay and pulled on her arm. For a minute, Phil held tight and I thought we were going to have a Lindsay tug-of-war, but then he dropped his arm.

"Sure you have to work, Lindsay?" Phil said. "I wanted to take you out to dinner."

"I promised Sarah I'd help her. Sorry," Lindsay said. She stepped around me and into the thrift shop.

I mentally reviewed everything Gennie had taught me in case Phil didn't give up easily. Instead, Phil sketched a salute and ambled off, hands in pockets. I hustled back inside, locking the door and throwing the dead bolt. Sobbing noises came from the main area of the thrift shop. I found Laura rubbing Lindsay's back as they sat on an old couch that was for sale. Laura raised her eyebrows at me like she had no clue why Lindsay was crying.

I sat on the other side of Lindsay and took her hand. "Did he hurt you?"

Lindsay babbled out something, but it didn't make sense.

"Take a moment," I said. I was wondering if I should call the security police but decided to wait until Lindsay told us what the heck was going on.

Lindsay closed her eyes and took a couple of deep, shuddering breaths. "I think Phil killed that homeless vet."

Chapter 33

"Ethan? You think Phil killed him?" That wasn't what I'd been expecting to hear. But I trusted Lindsay. She was a smart girl.

"Why?" Laura asked. We looked at each other over Lindsay's head.

"I met him in the woods over by the old thrift shop."

James had told me kids were hanging out there.

"He said there was going to be a big party." Lindsay shrugged. "I'd been hearing about them and decided to meet him. Ugh, I'm an idiot. He's one of those boys that says all the right things. I didn't listen to the voice telling me something was off." She sighed.

"You aren't the first it's happened to." It had happened all too recently to me.

"I got there, and no one else was around. Just Phil smoking some weed." Lindsay's face turned bright pink. "He had a bottle of vodka too. We drank part of it, and then he started bragging about all the money he had. He whipped out this wad of cash. He doesn't have a job and his dad is enlisted. I can't imagine him giving Phil lots of money. I asked him where he got it." She stared down at her purple, sparkly UGGs.

"He wouldn't say at first. I started teasing him, saying, 'What, did you take someone's lunch money?' Stuff like that. Then he got paranoid and asked me what I knew." Lindsay shook her head. "I told him I didn't know anything and that I had to go."

I took Lindsay's hand and gave it a squeeze.

"He said he couldn't let me leave until I understood it wasn't his fault. I asked him what wasn't his fault. And he said that the homeless man died." Lindsay took in a deep breath. "Phil said he hit him up for some heroin. Ethan denied having any. Phil shoved him and Ethan's head hit something. He got scared and ran off. Then he heard later the man had died."

"He left him there?" I asked.

Lindsay nodded. "When I grabbed my phone, Phil saw the look on my face. He snatched the phone out of my hand. I kicked him in the, uh, in a vulnerable place. When he doubled over, I ran. I could hear him running after me. He kept getting closer. I saw Sarah's car and came here. He caught up right after I knocked, tried to make it look like everything was fine." She shuddered.

"You did the right thing. Laura, call the security police. I'll call CJ."

* * *

Forty-five minutes later, the base had been shut down, troops were out searching for Phil, and gossip was flying, judging by the number of texts Laura and I were getting. From what I had overheard, it sounded like Phil was long gone. Even so, each car was being searched as it left base.

Luke hadn't killed Ethan. I'd wanted so much to believe the story he'd told me the night at the VA. The relief washing through me made me realize how many doubts had crept into my mind since that night. I'd started to believe what CJ was saying instead of trusting my gut.

James and CJ came over to where Laura, Lindsay, and I still huddled on the couch. CJ squatted down so he was eye level with Lindsay. "Do you have any idea where Phil might have gone?"

Lindsay lifted her shoulders and dropped them. "No. I don't know him that well."

"What's going on?" I asked.

"We can't find him." CJ blew out a frustrated puff of air. "He tossed his cell phone on the side of the road before he left base."

"Doesn't he have an aunt in Bedford?" I asked.

"The Bedford PD have already been over there. No sign of him." CJ stood.

"Maybe he still has my phone," Lindsay said.

CJ whipped out his phone and Lindsay typed in the locator information. A few minutes later, a map popped up, showing the phone moving south on Interstate 95.

"Thanks, Lindsay. Hopefully he's the one with your phone and he didn't pass it off to someone else," CJ said. He called the state troopers so they could track down the car. Then he turned to Lindsay. "James will drive you home if that's okay with you."

Laura rose. "Why don't I take her? She knows me better."

"It's up to you, Lindsay," CJ said.

"I'd rather ride with Miss Laura. My mom will freak if I get dropped off in a police car."

"I'll go in with you, if you want," Laura told Lindsay. We all exchanged hugs and James walked them out.

"Sarah, can I talk to you for a minute?" CJ asked when I started to head out after them.

I followed CJ over to a quiet corner of the thrift shop in front of the kitchenware.

"You realize you've been wrong about Luke this whole time, don't you?" I asked him. I'd never call him out in front of anyone, but I wouldn't hold back now that we were alone. "You're wrong about him killing Mr. Spencer too."

He looked down at me.

"What is it? Is Luke okay?" I asked. I wrapped my arms around my waist.

"We haven't found Luke."

I wasn't sure if I was relieved or disappointed. "Then what's going on?"

"I looked at the Purple Heart from the Spencers' garage."

"Was it his?" This could be the proof I needed that Mr. Spencer had faked being in the military. That something was going on and it centered on him. Purple Hearts popped up on eBay or at flea markets occasionally.

"No."

"I knew it. I told you he faked being in the service."

"He might have—we're looking into it. But the Purple Heart had Luke's name on the back. He was there."

No. None of my workouts with Gennie had hurt as much as this. "It looks bad," I said. CJ nodded. "He didn't hurt the Spencers. He might have been there for some reason, but he wouldn't have hurt them."

"Chuck?" Pellner came in the thrift shop. "You're needed."

CJ sighed and held up a finger. "Give me a minute," he said to Pellner before turning back to me. "I don't think I'll make it back to your place tonight. I hate not to be there."

"It's okay." I wished I meant it.

"Love you," CJ said as he walked away.

"You too," I said to his back. I had to find Luke.

Seeing Lindsay reminded me of the pictures she'd taken at the Spencers' yard sale. I had a lot more information now than I'd had the first time I'd gone through them. Maybe, if I looked again, something would click. I sat in my Suburban and scrolled through the photos. One stopped me. It was two men climbing into one of those extended-cab pickup trucks. The back of the truck was splashed with mud, and the license plate was obscured. Was it deliberate? I zoomed in on the photo to get a look at the men's faces. But both were in profile with hats low on their brows. One wore a plaid flannel and the other a long-sleeved T-shirt. Nothing unusual there.

But the more I stared at the picture, the more convinced I was that these were two of the men in the group of four I'd seen around town. I went through the photos again, looking for a group of four men, but Lindsay had only taken pictures at the end, when people were leaving.

As I stared at the picture a theory began to take shape in my head. Thoughts fell into place like coins being sorted in a change drawer. The men knew who I was because they'd come to the garage sale. I thought back to all the stolen valor videos I'd watched online. In most of them you never saw who the accusers were. Maybe an arm here or a back there but never a good look at their faces.

My brain buzzed like it was a hive full of angry bees. Liars. Stolen valor. Those four men in town. I'd overheard bits of their conversation at DiNapoli's. Out of context, it didn't make a lot of sense, but now I think it did. They had talked about hunting and veterans. I'd put it together wrong. They were hunting fake veterans.

What if they planned to expose Mr. Spencer that day, but things went horribly wrong. It wasn't much to go on, but I forwarded the picture to CJ with a short explanation of my suspicions. After waiting a few minutes, I realized I wasn't going to hear back from him.

I looked through the rest of the photos, enlarging each one to see if the other two men were in the background of any. My eyes almost popped out of my head. There, in the background of a photo of two women getting into a silver car, was the back of a man in a bomber jacket and newsboy-style cap. Just like the ones Mr. Spencer wore. *No.* Not *like* Mr. Spencer's—they *were* Mr. Spencer's.

Chapter 34

I thought back to the day of the murder. Mr. Spencer had had the jacket and hat on when he had taken Mrs. Spencer away. But he hadn't had them on when he and Mrs. Spencer had been found in the garage. I enlarged the picture as much as I could and saw the blurry outline of red hair. Tim Spencer. Tim, who was supposedly in Florida, who said he'd flown up as soon as he'd gotten the news.

I thought of him asking me to help him go through things in his dad's office. One that someone had obviously been in. I was so stupid. He wanted me to be there when he "found" the insurance policy. He had a history of violence and alcohol abuse. He'd mentioned worrying about paying for college for his kids.

But then there was the Tim who had cried because his dad was dead. His grief seemed so genuine. I didn't understand what all this meant, but I quickly forwarded the picture to CJ with a note. I tried calling him, but ended up leaving a message for him.

My phone binged at nine-fifteen, but it was Charlie asking me to meet her at the American Legion. There wasn't anything more I could do about Tim. I turned my attention back to finding Luke. Hopefully, figuring out what was going on with Herb would shed some light on Luke's whereabouts. I wrote her I could stop by in a bit. *Please don't let it be another karaoke night.*

The parking lot behind the American Legion wasn't very crowded, which was a good sign.

Charlie sat at the bar talking to Lesley, the bartender. I hitched myself onto the stool next to Charlie's.

"Can I get you something?" Lesley asked.

"A gin and tonic sounds great." I looked over the room. A couple of women sat in one corner, eyeing four men at another table. The turkey hunters who I suspected were hunting down fake veterans. The men ignored the women as they hunkered together in an animated discussion. Two other tables held groups of people playing cards. There was no DJ or karaoke machine in sight. I sighed with relief as Lesley put my drink in front of me. "Thank you. Cheers." After a deep drink, I told Charlie and Lesley about what had happened on base tonight. "At least I know my brother didn't do it," I said.

"Any sign of him?" Charlie asked.

"Nothing."

Lesley raised an inquiring eyebrow. I told her about my brother. "Have you ever met Luke Winston?" I asked her. "Has he ever been in here?"

Lesley grabbed a dish towel and polished a spot off the bar. She set the dish towel down. "Not that I can think of."

"How about Bart or Bartholomew Winst? He uses the name professionally sometimes." At least I hoped that was why he was using it.

Lesley tapped a finger on her chin. "What's he look like?"

"I wish I had a recent picture of him." I flipped through the photos on my phone and found the one of him right when he joined the Marines. I'd snapped a photo of a photo my parents had when I was out in Pacific Grove last Christmas. He was in his dress uniform, cap low on his forehead. He looked young. "His shoulders are broader now, more five-o'clock shadow."

"He doesn't look old enough to shave in that one," Charlie said as I showed them the photo.

"His hair his longer, brown." I looked hopefully at Lesley.

"Sorry. I don't think he's been around."

"Why'd you want me to meet you?" Charlie asked.

"I wanted to ask you about Herb Fitch," I said, lowering my voice.

"I heard about his house," Charlie said.

Lesley shook her head and made a *tsking* noise.

I guess everyone in town knew about the vandalism at Herb's.

"I found this photo of him from an event here." I showed Charlie the photo. Lesley leaned over to look at it too.

"What about it?" Charlie asked.

I enlarged the part to show Herb's belt. "That's not a regulation belt. Is it possible Herb faked being a vet, someone found out, and spray-painted 'LIAR' on his house?" I glanced back at the four men. I hoped I was wrong because I liked Herb.

Charlie shook her head, her Afro flowing around her. "His arthritis makes it hard for him to use his uniform belt." She pointed at the picture. "The one he has on is made for people with arthritis and is easier for him to work. Even then, it's not easy. A couple of months ago, I saw him come out of the men's room, still fumbling with the buckle. He misinterpreted my intentions when I told him I'd be happy to help him with his belt next time. I'm still trying to decide whether to take him up on his misinterpretation or not." Charlie grinned.

Lesley and I laughed. Thank heavens Herb was on the up-and-up. I quit laughing when I realized another door in my search for Luke had just slammed shut in my face.

Charlie frowned. "Trust me, Herb served, and if someone around here thinks he didn't, then we have a problem."

"I think it's those men." Instead of turning to

look at them, I hitched a thumb at them over my shoulder.

"Why them?" Charlie asked. "They seem harmless."

I tried out my theory on her and Lesley. Having someone older to talk to who'd served was a relief. If she bought my assumptions, CJ might find it believable too.

"Look at this picture." I flipped to the picture I thought might be of two of the four men. "Do you think that's two of the men sitting back there?"

Charlie and Lesley took turns looking at the photo.

"It could be," Charlie said.

"Then again, it could be anyone," Lesley said. She looked across the room. "Duty calls."

Charlie and I turned. The ladies were signaling they wanted another round so Lesley grabbed an order pad.

"Lesley, do me a favor. Look and see if any of the men's hands have black paint on them."

"Why? Oh, because of Herb's house. Got it."

"Be subtle," I added.

She nodded and headed over to the women first because their signaling was growing increasingly frantic.

Charlie and I looked over the crowd. Lesley took the women's order and then stopped by the group of men. She chatted and laughed. She dropped her order pad on the table. As Lesley picked it up, I watched her study the men's hands. On her way back over to us, she checked in with the card players.

"Any luck?" I asked when Lesley got back behind the bar and started to mix drinks.

"No painted hands."

Darn. "Thanks for trying," I said. "So do you think anyone else who's here will talk to me?" I asked Charlie. "Maybe the card players know something about those men."

"We can't interrupt the card players, and they'll play into the wee hours, right, Lesley?" Charlie said.

Lesley faked a big shudder. "Half the time, I'm afraid to ask if they want anything to drink. But it's hell to pay if I don't."

"Do you know anything about the men?" Charlie asked her.

"Not much, except they're here on vacation or something and they tip real good." Lesley smiled. She filled a couple of mugs with Sam Adams lager.

"What about the women in the corner?" I asked. "Should I talk to them?"

Lesley snickered and Charlie laughed.

"What?" I asked, looking back and forth between them.

"They get so loaded, they would tell you the Pope had been in here if you asked," Lesley said. "I have a cab on standby on the nights they're here. As soon as I see them gather their things, I send the cab driver a quick text." She smiled. "He hasn't let me down yet. They make it home safely, and the next morning when they come back for their car, they leave a huge tip. It's a win-win."

"You take good care of your customers," I said.

"I try," Lesley said.

Charlie nodded. "So have you heard anything new about who killed Mr. Spencer?"

"I haven't." I didn't want to tell her I'd found out he wasn't really a veteran. It still hurt that he'd lied to me because I had liked him so much. I also felt some empathy to Mrs. Spencer in a coma in her hospital bed, not knowing what was going on.

Lesley hefted the tray of drinks she'd assembled. We watched as she distributed them. At the card players' table, she slipped the drinks in unobtrusively. She chatted with the women for a few minutes, and they turned to look at Charlie and me. One held up her glass of wine to us. Lesley moved on to the group of four men. There, she tossed her hair and cocked a hip, smiling as she put down the drinks and chatted. I could tell she was flirting and the men were enjoying it. No wonder they were good tippers.

One threw his head back and made a strange hoot-like laugh. I'd heard that before, but where? It wasn't the night at DiNapoli's. They'd been pretty low-key there. It was too noisy for it to have been here on karaoke night. I closed my eyes to concentrate. The videos I'd watched about stolen valor. I opened my eyes. That was it and I was right about them.

I heard the hoot again and whipped my head around. I made eye contact with the hooter. His eyes narrowed and he leaned over to the man next to him, whispering something in his ear. That man looked over at me too and not in a friendly way.

"I have to go, Charlie," I said as I gathered my

stuff. What they were doing might not be illegal, but if they had something to do with Mr. Spencer's death CJ needed to know. I told Charlie good-bye and waved to Lesley as I headed out.

I stood outside, looking over the parking lot. Stars popped, a light wind blew, and light sweater weather was settling in. There were no big pickup trucks with king cabs like the one in the photo. I slid my keys out of my purse as I hustled to my Suburban. I clicked the locks open, tossed my purse across to the passenger seat, and heard a noise behind me. Before I could turn, something hard whacked the back of my head. The keys slipped out of my hand. My knees buckled. I tried to grab the car seat to stop collapsing, but my brain wasn't communicating commands to my limbs. My chin bounced on the edge of the runner, jarring me. I was a fast-forwarded version of the Wicked Witch of the West melting. That was my last thought as I hit the pavement.

Chapter 35

I woke to a gentle swaying, but I couldn't see anything. I tried to stretch out, to turn, but I was in a small space. My knees pressed against my chest as I was almost tucked in a fetal position. A picture of Mrs. Spencer flashed through my head. I fought back panic. *Focus, Sarah. Breathe.* I patted around me and touched rough carpeting below me and metal above.

The noise I heard was tires on pavement. I was in the trunk of a moving car. Again. A year ago, I'd been tossed in the back of my Suburban under very different circumstances. But no less scary. At least this time no duct tape was involved. I swallowed. Yet. I had to use that to my advantage.

I pounded on the interior of the trunk lid, but since I wasn't able to extend my arm, the noise was more of a light tap than anything that would draw any attention. It was too cramped to kick. How long had I been back here? I had no concept of time. Was this the car that had been seen leaving the woods the day the Spencers had been murdered? Or the one that had U-turned when I'd been parked in front of their house the first time I'd met Tim there?

I hoped not. I tilted as the car turned and bounced onto a bumpy road. It stopped moments later, and I realized I had seconds to decide a course of action. What would Gennie do? Fight.

The car rocked as two car doors slammed. But nothing else happened. It was quiet. Footsteps crunched on what must be gravel, but they went away from me. I tried to move, but the trunk was tiny. I couldn't stretch my legs out, let alone get into a crouch to spring out when the trunk opened. I moved my hand around, searching for a trunk release. I think I'd read somewhere all cars were required to have them now. But I didn't find anything. My luck, I'd get stuck in the back of an old compact car.

I laid there trying to figure out why I'd been grabbed tonight. I ran through the evening in my head. Then I pictured Lesley chatting with the men while she took their orders and served them. They must have done this. Maybe that's why they were such good tippers—she fed them information.

The crunch of footsteps headed back toward me. The trunk sprung open. Before I could move, some kind of heavy rope net was thrown over me. A blanket followed. I fought, but only tangled myself in the net. I yelled and screamed. The fact no one tried to silence me scared me. We must be somewhere remote.

Someone lifted me by the torso. Someone else grabbed my legs. I tried to buck, but it was as ineffectual as a June bug hitting a screen. Seconds later, I was lowered gently onto what felt like a floor. The arms released me and I heard something slam shut above me. I was screwed.

I clawed at the net and rolled around trying to shake free of the blanket. It smelled dank and cold seeped through the blanket. A muffled sound made me still. Had I heard a voice? I might not be alone. I managed to roll out of the blanket, but it was too dark to see anything. It wasn't the kind of dark one's eyes would adjust to. It was black and inky—no cracks of light came from anywhere. I freed myself from the net.

"Who's there?" a man's voice asked.

"Luke? You're alive." My voice cracked, but I told myself this was no time for emotions. I tried to stand but whacked my head on what was a very low ceiling. For a minute, I saw bright lights. But it wasn't actual light, just one too many whacks on the head for one night.

"Oh no. Sarah. I can't believe I dragged you into this mess."

"What is this place?"

"I'm not sure. I'm tied up and it's hard to move around."

I scrabbled around on the hard-packed dirt floor. It was cold down here.

"How did you end up here?" I asked. The dirt was hard on my hands and knees. I reached out a hand, patting the dirt before me as I inched along. "Talk so I can find you."

"Two men pounced on me the night I saw you at the VA."

A burn of anger warmed me up. "You've been down here since then?"

"Yes."

"I kept hoping you managed to get away."

"Don't you think I would have called you? Made sure you were okay?"

Sadly, I wasn't sure. Silky tendrils brushed across my face. I jerked back. "Yuck."

"Cobwebs? They're all over the place."

"Yes." I batted the air, hoping to pull the thing down.

"You've always hated them."

"Not as much as I hate the men that did this to you."

"To us. I tried to stall them that night, hoping you'd get away."

"One of them was dressed like a security guard and fooled me."

"They've had you since then?" Luke's voice was low and mean. I'd been on the receiving end of that anger during one of our phone calls years ago.

"No. That's the weird thing. I woke up in my apartment. They took me home." My hand touched Luke's foot.

"There's duct tape and rope around my ankles, so try my arms first. Then I can help with my legs."

I scooted along until I found his arms. Layers of duct tape bound his wrists. I picked at it, hoping to find the end piece.

It made me ill. "Who did this?" I asked. I might not be able to see anything, but at least I'd get some answers and maybe we'd find a way out.

"No idea. Do you know?"

I nodded and then realized he couldn't see me. "I'm not sure. But there've been these four men in town. At first I thought they were outdoorsmen, but I think they were here for something else."

Luke groaned.

"Did I hurt you?" I was still plucking at what felt like the edge of the duct tape with my fingernail. Good thing I had such strong nails.

"No. I got you into this mess. I didn't mean to."

"Stay still," I said when he moved his arms. I restarted my search to find the end of the duct tape. "I figured out you track down people who pretend they're in the military. Mom and Dad will be proud."

"They won't be, not once they know the whole story."

"Tell me."

Chapter 36

Luke was quiet for a long time. "I'm not the brother you'd hoped I'd be or one you'd even want."

"I love you. No matter what."

"I started out with this drug- and alcohol-induced rage. At what I'd seen, what I hadn't done. Then I found out someone was using my buddy Nick's identity. He died in Iraq."

"I'm sorry." I tugged on the duct tape and got a little piece loose.

"I wanted to be the hero. The one I never was over in Iraq. Nick was the guy who took one for the team instead of running."

I kept my head down and scratched and tugged and pulled on the tape. It was almost impossible in the dark. The cold made my hands feel like chunks of ice.

"I outted a couple of jerks who were getting benefits. They were scum in my book."

"In everyone's book."

"Then one day I tracked a man down. I was

broke and needed a fix. He told me if I didn't rat him out, he'd pay me. I figured if it worked with him it would work with others. Quite the way to make a living."

I sucked in a bit of air. My baby brother a blackmailer? I flashed back to the money on the floor of the Spencers' garage. My eyes blurred with tears, but I kept my fingers working on the tape. "You were blackmailing the Spencers?"

"No. I sobered up about five years into my con. It's why I stayed away from all of you, so you wouldn't know what a loser I am. The couple of times I called you? I wanted to tell you, but chickened out every time."

This was the most honest talk we'd had in years. How odd to be doing it in the dark, when we were in danger. But maybe the dark made sense since neither of us could see the judgment in the other's face. "What are you doing now?" I asked.

"I've been slowly paying people back. And only exposing them after giving them the opportunity to do it themselves. No one really gets any joy out of finding a faker. The good guys exposing frauds don't go around and leap out to have gotcha moments that make them look good. They turn people over to feds to deal with them. There's a difference between wearing a uniform and defrauding the government for veteran's benefits."

"I figured out Mr. Spencer wasn't in the service." I shook my head. "He was just in a movie about Vietnam. Were you planning to expose them?" I peeled back a layer of tape.

"I went to the Spencers to give them a chance to confess." Luke fell quiet for a moment. "I've learned over the years more about how people get caught up in things. It starts with a little lie someone tells and it snowballs."

I didn't want to ask the next question. "Did you hurt the Spencers? I told you that night at the VA that your fingerprints were there. Likely there's other evidence I haven't heard about. They found your Purple Heart medal in the garage too."

"The door into the back of the garage was open. Mr. Spencer looked dead and I thought Mrs. Spencer was. I heard a commotion in the woods and headed down to see if I could identify anyone."

"It *was* you I saw running in the woods." I quit picking at the tape for a minute and held Luke's cold hands in mine. We'd been close to coming face-to-face at the Spencers' house.

"I called 911 and then chased a runner. But it was a woman out for a morning run."

It explained why he sounded out of breath when I'd listened to the 911 calls. I started working on the tape again. "You should have gone to the police."

"I told you I was no hero."

"Why did you have your Purple Heart with you?"

"I kept it as a reminder of how I'd failed my friend and as a reminder about what I needed to do."

I unwound more of the duct tape. "How did you end up in Ellington?"

"About six months ago, I started investigating a group of men who were going around exposing fakers. They humiliated them as much as possible, posting videos, mocking them, ripping patches off their uniforms. But I wasn't sure who they were because they were never in the videos."

"What made you want to go after them?"

"They started getting it wrong. They went after a female officer who used a different name for her blog. She started getting death threats even though she served honorably."

"They got it wrong with Herb Fitch too." I explained what had happened at Herb's house and about his belt.

"I eventually found out none of them ever served."

"I think Lesley, the bartender at the American Legion, fed them information. She heard and noticed a lot bartending. Maybe they suspected Herb or were looking for other fakers there." I could see Lesley wanting to help in that case. "If they didn't serve, why were they doing it?"

"One of them lost a daughter in Afghanistan. They started off with good intentions. People touted them as heroes, but they went off the rails somewhere."

"Why did you have to keep it all a secret?"

"Because more than one group claimed they were the ones behind the videos. Every time someone got close, the men disappeared. I couldn't chance losing them and didn't want to accuse those four if they weren't the ones behind the videos."

"What do you think happened at the Spencers'? They confronted them and things went horribly wrong?" I asked.

"I don't know. As far as I know they've never been violent until now."

I ripped off the final strand of tape, the one stuck to his skin.

"Ouch. Jeez, that hurt. I think you took every last bit of hair around my wrists."

"Suck it up. Help me with your legs," I said.

"I don't have any feeling in my arms."

I briskly rubbed first one arm and then the other. "You stink," I said.

"Yeah, sorry, the shower facilities aren't the best here." He shook both arms.

"Did they find out about you? Is it how you ended up here?" I crawled down to where Luke's feet were and started tugging at the ropes.

"They must have."

"Did they hurt you?"

"No. They brought me meals, blankets, a pillow. I can't figure out what their end game is."

"I hope it's not to leave us down here to die."

"Me either."

For a while, we concentrated on loosening the ropes around his legs and our own thoughts. Our hands bumped each other and we didn't seem to be making any progress. My fingers were so cold, I stuck them under my armpits to try warming them up. It wasn't that the temperature outside was terribly cold, but given the dirt floor, we must be in some kind of underground room. "I'm cold, Luke. I've got to find the blanket they wrapped me in."

"Take mine," Luke said.

"No. You need it. Give me a minute." I crawled around, bumping into walls, until I finally found it. I dragged it back over to Luke. I wrapped it around my shoulders and leaned against him. My eyes closed. I snapped them back open, not that it made a difference. My hands shook so badly I was making things worse for Luke.

"Take a break and warm up." Luke sounded as tired as I felt.

"Okay. For a minute."

Sometime later, I jerked awake. There was no way to tell how much time had passed. It was still as dark as when they'd tossed me down here. Luke snored gently.

I shook him. "Luke, wake up. We've got to get out of here." I started back in on the rope. "How did you find out about the Spencers?"

"Their name came up during my investigation."

"From Ethan?"

"Yes. I went to their house and spotted you. I couldn't believe you were there. I ducked around the back." Luke yanked violently at the rope.

"Stop. That's not helping. It's only making it tighter."

"Do you have any idea where we are or what this place is?" I asked Luke.

"It doesn't seem like a barn—the space isn't big enough. And it doesn't seem deep enough to be a cellar. I can't stand straight up."

"When someone brings you food, how many men come?"

"Usually only one."

"Then we can take him," I said, and tried to believe it like Gennie had taught me. "We'll have to pretend you're still tied up. And that I'm asleep."

"I am still tied up."

"Hopefully, by the time they return, you won't be."

"What if they don't return?"

I hadn't thought of that. It wasn't an option.

Luke and I were both exhausted by the time we finally undid all of the rope and duct tape. I was pretty sure my fingers were bleeding.

"How are they coming in and out?" I asked.

"There's a trapdoor in the ceiling in the center of the room. They set something heavy on it though. Trust me I tried to get out of here."

"How? You're all tied up."

"I managed to get to my feet a couple of times and scoot around. Or I'd roll around trying to find another way out."

"They must have lowered me through the trapdoor. The weird thing is besides whacking me on the head, they were gentle with me. And if it was them at the VA grounds after they choked me, they took me home and put me to bed. I don't get it."

"They choked you?" The anger in his voice felt like a slap.

"Just enough to make me pass out." I put a hand

to my throat. What if they hadn't known what just enough was? "And that's it? There's not another way out?" There didn't appear to be any windows or if there were, they were boarded over.

"There's one other opening over in the corner. But it's too little to get out of. Some kind of chute. I couldn't get my shoulders through it. And with my hands and feet tied, no way to get any kind of grip on anything."

"Show me. Maybe I'll fit."

"I think it's blocked off too. No light shows through."

"We have to try."

Luke took my hand and we bumbled our way over to it. Under any other circumstances, we'd laugh at how ridiculous we looked. Luke guided my hand to the opening. I ran my hand around the roughly shaped rectangle.

"My shoulders are smaller than yours. Maybe I'll fit." I tried to peer up it, but didn't see a glimmer of light. "Okay. I'd better give it a try." I stood, raised my arms above my head, and searched for something to grab on to. Good thing I wasn't claustrophobic. I ducked back out. "You might have to boost me," I told Luke.

I tried again. My shoulders cleared, just barely, and I hoped my rear end wouldn't get stuck. I clawed around with my hands and found something to grasp. I pulled up. The space was small enough that I didn't have to worry about sliding back out. I did have to worry about getting stuck.

I reached again. My hand hit something scratchy but firm. I pushed on it. Dirt, hay, and dust cascaded down on me. I couldn't breathe or call out because my mouth was full of it. I made a choking noise.

Luke grabbed my legs and yanked me back out. My sweater ripped and something scratched my side. I spit out a mouthful of dirt, sneezed and coughed.

"Are you okay?"

I rubbed at my eyes, and when I opened them again, I could see Luke in a faint light coming from the chute. "I'm better. If the opening doesn't narrow, I think I can get out."

I pulled and wiggled, while Luke pushed and shoved. My hips stopped me briefly once. If Luke hadn't been there to push, I don't think I could have clawed my way out on my own. I was cursing like a sailor in my head. Only in my head, in case someone was here. I slowed as I reached the top. Luke couldn't reach my feet any longer.

I took a quick peek out. No one was around, at least not up here. Sun shone in through the large open door at the front of the building. It was daytime. Somehow, I'd expected it to still be dark out, kind of like when a movie lets out and the light makes you blink in surprise. I dragged myself out and onto the rough plank floor.

This looked like an old carriage house. I was in a loft that had probably been used for hay. I scrambled down a rickety ladder to the main floor. It would have been for the carriages and horses.

The lower level, where they'd stashed Luke and me, was for pigs. The place was empty except for an old wooden trunk in the middle of the room on top of the trapdoor. I ran over to it and started to inch it aside.

A car door slammed. Someone was here.

Chapter 37

I glanced around, but there was no place to hide and I wasn't going back down that chute. There wasn't anything to use as a weapon. Steps crunched toward me on the gravel. There wasn't time to scramble back up the ladder. And this place was spotless. My only option was to stand against the wall on the same side as the door. The corner was dark and hopefully whoever was coming in wouldn't expect anyone to be in here.

A man ambled in with a bag of food from McDonald's in his hand. The fries smelled heavenly. He shoved the trunk aside and lifted the trapdoor. He started to lower the food in when Luke yanked him into the hole. The man yelled as Luke climbed out and slammed the trapdoor down. I ran over, and together, we shoved the trunk over the door.

"Was he alone?" Luke asked.

"No," a man said.

We turned and spotted a man standing inside

the doorway. I ran at him and slammed my fist into his windpipe.

"Oof," he yelled.

My momentum tumbled us forward. We landed outside, in the gravel driveway leading to the carriage house. Before he had a chance to react, I started pummeling his face with my fists. He bucked me off and started to rise, but I swung a foot out and tripped him. Luke leaped on him.

"Take their truck and get out of here," Luke yelled as they wrestled.

A pickup with one door open idled fifteen feet away. I ran to it, hauled myself up, and shoved the truck into drive. Luke and the man struggled to their feet. Luke squinted in the bright light after being held in the dark for four days. The man swung his arm and punched Luke hard. Luke swayed but grabbed the man.

Instead of driving away, I drove straight at Luke and the man, praying Luke would get out of the way.

I punched the horn. Luke looked up and leaped away at the last possible second. I slammed on the brakes. The truck skidded to a stop and pinned the man against the wall of the carriage house. He pounded the top of the hood. I couldn't believe I hadn't killed him. By the way he cursed me, he must not be seriously injured either, just trapped.

Someone had left a cell phone in the cup holder. I scooped it up and managed to dial 911 with my trembling fingers. I gave the dispatcher a description of the carriage house and the bright white house in front of it.

"The whole place seems deserted," I told the dispatcher.

"It sounds like the old Ward place. It's up for sale. I'll have someone there in no time."

I leaped out of the truck as Luke raced over to me. He was bruised and filthy. His eyes were still squinted together, but I hugged him like my life depended on it.

"Are you okay?" he asked.

I nodded. "You jumped on the man and told me to leave. You are a hero."

Luke shook his head. "You're a nut."

Sirens sounded, and I could tell they were speeding toward us.

"I'm going to check on the other guy. Just to make sure he can't get out through the chute. Sit in the truck with the doors locked just in case."

"Wait a minute." I hugged him one more time. "Thank you."

Luke held me for a second and then ruffled the top of my head. "Keep an eye on him." He pointed at the trapped man, who continued to squirm and curse.

I climbed back into the truck. It was already nine in the morning according to the clock on the dashboard. I gave the man my best steely stare. He was one of the four men I'd seen around town. Seconds later, three squad cars screamed up. CJ leaped out of his official SUV and ran to me. I slid back out of the truck. We held each other for a long moment until he noticed the man I'd trapped. He shook his head.

"You managed that?" CJ asked.

"With Luke's help."

CJ looked around. "Where is he?"

"In the carriage house, making sure the other guy doesn't get away."

Keeping an arm around me, CJ told Pellner to go check the situation in the carriage house with Awesome. He asked another two officers to move the truck and cuff the man. We watched as the truck inched back. The man tried to run off but didn't make it far before he was tackled.

A few minutes later, Pellner and Awesome came out, each holding the arm of the cuffed man. He didn't seem to have any fight in him.

Pellner stuffed him in the back of a squad car before coming over to us.

I craned my neck looking around. "Where's Luke?"

Pellner looked at CJ. "No one was in the barn, Chuck. Except him." He pointed toward the squad car.

"But my brother. He was going to stand guard...." My voice trailed off. Luke had taken off again. "Is there a back way out of the carriage house?"

Pellner looked at his feet, dragged one in the gravel. "Yeah. There is, Sarah." The empathy in his eyes when he finally looked at me did me in.

"Find him," CJ said.

"He didn't murder Mr. Spencer," I said.

CJ nodded. "We still need to talk to him."

Pellner moved away and spoke into the radio on his shoulder. CJ led me to his car and helped me into the front seat. He got a blanket out of the back and tucked it around me. I shivered so violently, the car moved. CJ took an edge of the blanket and wiped at the tears I hadn't even realized were streaming down my face. If there was such a thing as a broken heart, I was experiencing it. Luke had promised me he wouldn't leave without telling me.

"I'll be back in a few minutes to take you home," CJ whispered in my ear. He kissed my temple and left. I sat there, mesmerized by the lights flashing off the white wood of the carriage house. What would I tell my folks? I leaned my head back against the headrest and closed my eyes. I'd tell them Luke saved me, even though, for whatever reason, I couldn't save him.

"Where's my car?" I asked CJ as we left.

He tensed his grip on the wheel. "Back at your apartment. They moved it again. It's one of the reasons no one realized you were missing. I'm sorry."

I waved my hand. "It's not your fault."

"I was up most of the night. I grabbed a nap at the station. If we lived together—"

"Not now, CJ. And if we did live together, you still would have been at the station."

"Do you want ice cream from Bedford Farms?" CJ asked.

It was eleven in the morning by the time they'd wrapped up everything at the carriage house. I'd given my statement to Awesome. I supposed Pellner was tired of taking them from me. CJ had been suggesting things to try and cheer me up as we drove home. I'd already said no to lunch at DiNapoli's, a lobster roll from West Concord Seafoods, and a stop to see Carol. His effort was so sincere and sweet, I finally said yes to ice cream. I did it to make CJ feel good, feel like he could do something in a situation where there was nothing to do. Despite the EPD's best efforts, no one had spotted Luke, but then I hadn't really expected them to. He was good at disappearing.

"Phil was arrested last night down in Foxborough," CJ said.

"That's good," I said.

"He was dealing again, and that's why he had the money he showed Lindsay."

"Did you ever find a connection between the money Ethan had and the money at the Spencers?" I figured this was as good a distraction as any and CJ was definitely in the mood to humor me.

"None. Ethan cashed his Social Security checks at the bank every month. He must have just preferred to carry cash."

"Hmmm." I closed my eyes and leaned back against the headrest. Those hours trapped in the carriage house with Luke were, in some crazy way, a gift. It was the most honest we'd been with each other since I married CJ. The first time we'd let all the shields down and the truth out. But I didn't understand why he'd left. There was a chance he would have been in trouble for leaving the Spencers in the garage, but he'd made one of the many 911 calls to the police station. Maybe the intimacy between us had been too much for him after years of roaming. The thought I might not ever know weighed on me.

"Did you find Tim Spencer?"

"Yes, but he's telling a very different story than his mom."

"Mrs. Spencer woke up?"

CJ nodded. "However, she's having difficulty communicating. It will probably be a few days before we sort out their stories."

CJ pulled into Bedford Farms a few minutes later. "You can wait in the car if you want."

I nodded.

"You want the usual?"

That made me smile and I nodded. CJ pulled his phone out of his pocket as he walked up to order. I watched as he stopped and chatted for a few minutes. He glanced back at me once and nodded a couple of times. After he hung up, I watched him order.

He returned with a kiddie cup of Almond Joy ice cream for me and a large Green Monster, which looked big enough to feed half the force. "Pellner called. Those four men turned on each other like buzzards after carrion as soon as he told them they were going to be charged with kidnapping."

I spooned in a bite of creamy deliciousness.

"They were under some misguided notion they were keeping Luke and you out of the way while they went after what they called a big fish."

"Do you know who they were talking about?"

"No one's 'fessing up yet. Ethan had been feeding them information."

I paused, spoon midair. "Do you think Ethan told them about the Spencers?"

CJ had polished off a dip and a half and started on the next one. "Probably."

"So it was them the night at the VA?" I frowned.

"Yes. And they were the ones who took you back to your apartment. Pellner said one of them kept apologizing."

I stared down into my almost empty cup of ice cream. "They thought they were doing the right thing. They started out with good intentions."

"You are way more forgiving than I am. Just this once, I'm really glad Seth Anderson is in love with you. He'll go after them hard."

I glanced over at CJ. He was looking out the windshield like he saw something out there. A piece of chocolate stuck to the corner of his mouth. We'd never really talked about my relationship with Seth. I was too tired to start now.

My phoned buzzed. I grabbed it out of my purse. It was a text from a number I didn't recognize. I'm no hero. But I love you. Luke.

"It's Luke. He sent a text." I showed it to CJ, then sent a quick text back. Love you. Come home. A few seconds later, it bounced back to me as undeliverable.

"We can go to the station and try to trace it."

I shook my head. "He'll have already gotten rid of the phone. Let's go home."

Chapter 38

On Saturday morning, a week later than planned, I roamed around Gennie's house one more time. When I'd read the *Boston Globe* at breakfast, I'd found a feature article titled GOTCHA by Bart Winst. It was an amazing story about stolen valor and the twisted tale of the four men who'd called themselves Honor Taken. I hoped, since Luke used the name Bart Winst, he was sending me a message that he loved me and he'd come back someday.

But I couldn't focus on him now because Gennie's sale started in a few minutes. I peeked out an upper window. There were plenty of people waiting to come in. I straightened a few more things, went down the stairs, and opened the door with a smile. Ryne O'Rourke stood there grinning at me.

"What are you doing here?" I asked.

"Shopping for my uncle."

Stella had told me Ryne's uncle owned an antique store in Concord. I stepped back to let him in.

He stumbled on the doorsill and grabbed me. My arms shot out to catch him.

"Oh, I think it's my ankle," he said.

"You're hilarious," I said, letting him go. "And a faker."

"It takes one to know one," he said as he headed down the hall grinning.

"And mature," I muttered. Ryne laughed so he must have heard me.

A crowd of people pushed in behind him. I spent the rest of the day whirling from room to room. The sale went well, and at the end of the day, nothing was left but drapes and curtain rods, which were to be sold with the house.

Ryne had bought a lot of stuff and argued over every price like it was a matter of life and death. And, trust me, he was getting close to death a couple of times with his outrageous offers. He was exhausting. But out of courtesy to his uncle and the amount he bought, I gave Ryne a bigger discount on some of the pieces than I normally would have. I saw the shrewd businessman hiding behind the jokester.

After the sale ended, Gennie came by and I pulled a bottle of champagne out of the refrigerator. I uncorked it and poured us each a glass. "Here's to you," I said. "Thanks for all of the business." We tapped glasses before taking a drink.

"Thanks for all of your help. You worked hard.

How are you doing now that things have settled a bit?"

I'd talked to Gennie throughout the week, first to apologize for not showing up last Saturday and then to arrange to have the sale today. "Better. My fighting skills are lacking." I'd tried to block the visions of me tackling the man at the carriage house, how wrong things could have gone.

"You're here. You did something right." Gennie sipped her champagne. "What happened to the Spencers? There hasn't been much in the paper."

I sighed. "It's such a wild tale."

"So who killed Mr. Spencer?"

"Mrs. Spencer." I'd been so shocked when CJ had explained it all to me.

"You're kidding. I'd heard around town that it was the son."

"Mrs. Spencer was furious her husband was going to give more money to Tim. She grabbed a wooden lobster buoy, and whacked him with it. He keeled over and cracked his head open on the floor. She had a stroke when she saw what she'd done."

"And their son didn't do anything?"

"His story is she grabbed the buoy and started swinging it at him. He ran back into the house to avoid it, knowing his dad was better at calming her down. When he heard the scream, he blended with the garage sale crowd. He saw his parents and because of his history he panicked and left."

Gennie fidgeted with the stem of her champagne glass. "Do you believe him?"

I lifted my shoulder and dropped it. "I don't know. He certainly tried to cast suspicion on other people." I thought about Brad, how I'd accused him based partially on what Tim had told me. Brad had ended up putting the paperwork together that showed Mr. Spencer had faked his military service and turned it over to the higher-ups. "When that didn't work, he tried to take the blame himself."

"How?"

"Tim acted like he was in Florida when the officer tasked with notifying him called."

"So he was already here?" Gennie asked.

I nodded. "The officer called Tim's cell phone because his family doesn't have a landline. Tim came up with an elaborate plan. As soon as he got the notification, he bought a one-way ticket from Tampa to Boston. Then he called a local florist in Tampa and arranged to have flowers sent to his mother. To further shore up his story, he went to one of those websites that caters to flyers and ordered something during the time he was supposedly flying up here."

"I don't get it."

"Tim showed all the charges to the officer questioning him during the investigation. No one looked beyond that because it all seemed legit."

"What good did that do?"

"Tim figured if all else failed, and he had this back-up plan, the officer would check his phone records and realize the calls were placed from here. He was willing to take the blame so his mother wouldn't have to go to jail. He said he owed her that and more."

"If he wanted to save his mom, why didn't he just confess?"

"Because he knew they suspected my brother. He hoped they would pin it on him."

"That's horrible."

I clenched my champagne glass. "I know. I understand trying to protect your family. But not by blaming an innocent person." I, at least, had been ready to turn Luke in if he'd been guilty.

"I wonder what will happen to her."

"I don't know. As DA, it's up to Seth to decide on the charges." I raised my champagne glass. "But this is supposed to be a celebration. Here's to you and your new adventure."

We clinked our glasses together. "Are you going to put your house on the market now?" I asked.

"Unless I can find a buyer without having to go through a Realtor. I'll give them a great price."

We toasted to that.

"What about you and CJ?" Gennie asked. "This house would be great for you."

I had fallen in love with it during the months I'd worked here. The kitchen was beautiful, really too nice for someone with my cooking skills, but maybe I could learn. I pictured CJ and I working side by side in here. He could have a gym in the basement. I could use one of the bedrooms overlooking the large backyard as an office. Maybe we could get a dog. I'd have a lot of fun scouring flea markets and garage sales for things to furnish the house with.

"I'll even leave the punching bag down there as a remembrance of me."

I laughed. "You're right. It's perfect. CJ and I are having dinner tonight. I'll talk to him about it. He's been wanting us to move in together to really restart our lives." I'd miss seeing Stella as much as I did, but at least I wouldn't have to share walls with the likes of Ryne O'Rourke.

Chapter 39

I zipped home. CJ's car was parked in front of the house. I ran up the stairs and pushed open the door.

"I have great news," I said.

"Me too." CJ picked me up and twirled me around. "I applied for my dream job. Chief of police in Fort Walton Beach, Florida. There's even a house for sale down the street from my parents. It's brand spanking, new. Not like the old creaky houses around here. With vaulted ceilings, a swimming pool, and a hot tub. And you won't have to run your business anymore."

I felt dizzy from the twirling and what CJ was saying. "My business?" I loved what I did.

"No more cold winters. Plenty of fishing. The cost of living is way cheaper." CJ put me down and looked at my face. I made no attempt to hide my distress. "We don't have to live by my parents if that's why you're upset."

"It's not. I love my business."

"Okay. Well, there you won't have to stop in the winter. You can run it all year." He looked so proud of himself.

"But you applied for it without even talking to me."

"Not just applied for it," CJ said. "I've had two interviews and I'm their top candidate. I wanted to surprise you. This will be the best assignment ever."

"It's not an assignment. Not like when the Air Force sent us someplace. You chose it." I walked to the window that overlooked the town common. The church bells chimed. I loved my friends here and Ellington, even with the terrible winters.

"You've always known I wanted to move back there someday. You always say how beautiful the beaches are, how it's a great place to go antiquing."

CJ had sacrificed a lot for serving in the Air Force. He deserved his dream job. He was right about the weather, antiques, and beaches. I turned back to face CJ. "But we've made our life here. I even found the perfect house for us. Gennie's. She said she'd give us a good deal. Call the department in Fort Walton and decline."

"That old house?" CJ looked perplexed.

Minutes ago, I'd been excited about life, about how things were working out. "I can't believe you'd do this to me. To us," I said.

CJ sat on the couch, arms resting on his knees. He stared down at his clasped hands and then shook his head. "I've tried to keep this to myself, but I can't anymore.There's something you've been keeping from me," CJ said, looking up at me.

I tried to decipher his expression: sad, frustrated, angry. All of the above. Yes, I'd been keeping something from him, but I stopped myself before I said it out loud.

"I know there is. I've felt it these past couple of months. I couldn't figure out what and wanted to give you the space so you could tell me, so you'd trust me." He closed his eyes for a moment. "I don't get why you can't trust me after all our years together."

"I made a promise to someone. You wouldn't want me to break a promise I made to you," I said. I had to talk to Mike Titone, to get him to release me from my promise.

"No, I wouldn't, but it's me. Your husband—" He held up a hand. "I know. We aren't married, but we should be. I want to be. Do you?"

Aargh, such a loaded question. Yes, eventually I did. I loved CJ, but I liked dating him.

CJ walked over to me and ran a finger down my cheek. "We need a fresh start. Away from the people here."

I shook my head. Was he talking about Seth? Seth who I'd hardly seen? Who I'd moved beyond. But who CJ had said loved me only last week. "I like the people here. I'd miss them."

"It's not like you can't come back and visit. You've always made the best of everywhere we moved. You didn't even want to come here."

Connect with U(s)

Visit us online at
KensingtonBooks.com
to read more from your favorite authors, see books
by series, view reading group guides, and more.

Join us on social media

for sneak peeks, chances to win books and prize packs,
and to share your thoughts with other readers.

facebook.com/kensingtonpublishing
twitter.com/kensingtonbooks

Tell us what you think!

To share your thoughts, submit a review,
or sign up for our eNewsletters, please visit:
KensingtonBooks.com/TellUs.

Acknowledgements

My deepest gratitude goes to my agent John Talbot of the Talbot Fortune Agency and my editor at Kensington, Gary Goldstein. Thanks for making this journey an adventure and for making me laugh.

To Barb Goffman, Donna Andrews, Clare Boggs, Robin Templeton, and Mary Titone—each of you added something special to this book and I'm so glad to call you all friends. Barb edits an early draft and, as I revise, continues to give me thoughtful advice. Mary not only reads but acts as my publicist. I don't deserve you.

To my Wicked Cozy Author and Wicked Cozy Accomplice blog mates—Jessie Crockett, Julie Hennrikus, Edith Maxwell, Liz Mugavero, Barbara Ross, Sheila Connolly, Jane Haertel, and Kim Gray—this wouldn't be as much fun without you. I love that when I write you saying I've gone completely bonkers with this book, you write back saying, "She's crazy. But mostly in a good way."

To my family, for sticking with me even when I'm at my grumpiest—I love you.

If you have something that you think might be very valuable, call in an expert. It's the only real way to find the actual value. But make sure the person is qualified and trustworthy. (I'm not asking much, am I?)

It's okay to mark FIRM on one or two items. But don't overdo it because most people enjoy the process of bargaining.

Are you an introvert? Ask an extrovert to come help you with the sale. They can bargain and welcome people.

People will buy almost anything. But don't put perishables out, and do check to see if your community has regulations about what can and can't be sold.

If you have a hard time parting with things, put the items you want to sell in black plastic bags so they are out of sight until the day of the sale. Have a friend come over to help sort. It's a lot easier for them to tell you if you haven't used it in five years, you don't need it. Be brave.

Garage Sale Tips

Pricing Items – there are a number of different ways to price your items. You can try to do it with a color-coded system like Sarah did at the beginning of *A Good Day to Buy*, you can lump like things together (all paperback books for fifty cents apiece, for example), or you can price every item individually. The first two save time, but as things get moved around, it can create confusion. If you have someone helping you (and you should) they must know your system as well as you do. Individual pricing takes a lot longer so you have to decide if the time is worth it or if you lose a little here or there from things being moved around, that it won't matter to you.

Lots of people check the prices of things on sites like eBay to determine how they will price things. This method is good to a point. However, some people will overprice things and some will underprice. So follow an auction to see what the final price is or if anyone even bids on it. If no one bids on a popular item, you know the price is too high.

"That's true." But people called Fitch the best kept secret in the Air Force. I'd always made the best of our assignments because it was either that or being miserable for a few years. It often became as much about the people as the place, but here it was the whole package. "Being stationed here wasn't a choice. Leaving is."

"There are two bases there. Which means two thrift shops you can volunteer at. You love doing that. Double the fun."

"You don't get it. You could switch Fort Walton out for London or Paris and I'd feel the same way. You didn't talk to me about a major change in our lives."

CJ took a step back from me. "What are you saying?"

"I don't know." I turned back to the window and looked across the common again. I could see Carol's shop, the DiNapoli's restaurant, and thought about how at home my friends here made me feel. I thought of my promise to CJ, not to let him die a lonely old man. I loved him. We had a long history of loving each other. Every couple had their problems to work through. Maybe I needed to dig deeper, to work harder on us.

But I'd also become my own person since the divorce. With my own goals and needs. Maybe my promise to CJ wasn't enough. Maybe sometimes love wasn't enough.

Should I stay? CJ came up behind me, put his arms around me, and rested his chin on the top of my head. Should I go?